Faults

Faults

A Novel

Terri de la Peña

alyson books
los angeles | new york

MANUFACTURED IN THE UNITED STATES OF AMERICA.
COVER DESIGN BY BRUCE ZINDA.

THIS TRADE PAPERBACK ORIGINAL IS PUBLISHED BY
ALYSON PUBLICATIONS,
P.O. BOX 4371, LOS ANGELES, CALIFORNIA 90078-4371.
DISTRIBUTION IN THE UNITED KINGDOM BY
TURNAROUND PUBLISHER SERVICES LTD.,
UNIT 3 OLYMPIA TRADING ESTATE, COBURG ROAD, WOOD GREEN,
LONDON N22 6TZ ENGLAND.

FIRST EDITION: SEPTEMBER 1999

99 00 01 02 03 **a** 10 9 8 7 6 5 4 3 2 1

ISBN 1-55583-478-7

LIBRARY OF CONGRESS CATALOGING-IN-PUBLICATION DATA
  PEÑA, TERRY DE LA, 1947–
    FAULTS : A NOVEL / TERRI DE LA PEÑA. — 1ST ED.
    ISBN 1-55583-478-7
    1. HISPANIC AMERICANS—CALIFORNIA—LOS ANGELES FICTION.
  I. TITLE.
  PS3566.E448F3 1999
  813'.54—DC21   99-29300 CIP

COVER ILLUSTRATION BY JULIANNA PARR.

Acknowledgments

Unlike Toni Dorado in this novel, I have very fond memories of the Pacific Northwest, especially of Whidbey Island in Washington State, where I wrote the first draft in Fir Cottage on Hedgebrook Farm. There, sister writers Ann Garrett, Dorothy Lazard, Pesha Gertler, Chris Halverson, and many others helped me mold a fragmented idea into a five-character narrative structure. My deepest thanks to the efficient Hedgebrook staff for providing nutritious meals and quiet space during the emotionally draining experience of creating this book.

On my return to California, las hermanas escritoras Therese Hernández, Tisha Reichle, Guadalupe Garcia, Irma Licea, Yolanda James, and Kathleen Bedoya guided me in delineating the characters' distinct voices. Melissa Capers in particular offered an honest, in-depth critique. Professor Sonia Saldívar-Hull, as always, analyzed the manuscript and pointed me in the right direction. Julie Trevelyan and Angela Brown at Alyson Books were empathetic and patient editors.

Gloria Bando shared that frightening morning of January 17, 1994, with me and spent the rest of that day walking through Santa Monica, Calif., and photographing the earthquake's damage. Her striking photographs served as inspiration for framing many of the events described in *Faults*.

Last but not least, without Mother Earth's jolting me awake that morning, I would not have had the impetus to write this book.

The Narrators

Antonia Maria (Toni) Dorado, 40

Sylvia Luz Dorado Brandon Anchondo, 37

Adela Ybarra Dorado, 72
(mother of Toni and Sylvia)

Gabriela Brandon, 18
(daughter of Sylvia)

Pat Ramos, 38
(Toni's ex-lover)

Prologue

December 29: Morning
Toni Dorado

Shards of rain strike the windows of the Coast Starlight, the Los Angeles–bound Amtrak. Crystalline drops glide down dusty glass, reminding me of tears streaking someone's cheeks. No point in being evasive: I am referring to *my* cheeks. Many lágrimas have slid down my face the past few months, with even more pent inside. I have cried over betrayal, ambivalence, indecisiveness—about the state of the world in general—and, these days, because I am going home.

Against the Naugahyde and plaid upholstery, I shiver and pull my wool-lined coat closer. The cold rain cannot touch me; only my fears can. No matter how I try to avoid them, will them away, they reappear like pounding raindrops. With my fingertips I wipe my eyes and lean back. I glimpse my brown face on the wet window, a smudged impressionistic image.

Was that how Amanda saw me? A blurry picture of what she thought a Chicana should be—an earthy, passionate, Spanish-speaking lover? If that is what she thought, she was dead wrong. With her I turned out to be the direct opposite of those stereotypes. We both had our signals crossed. I was her Technicolor fantasy; she was my ticket out, my escape route. No wonder none of it worked.

Now I'm returning to what I left behind. I have nothing to show for the past 18 months. How can I explain to Mama or anyone the misery of living in the woods with Amanda when I had been so eager—desperate, even—to leave the smoldering ashes of Southern California?

Even though I drove to the Northwest with Amanda, to begin una vida nueva, a grand adventure, I found I could not run from myself. I could abandon the land of my birth, but I could not disentangle myself from its familial roots, its myriad of conflicts, including my sister Sylvia, and especially Pat Ramos.

Sighing, I watch the raindrops splatter. They hit the window with increasing force and relentless rhythm. Whenever Pat cries, which is not often, anger lies not far beneath the surface. Her anger smolders, sizzles, and emerges as furious tears. Confronting her about my decision to go with Amanda caused an emotional shock wave, an enormous rift between us I hope to heal. Failing to make Pat understand my departure did not mean I loved her less. Her answer haunts me still: "I'd believe that, Toni, if you were going alone."

I catch a stray tear and bring that finger to my lips. Tasting the saltiness reminds me of the evanescent flavor of Pat's *piel morena*. Closing my eyes, I imagine lying beside her, my curious tongue roaming her delicious brown skin, her mocha nipples, the fine black hair curling around her female essence. I never wanted to hurt Pat. No, I only wanted to leave—and knew she would not go with me. Sometimes I wonder if someone besides Amanda had promised a way out, would I have taken it? Probably, yes.

Lulled by the train's sway, I begin to doze. My dreams do not linger on Pat; they center on my recent respite from urban life, those unfocused months among canopies of red cedars and firs, those unstructured days and nights with Amanda Wyler.

She came back into my life when I needed her most. Amanda was as pale as Pat is dark, her generous figure a definite contrast to Pat's well-muscled runner's body. Amanda's russet curls cascaded around her heart-shaped face, her sapphire eyes placid compared to the continuous indignation of Pat's sepia ones. Even Amanda's soothing voice, reasonable to the extreme at times, seemed tempting in light of Pat's often argumentative tone. When Amanda and I reconnected, I longed for her calm acceptance, not the constancy of a lover always demanding more.

It had been years since we had seen each other, but encountering her that cloudy afternoon in the San Francisco hotel lobby erased the time. She was among those milling near the registration tables while I scanned job postings on the bulletin boards.

"Thinking about relocating?" She stood beside me, her eyes quizzical. Her pink lips evolved into a smile.

"Oh, my God—Amanda Wyler."

"Yes. A little older, a little wider. You haven't changed, Toni. Haven't even cut your magnificent hair."

I glanced around, wondering if anyone had overheard. Years ago Amanda would snuggle and wrap my black hair across her breasts, stroking it possessively, as if it were glossy mink or ermine.

"Same hairstyle. Otherwise I'm being forced from my rut," I confessed. "Last month I was laid off. Believe it or not, I'm definitely thinking about relocating. I don't know if I belong anywhere near Los Angeles anymore."

Her voice grew tentative. "The riots?"

"I call them 'civil disturbances.' My lover says they were a rebellion. Whatever they were they brought the racial tensions out front. All of us are still reeling from that, no matter where we live."

Amanda blinked. "Toni, I'm sorry about your job. You were there...how long?"

"Fourteen years." I sighed. "Cities and counties are slashing their library budgets. Makes me wonder if we'll soon be obsolete."

"I know." Her cool fingers skimmed my arm. "Would you like to join me for lunch? There's so much I'd like to—"

"Yes," I said impulsively. "It's been a long time, Amanda."

The winter rain continues to beat the train windows. I remove a turkey sandwich from my knapsack. The wafer-thin meat is bland, almost tasteless. On Christmas Eve I bought it in a deli near the Seattle motel where I stayed alone before boarding the Amtrak. Five days ago. During that interval I spoke only to the monosyllabic motel clerk and to a Native American maid.

That wet afternoon, noticing me about to enter my room,

she pushed her work cart toward me. Her inquisitive gaze took in my brown skin and black hair.

When I passed her in the cramped hallway, she whispered, "Excuse me, miss. What…people are you from?"

Shifting the soggy grocery bag to my hip, I pulled the key from my jeans pocket. "I'm Chicana—you know, Mexican-American."

Her midnight eyes slanted with amusement. "You look like…us."

"Thanks." I smiled, then blurted, "I needed to hear that."

She became hesitant. Perhaps my unexpected admission embarrassed her. Rather than answer she shoved her cart toward the next room.

Watching her, I unlocked my door. "I've felt so invisible here," I murmured in her direction. If she heard, she gave no response.

At first I was not invisible to Amanda. We fell into conversation and into bed that foggy San Francisco weekend. Before that I had never been unfaithful to Pat, although my feelings for her had become increasingly ambivalent.

Pat had insisted my layoff portended I switch careers, become an activist, and combat the triple evils of racism, sexism, and homophobia by her side. My bewilderment at being jobless—and the resulting depression—irked her. Mentally and emotionally sidetracked as I was, Pat believed I lost valuable time. She seemed relieved by my impulsive decision to attend the annual American Library Association meetings. A previous commitment prevented her from going to San Francisco with me. For once that did not matter. I craved time alone and found Amanda's soothing empathy a tempting antidote.

"Come visit me." Her burnished ringlets fell forward as

she leaned over me, strawberry nipples inviting. "You'll like Fir View, Toni. You'll want to stay in the woods forever."

"Would you want me to?" I studied her eyes—jet pupils flecked with gray, surrounded by sapphire pools.

"Yes."

My fingers glided over her marshmallow-soft contours. How could I have forgotten the pleasure she had offered years ago? Moaning, I felt her indulging fingers part me. With no regrets I opened my thighs to welcome her.

"I've always wanted you, Toni," she whispered. "For me there's no one else."

I doubt if Amanda meant to lie. Over the years she had maintained an illusory image, remembering me as the first Chicana she had ever met—intelligent, with obsidian black eyes, hair flowing like a monochromatic serape. Amanda was the feminist classmate who proved my instincts correct: I loved women. We commiserated over the drudgery of graduate studies in library science and frequently indulged in sexual pleasures. After graduation she returned to the Pacific Northwest to take a position as a small-town librarian. Since then we had exchanged holiday cards, sometimes letters, nothing else.

As time passed Amanda had made references in her letters to a shadowy relationship that apparently did not last long. Although she avoided specifics, I imagined her life in Fir View must have been lonely. The cabin she inherited from her parents nestled amidst several acres of Douglas firs and red cedars in the emerald hills above the town. Meeting her in San Francisco years later, I listened to an enthusiastic description of her sheltered home. Its peaceful surroundings seemed enticing. Depressed, demoralized, I eventually fled

Pat and California to join Amanda.

Living with her in that secluded environment populated only by ourselves, forest birds, and other wildlife, I began to blend into the cabin's rustic walls. Without the California sun, my brown skin faded, as if dissolving into the varnished pine. The only Chicana in Fir View, I simultaneously stood out and disappeared. Amanda seemed unaware of my gradual metamorphosis. Happy to share her life with me, she didn't recognize my increasing isolation. In tandem with that came my own realization that I am, without a doubt, an urban creature. I felt stifled in that emerald paradise.

The steady rain ebbs. Through the wintry sky a luminous sun emerges. Its muted glare aims at the train windows. I pull the plaid curtain to shield my eyes from the sudden brightness. A lengthy afternoon looms, and although I have a couple of novels in my knapsack, I decide to listen to music. Headset secured, I relax. The Chicano sounds of Marcos Loya's "Queen Calafia/Linda Mexicana" punctuate my drifting thoughts.

Gabriela Brandon

My Aunt Toni phoned a couple of weeks ago to say she was coming home. Right away I started crying.

"Gabi, you've really missed me that much?" she teased. Toni has no clue what she means to me.

I was too choked up to answer. Without Toni I wouldn't be living with my dad or going to college either. Without her advice, without her listening to me during bad times with my Mom, I could be like so many kids I grew up with—high school dropouts, potheads, gangbangers, single moms. Toni put me on the right track. Weird how such an inspiring woman can be so fucked up herself.

When I stopped crying and could talk again, I asked her why she wouldn't be home for Christmas.

"That would be too emotional, Gabi. I need to make a slow transition. The holidays are intense enough." She sounded worried about me. "Are you all right?"

"Yeah. Just happy tears." I grabbed a pencil from Dad's desk to scribble her arrival time. "See you at Union Station on the 30th."

"Good. Do you suppose anyone will go along with you?" She tried to keep wishful thinking out of her voice.

"Like?"

"Well—anybody."

I knew she was thinking about her ex. Probably too much to ask, but I offered anyway. "I'll tell Pat—if you haven't already."

Toni let out her breath. "Thanks, Gabi. Otherwise, it's very...awkward."

Like everybody else in the family, I never could figure out what Toni saw in Amanda Wyler. Old times' sake, maybe. Toni doesn't tell me too much personal lesbian stuff. Maybe she thinks she's being protective of me—or private about herself. It doesn't matter. I have ways of finding out.

According to Pat Ramos, Amanda was Toni's first love—or at least the first woman she got it on with. When my aunt was in grad school studying to be a librarian, I was a little kid, so there's a lot of stuff I don't remember. Whenever I'm in a snoopy mood, I ask Pat to fill in the details about Toni, things I was too young to know. It gives us both a chance to talk about those days.

I've tried to make up my own mind about Amanda Wyler, though. Pat can be pretty damn snide when it comes to her. That makes sense since Toni left Pat in the lurch and skipped town with the Wyler chick. Pat tries to pretend none of that matters anymore. She thinks Toni doesn't love her. That's not true.

Toni really took off 'cause she was so unhappy about Sylvia, my mom. They used to be close, when I was little, but not anymore. Sometimes I wish I could have left town too. The farthest I've gone is Dad's place. If it hadn't been for Toni, I wouldn't have gotten there.

Pat Ramos

The smartest move is to stay away from Union Station when Toni rolls in tomorrow night. Gabi phoned me at work to hint that she'd like me to go with her to pick up Toni. Not a chance. I can understand why the kid's edgy about driving into downtown Los Angeles at night, but I'm not into pulling a codependent number. In the first place, I have enough mixed emotions about my ex coming back. I'm half wanting to grab Toni tight and kiss her so hard she can't breathe and half wanting to flip her off to hell.

I'm at my desk, drafting a press release for Media OutReach for Equality about an upcoming boycott of companies that sponsor right-wing homophobic programming. No way can I concentrate. All I'm thinking about is that damn Toni Dorado. It's crazy-making, you know? A year and a half ago she took a hike. I'm barely starting to get used to that. Now she decides to come back 'cause country dyke livin' ain't what it's cracked up to be. Yeah, sure. Don't expect me to meet her on bended knee.

Ay, mujeres—especially this one—make me loca!

Whether she agrees or not, Toni's still going through midlife-crisis shit. She and Sylvia have given up seeing eye to eye—what else is new? The kicker was Toni's getting laid off. A big chunk of her identity was being the town's only Chicana librarian. All of a sudden she's looking for work for the first time since she got her degree. That really did a number on her.

She used the L.A. rebellion as an excuse to split. I wasn't buying that. Santa Monica sure wasn't burned down— just a few broken windows. Racism never defeated Toni before. She's always been a fighter, a quiet one, but a soldadera all the same. Truth is, things had been edgy between us for a while. I'm a little too "out" for her. I pushed too hard sometimes, wanting her to be more open than she was willing to be.

Why did she believe in a white dyke more than in me? Hell, is it my fault I couldn't offer her a dinky cabin in the Northwest, some so-called peace and quiet, time to reflect and all that shit? All I could give her was mi cuerpo, mi alma, my vida. Obviously that wasn't enough.

La Navidad was four days ago. No lie it was one of the worst ever. Last year's wasn't terrific either. This time I hung out with las amigas, tried to get into the Christmas spirit. Damn hard. Knowing Toni's coming back really has thrown me for a loop. Where do we go from here, if anywhere? I don't even know if I can trust her again. I'm scared to see her—even more scared not to.

I want to look deep into her fawn eyes, wind my fingers around that long black hair, caress her tawny body, her cuerpo de mujer. If—or when—I see her, I can't let her know any of that.

"How's it coming, Pat?" Jackie, my coworker at Media

OutReach, drapes her skinny form on the desk opposite mine. She's a towhead with a buzz cut and a great pitching arm. In the months after Toni left, we had a couple of quickies. We both decided we'd rather work or play softball together than be lovers.

"It isn't." I stretch and lock my hands behind my head. "Toni'll be in town tomorrow night."

Jackie takes a sip of coffee before asking, "A holiday trip?"

I shake my head.

"Returning to the scene of the crime?"

"You got it. Looks like for good."

"Hey, girl. Hope you have New Year's Eve plans."

"Nothing in particular."

"Make some, Pat. Go to a movie, clean out your fridge, rearrange your furniture. Be damn sure to screen your phone calls."

"More likely I'll curl up in bed and hide under the covers."

She eyes me. "You're really hung up on her."

I shrug. "Figured she'd be back sooner or later."

"What's your game plan?"

I grin. "Avoidance for the time being. Won't be easy. She'll be staying with her mom."

"A few blocks from you."

"Yeah. I drive by there every day on my way to work."

"It'd be easy to stop."

"Jackie, she knows where I live. I'm not about to make the first move."

"Hope you're right." She comes closer to stare at the sketchy paragraph on the computer screen. "In the meantime, you've got a deadline, Pat. Quit thinking about her body and flesh out this piece."

Adela Ybarra Dorado

Ay, I never thought it would be like this. My daughters are supposed to love each other, not fight every chance they get. I saw the ugly face Sylvia made when Gabriela said Toni would be home in a few days. Christmas Day was not the time to get into an argument over Toni. I tried to ignore Sylvia's jealous fit. Ever since, I've been busy getting the extra bedroom ready for my older daughter. Que bueno Toni will stay with me. Ojalá que she can live here a while. I've missed her so much. No se if she's missed me.

When my daughters were born, I was already past 30. Las muchachitas were the answers to my prayers. Antonia Maria is two and a half years older than Sylvia Luz. Sometimes those girls behave as if the sun, moon, and stars are between them. They were so close when they were chamacas. Toni always gave her little sister advice. Even if Sylvia didn't listen, she seemed to know her sister cared enough to say something, even if it wasn't always what she wanted to hear. Now Sylvia tells me otherwise, that Toni always butted into her life and taught her some bad habits. Eso no es la verdad. I remember as only a mother can.

When Toni went away over a year ago, she told me she needed a fresh start. Losing her library job hurt her more than she could say. Like her father, Toni holds her feelings inside. And I imagine que la Pat Ramos could be hard to live with sometimes, even though I think Pat was muy buena con Toni, better que esa Amanda. But when my older daughter gets an idea into her head, it's hard for her to let it go. Amanda promised her una vida nueva, a brand new life. Toni believed her. Maybe she thought she had no other choice.

I thought my heart would break when I saw them drive away in the U-Haul truck. I thought mi familia was falling apart. First mi esposo Juan died, then la Sylvia married that good-for-nothing Gonzalo Anchondo. And then Toni was gone too. Only my granddaughter Gabriela brightens my days. That girl is a treasure. Who would think a child who grew up with so much sadness could make an old lady like me so happy? Gabriela es un milagro, bendito sea Dios.

Tonight Gabriela will eat dinner with me. She visits two or three times a week. When Toni comes, Gabi will probably be here even more often. In some ways I think she has more in common with Toni than with her own mother, Sylvia. Not that Gabi is completely like Toni—tu sabes, she has boyfriends y todo. Pero she is smart como la Toni—they talk about books and ideas. Sylvia only likes to gossip about talk shows y el *National Enquirer*.

El Padre Huerta at the parish tells me parents have no control over their adult children's lives. He tells me I raised both girls to the best of my ability. No es culpa mia how they've turned out. But Padrecito Huerta has no children. How can he really know?

Sylvia Dorado Brandon Anchondo

Toni would never tell me her plans. No news is good news, if you know what I mean. I was ready to throw a party when she left. Such a relief to finally get her off my back.

Having her for an older sister hasn't exactly been fun and games. Toni has a righteous streak a mile wide. Never hesitates to let me know what a loser she thinks I am. Sure, it's fine and dandy for her to be a free-loving lesbo, gallivant out of state and whatever, but I never should have remarried, especially a guy younger than me. Since I don't have her education, her so-called sophisticated way of looking at things, everything I do is one big mistake.

I really don't have time to think about this mess. I'm getting ready for my shift in the maternity ward at St. John's, a few blocks from here. It's bad enough I'm probably going to be thinking about my damn sister all the way to the hospital. I'll never have a moment's peace when Toni's back.

Like when I was pregnant with Gabriela. Toni wanted me to consider all the options. Right. Maybe nothing else our parents taught me took, but there was no way I'd have an abortion. I dropped out of my first semester at Santa Monica College and married Jeff Brandon, Gabi's father.

He was a surfer hunk, living off his ritzy folks in Pacific Palisades. Jeff and I met at the beach. I'd saved up to buy a bikini—Mama and Daddy would've puked if they'd seen me in it. Jeff noticed me, though.

The marriage went nowhere. The Brandons weren't happy their number-one boy was a career surfer. To rub it in their noses even more, he had a brownie wife who couldn't pass muster with the country-club set. After a few years of waiting for Jeff to grow up, I got tired of that whole scene and wound up alone with my daughter, Gabi. Toni said I wasted myself by going into practical nursing instead of becoming an R.N. Like I had the money to support a kid *and* be in nursing school for years. The Brandons weren't going to help me. I did what made sense, and I'm not ashamed of that.

Now that I'm married to Zalo, Toni's panties are really twisted in a wad. Zalo grew up in a tough San Fernando Valley barrio. He still can't believe I have a dyke sister. He never lets me hear the end of it. He doesn't like Toni at all and sure doesn't keep it a secret. He thinks she's some kind of pervert. Hey, he has a right to his opinion. My parents were so damn understanding about Toni being gay. Figures. In their eyes she could do no wrong.

The way I see it the party's over. Toni's down on her luck. Why else would she be coming back to live with Mama? She can't exactly move in with that smartass Pat Ramos again. Things are like an ice age between them.

My sister really blew it this time, traipsing off with a white girl. When they were in grad school, it was always "Amanda this, Amanda that." Now Amanda's history too. What goes around comes around, huh? This time I think Toni got hers.

Part I

*[Her] professional opinion ran along the lines of
fault, and nobody saw things that way anymore, at
least she thought they didn't, and that anyway the
more she tried to figure where the fault lay the less she
understood what the question was.*
—From *Faultline*
by Sheila Ortiz Taylor

⤳ CHAPTER ONE ⤳

December 30: Morning
Toni

The black merlin flies bullet-fast through the twilight forest, undulating silently beyond outstretched fir branches. Its rapid flight frightens an unsuspecting flock of chestnut-backed chickadees in a scrawny cedar. The chickadees scatter in all directions. A young one lags. Crazed with fear it heads erratically toward the cabin's kitchen window, where I stand washing dishes. Mesmerized, I stare at the pell-mell approach of the merlin and the chickadee. The falcon's sharp talons grasp the chickadee at the same moment the two crash into the window.

I jerk awake, my heart beating as wildly as the captured chickadee's wings. Disoriented, I sit up, realizing I am on the train, not alone in Amanda's cabin. I push the plaid curtain aside. The damp window offers not a forest view but a dim glimpse of farmland broken by neat irrigation rows. The glowing hands of my watch read a few minutes past 6 in the morning. I rub my eyes, pull the coat over me, and recline again. I have a clear memory of the merlin's dark plumage, its deadly talons and lethal beak, the unfortunate chickadee strewn amid crushed fir needles.

Two months ago, alone in the autumn twilight, I had witnessed the merlin's actual attack. Only the cabin's window pane separated us. I screamed when the birds smashed into the glass. I remained motionless for several minutes, wondering if they were both stunned—or dead. At first I was too wary to check. When I heard no sounds, not even a rustle, I gathered my courage, threw on a jacket and sturdy work gloves, and crept through the back door.

Around the corner of the cabin, I found the birds silent and still, the chickadee surely dead, a flurry of tiny feathers surrounding it. The merlin lay on its side, talons curved, beak slightly open, its unblinking eyes gazing into nothingness. With the tip of my boot I lightly outlined its sleek body. I had never seen a falcon up close and could not wrench my eyes from its beauty. I shivered in the dampness. Backing away, I went to the shed to look for a shovel to bury the birds.

I was gone only a few moments. When I returned, little evidence of the birds or even their collision existed. A haphazard collection of chickadee feathers lay scattered, but not a trace of the merlin remained. Baffled, I leaned on the shovel and scanned the branches above. I neither saw nor heard anything. A chill ran through me. Could there be someone else in the woods, watching my every move, unnerving me by snatching away the birds' bodies? Leaving the shovel against a fir trunk, I ran to the cabin and locked the door.

"Excuse me." Toiletry bag in hand, I brush past passengers chatting by the narrow steps leading to the downstairs rest rooms. Other sleepy-eyed travelers wait in line next to the luggage area. Everyone looks as if they've gotten no sleep.

Yawning, I lean against a wall and adjust the collar of my wrinkled flannel shirt. I sway with the train's movements and try to read the posted Amtrak schedule. The Coast Starlight crossed the California border during the night. We are somewhere between Sacramento and Davis. Tonight I will be in my mother's house.

Shaking that thought aside I ponder my dream. This morning is not the first time that bird of prey has zoomed into my mind. According to Amanda the falcon is a totem. In dreams it instructs me to be agile and swift in capturing my needs and desires. I have a hard time believing in a bird that crashes into windows while pursuing prey. Amanda calls that attitude my "urban cynicism."

She constantly searches for hidden meanings and New Age interpretations for everyday events. To me, this smacks of some feminists' penchant for borrowing mystical concepts from Native American beliefs. While that can provoke fascinating discussions, I have grown up with Mama's "si Dios quiere" philosophy. Raised as a Chicana Catholic, I tend to adhere to my mother's advice: "If it's God's will, mija, it will happen." Even so, my own philosophy is a combination of "si Dios quiere" and logic. If two birds seem dead one minute and suddenly they are gone, I am more likely to believe someone took them away. Amanda, on the other hand, has no trouble accepting that the falcon was momentarily stunned; when it recovered it snatched the chickadee and flew away. While I was unfolding that afternoon's mystery, she studied me. "Did you find any footprints by the cabin?"

"Amanda, don't you get it? I freaked." Serving a hefty bowl of salad, I sat in the opposite pine chair. "Being alone in these woods can be very scary."

"I lived by myself before you came here, Toni." She

squeezed my hand to calm me. "If you feel better locking yourself in, that's fine. A better idea might be to walk into Fir View before dark. You could meet me at the library, and we could come home together."

"Finding a job would be the best answer," I muttered, dousing my salad with poppy-seed dressing. "I have too much time on my hands. There's nothing for me here, unless I want to clean cabins, waitress, or baby-sit." I met her gaze. "I'm bored."

"Oh, Toni. At the end of the month you can help with the library's used book sale." She popped a plump tomato into her smiling mouth. "What else is for dinner?"

Settled in my seat, I watch the rolling farmland. Red-winged blackbirds flutter through tall reeds at the edge of irrigation ditches. The dazzling scarlet patches on their wings brighten the gray skies—an otherwise dreary landscape.

At the Davis rail station, a stout woman with a ruddy face and pale braids forming a crown takes the empty seat next to me. She is the quintessential farm wife. With a grim expression she glances at the Marcos Loya cassette on my lap—the one where his bearded face and closed eyes evoke a Chicano Jesus—and doesn't utter a word to me.

I'm not on this train to make friends, although I had an amusing conversation in the dining car with an apparent dyke the night before. She was a butch ROTC instructor with a fervent interest in mystery novels, particularly those penned by women. When I told her I was an erstwhile librarian, she grew even more enthused about her favorite subject. She went on and on about her "partner" Norm's huge mystery collection. For good measure she threw in the names Forrest, Wilson, and Wings. The heterosexual couple at our table seemed oblivious to the innuendo in our conversation. We talked around them, never mentioning "the L word." Neither of them had a glimmer that *Norm* was the code word for *Norma*.

Martinez, Richmond, Emeryville, Oakland, San Jose: The California scenery changes from farmland to industrial to urban. The boarding passengers are different from those in Washington and Oregon. More Latinos and African-Americans, bound for Southern California, join us at each stop. I wonder if anyone will come with Gabi to Union Station.

Noon
Gabriela

"Why won't you come with me tonight?"

My boyfriend Phil picks up a fat inari roll and crams half of it into his mouth. He swallows most of it. Meanwhile he scopes the selection of sushi on his plate. He has habit of eating them in some weird ritualistic order: sashimi, California roll, inari, shrimp.

"You didn't answer me, Phil."

He gulps down the last bit of inari. "Maybe your grandma should go with you. If I show up, Toni might think I'm bein' a spy."

"Get real." I tap my chopsticks on the edge of the styrofoam rice bowl.

We're grabbing a bite at Eatz in the shopping mall. Screaming kids and loads of hungry after-Christmas shoppers squeeze around us. In a few minutes we're due back at the Warner Bros. store where we're having a Looney Tunes sale, but I want to settle this first.

"Look, I'd feel safer with you there, man. My grandma

wouldn't be any help if some cholo tries to jump us in the parking lot."

Phil laughs and pushes back his longish strands. His black hair is shaved on the sides and combed straight back on top. I cut it for him on Christmas Eve. We both like the way it looks. He's *fine,* my Phil, and just about as stubborn as me.

"What's so funny?" I act superannoyed. "That some cholo would take a grab at me?"

"Girl, you'd flip him over." Phil makes his fingers fly like little people across the table.

"You'd stomp on that sucker dude with your Timberlands and flatten his cojones."

We both giggle at that graphic image. I nudge him hard. "In other words you're not coming with me."

"Hey, Gabi." He props one long leg on the polished chair next to him. "It's your family business."

I narrow my eyes. "You have something else lined up?"

"I promised Veronica I'd help her wash her windows. She's having a spur-of-the-moment New Year's Eve party." He reaches into the front pocket of his jeans. "Before I forget, here's the invite for Toni."

I take the small envelope and move my chair closer. "Okay. You're off the hook this time. Is Pat invited?"

He leans over to curl a muscled brown arm around me. He eats sushi with his other hand.

"Why wouldn't she be? She's good friends with René. But like Veronica says, some of the people they've invited might already have plans."

I snatch the last of his shrimp. "Maybe you'll have to be my spy and find out for sure."

Pat

The Media OutReach for Equality is closed for the holidays, but I'm in the office anyhow. Might as well clean out my desk drawers and tidy the office to start off the new year. I have a friend who volunteers at the local lesbian archives. Now's as good a time as any to fill up a box or two of dyke-related press releases and old brochures for her.

I don't want to be home in case Gabi phones again. Trying to keep a Toni-free mind ain't easy. I couldn't sleep last night, thinking about her. Her fawn eyes weren't soft the last time I saw her. She wanted to be gone and didn't hide it. Wish I could forget all that, but the best thing to do is keep busy.

Around noon I'm making good progress when I hear a knock on the office door. I shrug it off. Holiday hours are posted outside. Today I'm not about to do any real work.

"Ramos, are you in there?" René Talamantes yells between knocks.

"Shit," I mutter. Can't shine *her* on. She's seen my Mazda out front. "Keep your damn chones on."

As soon as I unlock the door, Talamantes slides in, black eyes darting. "How come you're workin'?"

I eye her rangy body. She stands with one hand on her hip, endless legs apart in faded jeans and cinnamon-colored boots. Her shiny black hair falls over her royal-blue turtleneck.

"End-of-the-year clean-up." I lift one of the boxes to an empty chair. "Why'd you track me down?"

Her wide lips shift into an easy grin, the kind that captures everyone who sees it. "Ay, Pat. Don't be so defensive. Thought we could shoot the breeze about the Chicana activism documentary."

I'm skeptical. "You ought to be helping Veronica get ready for the party."

"Pues, I am," she insists. "On my way to Trader Joe's for blue corn chips, jugo y cervezas. Thought you might want to tag along."

I open another drawer and start removing file folders. "You just want to be sure I'm going to your party."

"Are you, mujer?" René squats beside me. "Mira, I'll run interference if Toni shows up. I promise, eh?"

On the carpet I spread the file folders and open the one on top. It's full of correspondence that might overlap into next year. I put it aside and go to the next one.

"You deaf, Ramos?"

I meet her steady gaze. "I'm not scared of Toni."

"Hell, I know that. She's the one who ought to be scared." René grabs a Hershey's kiss from the candy dish on my desk and unwraps it elaborately. "I've already told Veronica not to be surprised if Toni doesn't show. Pero, if she does—"

"René, I don't want to see her yet. Too soon."

"I disagree, mujer. Listen, you'll be among amigas, verdad? Say 'hi' to her and move on. You don't have to get into a pinche dialog."

I smile at that. "You make it sound so easy."

Chewing the candy she plops next to me on the floor. "Just tryin' to break it down: She threw you over, she's coming back. Sooner or later you have to deal with that."

I flip through the correspondence and put it in date order. "To be honest, I don't even know how I'll react—whether I'll cuss her out, throw my arms around her, or what."

"Ya lo se." René nods and reaches for another Hershey's. "The medium was the message."

"Huh?" I frown at her. Is she switching subjects on me?

"You know what type she went for. Toni got a bum deal from the library and went into a tailspin. She really needed consolation, mujer." She wraps her arms around herself to illustrate. "She went for warm and cuddly, one of those pillowy country dykes, not for your homegrown fiery activism. Toni couldn't have been happy in that hick town. Probably couldn't even buy tortillas in that there Mom 'n' Pop general store."

I glance up from shuffling papers. "How do you know?"

"Just guessin'." She unfolds herself in one motion and rises. "You comin' with me, Pat?"

"On one condition: Put these boxes in your van and take them to the archives next time you go. It'll save me a trip."

"No problem, esa." She hoists one box to her hip. "I'm showing a video there in January anyhow."

"I know." I stick several files in the drawer and shut it. Right now I need an amiga. Grabbing my jacket and keys, I follow René out.

Twilight
Sylvia

"Mama, I'm not going to the train station. You're the one who should," I whisper. I don't want Zalo to hear me. He's on the other side of the screen door. Mama caught me right when I came home from work.

"It'd be nice if we went as a family, mija," Mama says. She turns the hose on the hibiscus bush. She's disappointed by my answer. That's too damn bad.

"Mama, when are you going to realize Toni and I don't get along? She doesn't want to see me. She'll really be pissed when she finds out me and Zalo live next door. Did you tell her Doña Filomena died?"

"Pues, no." Mama squirts a trickle of water on the geraniums bordering my steps. "I never got around to it. Toni knows poor Filomena was very old. The duplex would have been for rent sooner or later."

I stick my hands in my sweater pockets. "The only good thing is that when Toni finds out we're neighbors, she'll move to her own place in no time."

"Don't be so mean, hija," Mama scolds. "Your sister's going through a bad time. Try to be nice to her, eh?"

"Tell *her* that," I mumble over my shoulder.

"What the fuck's going on out there?" Zalo comes out of the bathroom in striped boxers and a beat-up T-shirt that says SHIT HAPPENS. His thick arms and legs remind me of chorizos—hairy ones. He acts like it's summer all the time. I'm still shivering from standing outside with Mama. Maybe Zalo's hairiness keeps him warm.

"I was talking to my mother."

"About what?" He grabs the remote, zaps to ESPN, and raises the volume.

"If you turn that down, maybe you can hear me." I step closer. "My sister's due in tonight, remember?"

"Fuck her." He glares at me and slumps in front of the TV. "That sicko better stay outta my face. You hear me, Sylvia?"

"The feeling's mutual. Toni won't go out of her way to see you."

He makes a fast move and yanks me into his lap. Zalo hasn't taken a shower yet, and he has that sleepy, sexy smell to him. He rubs a big hand across my belly. He touches me like he owns me. After hearing squalling brats and cleaning baby shit in the nursery all day, I don't even mind if he's kind of rough. It feels damn good to have mi hombre show his want for me.

"When the kid's born I don't want her near it. Understand?"

"She doesn't even know I'm pregnant."

His groping hand forces apart the buttons of my white uniform. The screen door is open. I feel cold when Zalo's fingers spread into my panty hose. I hope Mama has gone inside.

"Does your dyke sister do it like this?" He breathes into my ear.

I shake my head away. I hate it when he talks like this. I've lost interest but don't say that. "Let's do this in bed, Zalo."

He grunts and pins me down. The screen door stays open.

Adela

Ay, Dios, whatever got into my head? Why did I rent the duplex to them? Sylvia hasn't been the same muchacha since she took up with ese Zalo malcriado. Gracias a Dios that Gabi went to live with her father. There's no telling what could have happened to her if she had lived with Sylvia and that pig Zalo.

I roll up the garden hose and leave it lying like a shiny snake, a coiled vibora, by the side of the house. I wish it was a snake. I would throw it at Zalo. Maybe it would bite him, kill him. Ay, Jesús, what am I saying? I have to remember to keep these awful thoughts to myself when Toni comes home. She can't stand Zalo either. Together we could dream up horrible fates for that useless one.

Inside, I kick off my chanclas. They're full of mud. No sense in tracking all that through la casa. On my way to the bedroom I hear the phone ring.

"Hello?"

"Hey, Grandma."

"Dónde estás, Gabi? Still at work?"

"I'll be leaving pretty soon. Do you want me to pick up anything for you?"

Ay, esa muchacha es una angelita. "Maybe some ice cream, eh? I made a pumpkin pie. You know how Toni loves that. She might be hungry when she gets home. Quien sabe if she'll have dinner on the train? I'll save some tamales for her. We can't eat too many ourselves, Gabi."

She laughs. "That's fine, Grandma."

"Your mother won't be coming with us."

Gabi sighs. "Didn't think she would. Wish you hadn't asked her."

"She's my daughter too, chula." I turn on the lamp beside the sofa and sit. "I don't like this feuding."

"Neither do I." Her voice sounds tired. "We should leave for Union Station around 7, OK? See you in a little while, Grandma."

"Bueno, mijita."

I hang up the phone. For a few minutes I sit in the quiet living room. Except for traffic outside, the chirping of Nopalito, my little parakeet, is the only sound. Soon my daughter will be home. I smile at that thought. After tonight I will hear her voice too en la casa, not just mine and Nopalito's. It will be good to have her to talk with. My older daughter, my first baby, will be here with me once more.

Ay, Dios mio, I have to start dinner. No time to cry. Gabriela is already on her way.

CHAPTER TWO

December 30: Night
Toni

The Coast Starlight speeds past the sprawling El Capitan campgrounds south of San Luis Obispo. While the ocean shimmers like a liquid aquamarine, a wave of homesickness encompasses me. How I have missed the immense California coast, its rocky reefs, its seaweed-decorated beaches. The afternoon sky reveals the Channel Islands in the distance. I have always taken these natural elements for granted. Being away from them has been more wrenching than I could have imagined.

In Santa Barbara the Amtrak's schedule is delayed by the evening rush hour. The rail tracks cross through the commercial State Street district, and the train halts to allow traffic to pass. We leave the city slowly and weave through the towering eucalyptus groves of Montecito.

A nonnative tree transplanted from Australia, the eucalyptus is plentiful in Southern California. It thrives there, tall and aromatic, yet dangerously flammable during dry seasons.

Like other aliens in the Golden State, it is both welcomed and reviled. Seeing all these eucalyptus trees proves I am almost home.

Daylight ebbs and a violet and magenta sunset replaces it, creating a kaleidoscope of colors reflected in the Pacific. The Coast Starlight winds by the seaside homes of Summerland, the seacliffs of Muscle Shoals, and inland into Ventura County.

The darkness brings another bout of insecurity, more ambivalence, much apprehension. What am I returning to? A bewildering year is ending. What will the next one bring?

I cross my arms and stare into the black night. I sold most of my possessions when I left California; I return now with bare necessities. I shipped a few boxes of books to my mother's house the day after Christmas. Will I bother to unpack them? I don't plan to stay with Mama long, but if finding a job proves difficult, I will have few options.

In Simi Valley the Coast Starlight glides to a side track to make way for a Metrolink commuter train. A lot has changed while I was away; I realize some people in distant suburbs actually ride the train to their workplaces in downtown Los Angeles. Simi is north of L.A.—in Ventura County—infamous for being the site of the first trial of the Los Angeles police officers who brutalized Rodney King. Beyond me in the night lie unfamiliar neighborhoods, white-populated enclaves whose residents don't know much about inner-city life and people of color. Have the long months since the second trial helped them to understand why the acquittals caused south-central Los Angeles to detonate?

Although I can't prove it, I was probably laid off because I was so outspoken after the L.A. riots. For the first time in my employment history, I began to lobby in earnest for community outreach, multicultural and bilingual library programs,

more books in languages other than English. My coworkers
were accustomed to my low-key approach of dealing with
racial-ethnic issues (such as a leading occasional bilingual
children's story hour). After the verdicts I could neither de-
emphasize the inequities of life people of color suffer nor
could I justify their continuance. I stopped keeping quiet.

Speaking up does not come naturally for me; I'm no born
activist like Pat Ramos. A librarian for most of my adult life,
I am accustomed to insisting on silence. When my sudden
transformation resulted in supervisors' and coworkers' dis-
trust and outright disagreement with my views, I eventually
found myself out of work. "Budgetary cutbacks" was
the official reason. I had been in line for the next supervisory
position in the reference section. With the layoff I lost my op-
portunity to advance. By then, of course, I only wanted
to flee.

The train meanders through a series of narrow tunnels in
the Santa Susana mountains. Some passengers get ready to
disembark at Glendale, the next stop. They gather duffel bags
and cram paperbacks and snacks into side pockets. Watching
them, I grow restless, impatient, and wary of facing my
family.

After Glendale time drags. I grab my knapsack and stick
the Walkman and cassettes in. I want the reunion over and
done with. Parallel to the concrete arroyo of the dissipated
Los Angeles river, the train travels sluggishly. It moves along
the edges of the Eastside, past wooded Elysian Park and
Dodger Stadium, toward the behemoth Los Angeles County-
USC Hospital and the county jail.

Glowing lights announce the Los Angeles Civic Center.
Next stop: Union Station. Rising, I sling my knapsack over
my shoulder and reach for the bigger bag overhead. Like the

other weary passengers, I stand in the aisle until the train halts. But unlike them I am full of dread, not anticipation.

Gabriela

Grandma's bundled in her navy wool coat. Her gray hair's fluffed over the thick collar. It reminds me of angel hair on a Christmas tree, but Grandma's is much softer. She seems so little and round on the wooden bench, almost like she's in church listening to one of Father Huerta's sermons. Only difference is she looks nervous tonight, all the time checking her watch on the huge overhead clock at Union Station.

This train depot has been in lots of movies. It has that "Spanish-style" architecture you see all over Beverly Hills and Santa Barbara. Too bad Los Angeles didn't stick to that same kind of building code. Spanish style might be phony and, like Toni says, "overly romanticized," but it looks pretty. Most buildings downtown seem like a crazy mishmash, thrown together like hundreds of Monopoly pieces scattered across the L.A. Basin.

Union Station inside has a real old-time feel—at least, the way I imagine old times were. I can picture Barbra Streisand in *The Way We Were* sweeping through those wide doors like Toni will in a few minutes. I'm trying to distract myself 'cause I'm as jumpy as Grandma.

"Want some gum, Grandma?"

"No, mija. You get some if you want."

"Do you want anything?"

She shakes her head. I walk away and turn to check her out once more. I think she's praying. Grandma has one hand in her coat pocket. She usually keeps a rosary in there. She has a faraway look like she gets when she's saying Hail Marys.

She's worried about what Toni will say when she finds out my Mom's living next door with that scumbag Zalo. Grandma's like everyone else in this family. We procrastinate about telling each other yucky news, then end up backing ourselves into corners and dealing with someone's anger, disappointment, disgust—you name it. Come to think of it, we probably all learned that goofy strategy from Grandma.

I'm positive I learned it from my mother; she must have gotten it from hers. Even Toni does it, which is why Pat is so pissed. If Phil split with my direct opposite, leaving me clueless, I'd be furious with him too.

Toni's really into wishful thinking if she expects Pat to meet her tonight. Sheesh, they need to take their time. They have a whole mess of talking to do. Who even knows if anything would come out of that?

I loved it when they were together. It was like having two zany aunts. I used to sleep over at their apartment a lot when I was little. They would read me stories and take me to the L.A. Zoo, Disneyland, Magic Mountain, Knott's Berry Farm. No matter what, Pat says she'll be my friend forever—and she has been. She helped me pick my fall semester classes. We've gotten even closer, I think, since Toni's been gone, and my mom doesn't like that. Sheesh, there's plenty I don't like about my mom. Like the way she acts so crazy over her ugly husband, for one thing.

In the little gift shop I buy some Wrigley's and twirl the postcard rack a couple of times before strolling back to Grandma. She's giving me the old-lady-versus-kid look when I walk up.

"Esos pantalones are tight, mijita."

"They're blue jeans, Grandma. If I wear 'em baggy, everyone'll think I'm in a gang."

Grandma gives me the once-over again. "Maybe I'm viejita, but there's nothing wrong with my eyes. Those pantalones
are too tight."

"You think that's why I've been standing up for the past
half hour?"

In spite of herself Grandma laughs. "Ay, muchacha. You
have an answer for everything."

I slide next to her on the bench. "I hope we'll both have
some answers for Toni tonight."

Adela

"Dios te salve, Maria, llena eres de gracia." My cold fingers grasp the rosary's glass beads and silent prayers fill my
head. I am glad Gabi has gone to the gift shop for a while.
Her pacing in front of me has made me even more jittery.
Instead of being anxious about Toni, I decide to pray or concentrate on memories.

Mi esposo Juan and I left for our honeymoon from Union
Station more than 40 years ago on our way to San Diego. Not
too long after that, I found out I was going to have my first
baby, la Toni. Ay, she reminds me so much of Juan it hurts.
Her quietness makes you wonder what she's thinking. Juan
was like that, but our daughter is much more complicated
than her father.

He and I cried together when she told us she is "una de las
otras," one of the others. Toni herself would rather use the
word *lesbian*. We thought we were to blame for the sadness this
brought to our family. When Toni was a teenager, we never insisted she have boyfriends. We knew she was a smart girl busy
with her studies and hoped someday she would meet someone
and marry. Instead, during her 20s, she was una soltera.

When Toni told us the truth about herself, it was already years after her college days with la Amanda. In between Amanda and Pat there were a couple of women Juan and I never met. Maybe they were people Toni knew at the library. She doesn't talk about them, only to say "they did not work out." She confided in us when she realized she was in love with Pat.

This Patricia—at first I was suspicious of her. Now I think of her as another daughter. All the time Toni was away, Pat would still come to see me, to be sure I was all right. She helped me put up the Christmas tree this year and last. Since her parents are with God and her brother Carlos is in San Diego, she considers me her family. Si, la Pat es muy buena gente. Too bad she stayed home tonight.

Y sabes que? She is one of the few I can talk to about la Sylvia. I don't like criticize Sylvia in front of Gabi. Sometimes I forget and say something I wish I hadn't. If Gabi asks me about it, fine. She is old enough to know. But most of the time I do not want to cause bad blood between my granddaughter and Sylvia.

Gabi and I sit together until a few minutes before 8 o'clock.

"Mijita, do you want to wait by the doors? So many people here. If we stay where we are, Toni might not see us."

Mi nieta springs up and takes my arm. "Be sure to tell me if you get tired standing, Grandma. The train might be a few minutes late."

By her quick movements I know she is worried like me. We don't know what to expect. Toni did not say much in her letters. When she decided to come home, she called Gabi.

We make our way to the row of doors at the far end of the station. In ten minutes, si Dios quiere, Toni will pass through them. After such a long time, we are ready to hug and kiss her, to welcome her home.

Toni

The Coast Starlight spills its passengers into the cavernous terminal at Union Station. While I haul my bags to follow the others, the wide corridor flanked by pale brick walls seems endless. A rush of chilly air hurtles through. Los Angeles in December can seem cold to its natives, but it's warm compared to where I have been.

Gabi is behind those faraway doors. I trudge toward them, pondering my deep-rooted kinship with my only niece. Since her infancy I have spent countless hours with her, taught her the alphabet and word identification, read her bedtime stories, and introduced her to the children's section of the library. I am old enough to be her mother, but I consider her both little sister and trusted friend. Often I wonder if I have tried to recreate my sibling relationship with Sylvia through her daughter. With Gabi there is no intense rivalry surfacing at unexpected moments, no smoldering resentments, no sudden betrayals. At times Gabi seems older than her years and, at others, the ready-to-laugh teenager she actually is. It seems incredible, but she is about to finish her first semester at Santa Monica College. At this moment I am quite aware of the 22-year age difference between us. My whole body aches with fatigue.

Directly before the double doors, the family walking in front of me separates. The African-American father has a drowsy toddler riding on his broad shoulders. He glances around to search for his wife and their lollygagging little boy. He waves to them and pushes the heavy wooden door wider to allow them easy passage. I take advantage of the momentary gap to slip through, the edge of one bag bumping against the scarred jamb.

After the dimness of the corridor, the train depot's lights seem glaring. I squint to get my bearings.

"Toni! Toni!" In her rush, Gabi almost collides with the father and sleepy toddler. "Oh, Toni, I'm so glad you're back."

My niece grabs me in such a hug that I nearly lose my footing. Tossing one bag to the linoleum floor, I keep the other slung over my shoulder as I squeeze her near. She is no longer gawky; in fact, her body feels womanly against me. It's startling, yet moving. She has really grown up while I was gone. My eyes well up with tears. I exhale slowly. I don't want to cry, not now.

Then I see Mama, standing on the sidelines, as if bashful about approaching. She, too, has changed; she's grayer and plumper, her black eyes shiny as marbles.

Rubbing Gabi's back once more, I let go of her. Mama's dark eyes do not leave mine. She blinks rapidly. When I lean toward her, we embrace without words, with silent tears. All our lives Mama and I have had our share of disagreements, but I have never been so relieved to see her, so touched by her affection.

"Ay, mija," she whispers at last. "You look tired." Mama steps back for a better appraisal.

At once I am conscious of my appearance. For convenience's sake I have coiled my waist-length hair into a single braid. My forehead is oily and so are the surrounding strands of hair that have become disarrayed. I look a mess. My plaid flannel shirt and faded jeans are wrinkled and travel-worn.

I wipe my eyes with the back of my hand. "I could really

use a shower. Being on the train for two days—"

"So that's what the funky smell is," Gabi teases. She lifts my bag. "Come on, Toni. Let's go home."

The small trunk of Mama's Ford Escort is crammed with a hoard of items: old clothes for the parish rummage sale, a complete set of loteria cards, papier-mâché angels, a tangled set of Christmas lights, a plastic bag of corn husks for tamales. I stuff myself and the luggage into the backseat. Mama sighs and sits in front, unwinding the shoulder harness and clicking it shut.

"It would have been nice if you had come home in time for Christmas." She half turns her gray head toward me.

"Mama, I wasn't much in a holiday mood." I gaze out the window at the orderly rows of cars in the parking lot, a fitting glimpse of downtown Los Angeles. Craving more rest, I yawn again. I doubt sleep will come soon.

Mama aims for a more direct tactic. "Did la Amanda treat you bad, mija?"

"No, Mama."

While her baffled eyes try to connect with mine, I do my best to avoid them.

Gabi hunkers behind the wheel and starts the car. No doubt she has plenty of her own questions. "How're you holding up, Toni?"

Another yawn answers for me. "Hardly slept on the train. Beautiful scenery, though."

"Reality check: You're back in the City of the Angels. Concrete, smog, and amplified noise await," Gabi retorts. In the rearview mirror she smiles with some irony. She is as curious as Mama, but she is biding her time.

Adela

She is in the backseat, pretending to be asleep. Once in a while I turn to stare at my older daughter. It looks like Toni gained some weight while she was living in those woods. This is good. Her face is rounder, and she has much more gray in her black hair. Ay, but I don't like it in that long braid. She looks like an immigrant who just crossed the border, instead of the librarian who used to work in the main branch on Sixth Street.

Mi hija has never cared much how she dresses. Being away has made her even worse. Pues, she was on the train, after all, but she looks muy reborujada. Maybe, like she says, all she needs is a hot bath. A good shampoo and a firm hairbrush would help too.

Toni likes to be mysterious. She's leaning against the seat with her eyes closed. She knows I have muchas preguntas about la Amanda and what happened. Toni's worried I'm going to ask a million questions tonight. For once I can read my daughter's mind. She thinks I won't give her a moment's peace. Eso no es la verdad. I can wait until tomorrow.

"Grandma, let her take a nap." Gabi nudges me. "She's beat."

"I'm only looking at her, mijita. You know, Gabi, when your mother and Toni were little, Juan and me would take them on vacation trips. He liked to travel at night so we wouldn't have to rent a motel until the next afternoon. The girls would fall asleep in the backseat, just like Toni's doing now. I would turn around and check mis muchachitas during the night. They were so pretty, so peaceful when they were sleeping."

Gabi giggles at that. "The only time they weren't at each other's throats, I bet."

"They didn't use to fight that much when they were little. That came later."

"During their moody teenage years."

"Ya lo se. It's true, Gabi. When Sylvia got interested in boys, trouble between them started."

"I can hear every word, Mama," Toni murmurs from the back seat. "I hoped I wouldn't have to hear about Sylvia tonight."

Gabi glances at me. She expects me to say something about where Sylvia is living these days. Ay, I know Toni won't take that well.

"What?" Toni sits up fast. She leans forward. Her cabeza is almost between Gabi and me. "What's that look about?"

"You'd better tell her, Grandma. She's going to find out anyway," Gaby whispers.

I offer a quick prayer to Saint Jude, patron of the impossible, before I face my suddenly wide-awake daughter.

"Toni, if you had phoned me instead of Gabi, I would have told you right away. But I didn't know where to get hold of you anymore, sabes? Then I phoned Amanda, and she said you had already gone. She was crying—"

"Amanda is not the issue, Mama. What about Sylvia?" Toni's black eyes bore into mine.

Por un momentito, I hesitate, then spill it out. "She's living next door, in the duplex."

Toni sucks in her breath. "With—"

"Si, with el Zalo cochino."

"Shit, shit, shit!" Toni pounds the back of Gabi's seat. My granddaughter almost flies forward. "Why? Don't tell me you evicted Doña Filomena to let them live there?"

"Doña Filomena died, Toni," Gabi murmurs. She keeps her eyes on the Santa Monica freeway traffic. "That stupid

Zalo, of course, doesn't have a job, so Grandma—"

"Ay, Mama! You're such an enabler!" Toni glares at me with a fierceness I've never seen before.

I am confused. " 'Enabler?' Que quiere decir 'enabler'?"

Gabi gives a quick answer before Toni can cut in. "Psychology talk, Grandma. An enabler is someone who lets things go on—like you letting my mom depend on you. Toni's right. Instead of encouraging her to stand on her own two feet, you keep helping her out of jams."

"And that's wrong?" I move my eyes from one to the other. "Sylvia's my daughter. Now you're criticizing me for helping her. If I don't help her out, who will?"

"Mama, you won't be around forever. Sooner or later Sylvia has to learn to take care of herself." Toni has an elbow on each knee, her legs spread apart. Blue jeans or not, I never allowed her to sit like that when she was una muchachita. So unladylike.

"Ay, your sister makes so many mistakes. Pobrecita." I want Toni to understand why my heart goes out to Sylvia. "Her judgment isn't always the best."

"Exactly. Don't you think she ought to learn to figure things out once in a while?" Toni shakes her head. "I can't believe I'll be living next door to them." She rubs her eyes and stares at the cars whizzing by in the next lane. "All the motivation I need to find a job and my own place in record time."

"Look, Toni—" I don't like that we are getting off to a bad start already. "I want you to feel at home, mija. Don't run off again, eh? Take your time deciding what you want to do. I won't let Sylvia bother you."

Toni looks very tired, but I don't think her anger has melted. "Mama, no matter what you say, being next door to them is going to bother me a lot."

Gabriela

This isn't turning out how Grandma wanted. I zoom along to Santa Monica, Toni sulks in the backseat, and Grandma stays real quiet. Good thing Phil didn't come with me. He'd be bouncing out of his skin by now because of all this family tension. I've gotta keep the conversation rolling.

"Last time I spent the night, Toni, I left some bubble bath at Grandma's. If you're in the mood for it—"

"Gabi, that'd be the ultimate luxury. Thanks." My aunt sounds grateful I've changed the subject. Hearing about my mom automatically makes her uptight. Can't say I blame her.

Toni's aware I'm watching her in the mirror. Once in a while she gives me a "what am I doing here?" smile. It's an expression I'm not used to from her. Toni seems sadder than I can ever remember.

"How's Phil?" Right now I can tell she'd rather talk to me about my boyfriend than deal with Grandma.

Her question loosens me up some. "He's fine. I wanted him to come with us tonight. He thought it'd be too much a family thing. He knew what he was talking about, huh?"

"In a way. Isn't he practically family, Gabi?" Toni kids.

"He's a buen muchacho," Grandma adds.

Neither of us would argue with Grandma about that. That gives me something to be happy about right now. It's great that Grandma and Toni both approve of Phil Melendez.

"Speaking of Phil, he asked me to give you this." I pull out the New Year's party invitation.

When Toni recognizes the handwriting on the tiny envelope, she hesitates before opening it. Seconds later she frowns. "Who told Veronica and René I'd be back?"

I gulp. "Well, I mentioned it to Phil and—"

"Ay, Toni." Grandma turns to look at her. "The boy is close to Veronica. Of course he told her you'd be home. You should be glad that friends care enough to invite you to a—"

"Pat will be there." Toni drops the invitation. "If I went, I'd make things awkward for everyone."

Grandma gets impatient. "Muchacha, you can't avoid everyone you know! Start seeing your amigas, eh? Make new ones if you have to. I don't know what happened in those woods, but I don't want to see your face so sad every day."

Toni knows better than to answer. She shuts her eyes and keeps quiet for the rest of the way to Grandma's house.

⭑ CHAPTER THREE ⭑

December 31: Morning
Toni

A monotonous hum wakes me, but I'm afraid to open my eyes to verify my surroundings. I lie still. Am I on the train? Did I simply dream I came home? I am stationary, not rocking with the ceaseless motion of the railway car. I smell coffee and the down-home aroma of freshly made tortillas de harina. If Mama is here, she is being unnaturally quiet.

I wonder if the continuous mechanical sound is the echo of the Santa Monica freeway a few blocks south. As if to test my speculation, the hum intensifies, falters, wheezes, and grows monotonous again. It is much too close to be the freeway. Eyes closed, I reach one hand behind me to feel the rough plaster of the bedroom wall. It's warm to the touch, and it vibrates. The hum must be coming from Mama's ancient refrigerator on the other side of the wall. Her duplex is noisy and creaky, unlike the unyielding silence of Amanda's cabin.

I snuggle within the fragrant scent of pink flannel sheets. Mama has made the extra bedroom cozy, tempting me to stay. When I turned in last night, I found a bouquet of daisies beside the bed, before the framed picture of Our Lady of Guadalupe. Little sachet packets lay in the dresser drawers, and cedar blocks are in the narrow closet. Mama has welcomed me into her home.

She has been lonely since my father's death. Realizing that, I try to understand why my sister Sylvia and her brute of a husband are living next door. No matter how much I rationalize Mama's circumstances, I still resent my sister's proximity. She must have manipulated Mama's emotions with a familiar tactic: a hard-luck story. At least I have heard nothing from Sylvia—yet.

Rolling my head on the pillow, I notice my hair is still damp. Last night, following Gabi's suggestion, I took a relaxing soak and shampooed and conditioned my hair, mostly to avoid arguing with Mama about Sylvia. Before I escaped to the bathroom, Gabi seemed eager to leave. She knew I was tired from the trip and promised to see me over the weekend. I half hoped she would offer me an alternate place to stay, but I didn't want to impose on her and her father. Jeff doesn't need to be reminded of Sylvia anyway.

I reluctantly get up. The tedious hours on the train and the fitful night's sleep have made my muscles tight. I am physically and emotionally taut. Maybe a brisk morning walk will unkink the knots and prepare me for the worrisome holiday weekend ahead.

Before leaving I down a cup of coffee and wrap an impromptu breakfast burrito in a paper towel. Mama left me a note; she is at Mass. I don't want to be here when she gets back. I need some time alone. Last night was very tense, and I am a bit remorseful. Even so, I'm determined to be self-protective.

I know I will see Pat if I go to Veronica's party. I have to think about whether I want to face her so soon. I can deal with Mama all weekend.

I walk along Arizona Avenue, a residential neighborhood wedged between bustling Wilshire Boulevard to the north and Santa Monica Boulevard, the westward link of legendary Route 66, to the south. Tiny bungalows nestle beside sprawling apartment complexes, some old homes unrecognizable after being gentrified into two-storied versions.

Arizona is a shady street, its shielding trees adding to the morning chill. In the Northwest, scrawny palms swaying next to Jeffrey pines and eucalyptus trees towering over prickly pear cactus would be an incongruous sight. Here they characterize the surprising scenery of Southern California, the infusion of nonnative plants a living metaphor of the multicultural human population of the region.

Finishing the savory burrito, I stride faster. In jeans and my Seattle Aquarium sweatshirt, I shiver, my hair too damp to offer warmth. Above a row of pines I spot the seventh-floor stained-glass windows of St. John's Hospital chapel. The serenity of the chapel is a familiar haven. I used to go there often to ponder, to meditate, to question my motivations and choices.

Next to the chapel stands the hospital auditorium where my parochial schoolmates and I attended annual Christmas parties. We did not realize, in our innocence, that the Catholic hospital administrators considered the Mexican-American student body "underprivileged." As kids we thrilled in those lavish parties, never suspecting the hospital's charity until Sylvia and I read a description of the annual event in the local newspaper.

In light of our shared history with St. John's, I wonder if Sylvia finds it ironic to work on its maternity floor. Does she remember the "underprivileged" label as she bottle-feeds and diapers the progeny of the Westside's elite? Is she on duty at this very moment? Scurrying past the hospital's gleaming white 1940s architecture, I continue west.

Lincoln Boulevard's traffic is deafening. This winter morning I find my hometown much noisier than I remember—such a contrast to the stillness of Amanda's woodsy acres. On the corner of Lincoln and Arizona, the Something Old/Something Nouveau antique shop squats as usual. Newer structures have sprouted elsewhere, while many less fortunate sights remain. When I passed Eleventh Street I noticed the "cat/car lady"—as Pat dubbed her—at her regular parking space. A thin blond, she lives with two beautifully groomed Persian cats in a beat-up Pontiac Bonneville. A few blocks beyond, familiar homeless men, protected from the cold by dirty sleeping bags and makeshift cardboard barriers, nap in doorways of commercial buildings. If I had no one left, no surviving family, no friends, would I be desperate enough to curl into one of those smelly corners? I shake off the chilling thought and move on.

Past the brown brick First Christian Church and the currently unoccupied telephone company, I dash across Sixth Street. My hometown appears schizoid, a dizzying combination of prosperity and homelessness, property development and failed dreams. Amidst these contradictions I remember why I felt hopeless enough to leave it.

Sylvia

I tiptoe around the bedroom and grab a white uniform from a wire hanger. I'm careful not to wake Zalo. He's sprawled on our bed, mouth half open, snoring so loud you'd think he's in some kind of contest. He looks like a hairy brown animal, like a hibernating bear, except he's smack dab in this teeny room instead of a cave.

The cracked dresser mirror shows the uniform pulled tight across my tits and hips. Creases stretch the white polyester to the seam's limits. I try to smooth out the wrinkles. No use. Zalo snores even louder, razzing me in his sleep. His beefy chest goes up and down with each snore. Being out of work makes him fat and flabby; he needs to exercise.

Mama's older brother, Tio Manuel, had a build like Zalo, burly but more muscular. He used to make the most delicious barbecue. Whenever someone in the family was getting married or baptizing a baby, Tio Manuel would dig a pit in his backyard in Mar Vista to prepare for the barbecue. Sometimes my Daddy and my cousins or uncles would chip in to help.

Usually Tio Manuel liked to work by himself. He would take off his khaki work shirt and lean against a shovel to plan his strategy. Then he would rub dirt between his palms, his huge, hairy arms rippling with muscles, before starting his work. His husky body developed an easy rhythm, bending to loosen the hard ground, swinging the shovel back, heaving dirt over his wide shoulders.

His white undershirt would get blotchy with sweat. He'd sing at the top of his lungs, bellowing "Pancho Lopez" to the tune of "The Ballad of Davy Crockett," until my Tia Luisa would run out of the house to tell him to pipe down. Tio Manuel would laugh and shut up for a while, drink half a can of Budweiser, and start digging and singing again, making up crazy lyrics. All of his kids and the cousins like Toni and me would sit in a circle and watch, cracking up at his version of the tune.

When the pit was deep enough, Tio Manuel would round us up. We'd climb into the back of his Chevy pickup and go with him to the meat market. Back home he would prepare the pig, wrap it in burlap with spices, and bury it in the pit. He would cook el marano over hot coals. Days later we'd have a delicious pork barbacoa for the boda or bautismo.

I coil my hair into a twist and stick bobby pins in it. Due for another dye job soon. Zalo keeps snorting in his sleep.

When I was little I imagined the pig Tio Manuel buried would come alive in the pit. It would wake up in that dark hole and wonder why it was underground, all hot and smoky. Furious at being trapped, it would groan in despair. Finally, after so many struggles, snorting and grunting, it would crash out of the pit, ready to find Tio Manuel and get even.

While I watch Zalo sleep, I replay that kid fantasy. Zalo makes a lot of noise, but sometimes it's muffled, like the grunts I imagined the buried pig to make. He sounds like that angry boar underground, trying to break free, plotting its revenge. I would never say this to his face. He doesn't like to hear any of my growing-up stories, about how happy things were when Daddy was alive. Zalo would rather hear me bitch about Gabriela or Toni. It makes me nervous as hell to know she's next door. I don't want Zalo and her to tangle. Toni could make trouble for him, and she would, just to spite me.

Speak of the devil. Right after I leave the house and go up Arizona Avenue to the hospital she comes strolling along, her black hair the only straight thing about her. She doesn't seem to recognize me. She's looking down, like she's counting the cracks in the sidewalk, the way we did as kids.

"Step on a crack, break your back," I call out. Might as well be sassy.

"Sylvia?" Toni squints in the pale morning sun. She seems caught off-guard, maybe wishing she'd gone down Wilshire Boulevard instead. "Do something to your hair? You look different."

"A henna rinse." I pat my head to show off the reddish highlights.

"That guy's probably given you plenty of gray to hide."

"*You* should talk."

She shrugs. "I'm not interested in hiding mine."

I'm next to her, in no mood to give her a welcome-home hug. She looks worn out. "So…you're back. What happened?"

"Didn't work out." She shrugs again, no way ready to give me the lowdown. She rubs a hand across her eyes. Maybe she's trying to cover up tears.

"The amazing Amanda turned out to be a dud, huh?"

"Sylvia, let's get one thing clear," Toni says. Her eyes have a glisten to them. "Stay out of my life, and I'll do the same for you. If I'd known you were living next to Mama, I would've stayed some place else." She starts moving past me.

"I'll tell *you* something."

She keeps walking like she doesn't give a damn about what I'm about to say. I talk faster before she gets out of earshot.

"You've always thought you were better than me, Toni. Well, you're nothing anymore. Nada. You don't have anyone. You don't even have a job."

She doesn't answer. Her head is down like she's counting the cracks again. She hurries to cross 23rd Street. I watch her go. I'm breathing hard, trying not to think how happy Mama and Gabi are to have Toni home.

Adela

Toni is quiet when she comes in the kitchen door. Maybe she has been crying, but I don't want to be snoopy. I was worried when I came home and she was gone. If she feels up to it, she will tell me where she went, what is bothering her.

Ay, it must be hard for her to be back after so long, to be forced to give up her independence and stay with me. Last night Gabi reminded me to give Toni "space." All these new-fangled ideas. I lived with mi mamá until I married. But la Toni—well, that's another story.

She goes to the coffeemaker and pours a cup. Toni drinks it black, like her father did. "I saw Sylvia," she says.

"Y qué paso?" I touch her shoulder, stroking her wild hair from her bent head.

"I walked all the way to Palisades Park and back. When I saw her near St. John's—" Toni's voice becomes shaky. She puts her cup down and stares at the freshly scrubbed sink. "She's gained so much weight, Mama. And her hair—she looks awful."

"Es verdad que no se mira bien," I agree.

Toni comes closer. Como una muchachita, she puts her arms around me. I hold her while she sobs. She is much taller than me, pero no le hace. Ay, these days there is so much sadness in this family.

Toni takes a quick breath. She inhales again to control herself. "I can't stay here, Mama. Sylvia looked at me with such disgust. It's hard for me to be near her too. Why did she turn on me? What did I ever do to her?"

"Nada, mijita. Ese hombre cochino wants to turn her against all of us. He wants to rule her mind, eh?"

"And she's letting him," Toni says, shaking her head. She steps back, closer to the sink. "Oh, Mama, I wish you hadn't let them move next door. How can you stand that?"

"Pues, Sylvia's my daughter. She needed a place to live. Both of you will always have a home with me."

I know she does not like to hear that. She sighs and picks up her coffee cup. She moves to the table. The Santa Monica *Evening Outlook* is folded there. Toni removes the rubber band from the newspaper. She stares at the front page for a few seconds. She is not really reading it. She drinks more coffee. Then she pages through to the classifieds.

"I have to find a job and be on my own. Any job—it doesn't even matter. I could work in a bookstore, verdad?"

"Ay, Toni. You have so much education."

She looks at me over the newspaper. "Nobody at the library cared about that when I got laid off, did they?"

Dios mio, I don't know what to say. She is bitter and sad. I wipe my hands on a dishcloth and open the refrigerator.

"Tienes hambre, hija?"

"Don't wait on me, Mama. Do you have any cereal?"

"Cornflakes."

"That's fine." She gets up to take the cereal from the pantry shelf. She pours some into a bowl and removes the milk carton from the refrigerator. Pushing the newspaper aside, she sits and begins to eat. "How about you, Mama?"

"I'll have coffee with you." I pour un poco and sit across from her. "Quieres un pan dulce?"

"That'd be great."

I cut one in half to share. For a few minutes we eat in silence. There is so much I want to ask but do not dare. Toni will tell me when she is ready.

She finishes the cereal. She refills her coffee cup and mine too. When she joins me again at the table, she lets her eyes find mine.

"She wanted a baby, Mama."

"Eh?"

"Amanda. She wanted a baby." Toni takes un poquito de café. "That's why I left. One of the reasons, anyway."

"No entiendo. She had a boyfriend? Y qué? You found out?"

Toni smiles, that funny sonrisa I have always loved. Her mouth takes on a crooked shape, and her pretty teeth wind up in the middle.

"Mama, you watch TV. You've heard of artificial insemination, verdad? No man involved. Amanda planned to go to a sperm bank to be inseminated. She expected me to raise the baby while she continued working at the library."

"She wanted to you be—like a nanny? Que barbaridad!"

"Yeah, that's what I thought too." Toni traces the letters KCET on the coffee mug. It is from the public TV station. I kept it when she went away. "I always figured Amanda and I could have an equal partnership. She seemed to love me as I am. She never said anything about wanting to change me. She never mentioned wanting a baby until months after I moved in. I kept complaining about being bored, Mama, about not having a job. She came up with the 'perfect' answer: She would have a baby, and I would devote myself to raising her child."

"Ay, Toni." I reach across the table to pat her hand.

Confused by what she has confided, I do not want to say much, too afraid of hurting her feelings. I am a simple woman. Most of the time I do not understand her deepest thoughts and beliefs. I raised her one way, and she became something I know nothing about. This artificial way of getting pregnant—que barbaridad! If lesbians don't want men, why do they want babies? No comprendo. Pero I have never heard Toni say she does not like niños. I know she loves her niece Gabi. I think she feels la Amanda fooled her. Yo no se. I decide not to question whatever she tells me. What matters is she has trusted me enough to tell me something.

I hold her hand across the table. She cries again. Murmuring to her, I do not have the heart to tell her a baby will be en la familia soon. I think Sylvia is pregnant.

December 31: Night
Toni

On Amherst Avenue I park Mama's Escort. I do not leave it, as if immersing myself in the surrounding neighborhood before stepping out. Like everything else I have seen on the Westside today, this street has changed. An identical batch of townhouses nudges unfamiliar condominiums. The Spanish-style apartment building where Veronica and René live is one of the few originals remaining on this block near Santa Monica's eastern border. Pat's car is nowhere in sight. Maybe she has made plans for tonight, perhaps a New Year's Eve date with a new lover.

On the last night of the year I am by myself on a dark street. With a sigh, I contemplate whether to catch a late film in one of the Promenade's movie houses instead. Would I rather be alone among strangers or among erstwhile friends? After some minutes of indecisiveness, I grab the plastic bag with its bottle of merlot and slowly leave the car. Coming home means retracing footsteps. Might as well skitter across the dance floor and face the music.

Treading the damp lawn, I am very unsure of myself. Tonight most of the guests will be mujeres who no doubt side with Pat. I am persona non grata in this crowd. My friendship with Veronica—combined with a dose of curiosity—has prompted me to come to her party.

On the second-floor landing I find the screen door unlocked. Tish Hinojosa's gentle soprano floats from the stereo in the corner of one bookcase. A hair dryer buzzes elsewhere in the two-bedroom apartment. Hesitating, I ring the doorbell instead of barging in.

Veronica's curly head peers around the corner of the kitchen. "Hey, mujer," she exclaims. She swings open the screen door and throws her arms around me.

Standing back, I admire her. "You look wonderful," I whisper.

Veronica Melendez is no longer the shy teenager lingering by the library reference desk for a chance to chat. Her morena face is flushed, and I know her sudden color is due more to pleasure than to the reflection of her open-necked fuschia silk outfit.

"Because I'm thrilled to see you, Toni. Please, come in."

I hand her the merlot.

"Gracias."

"Looks like I'm the first guest."

She nods with a smile. "Gives us a chance to talk alone."

Veronica leads the way into the tiny kitchen. She lifts the Crock-Pot lid and stirs the simmering beans. "René's in the shower. She had her hair cut today—spikier than I like it. She's trying to fix the damage. The shower goes off, the hair dryer goes on. Un poco de silencio, and the cycle starts over." She laughs. "Surprised we're still together?"

"Not at all, Veronica. You two blend."

She replaces the lid, setting the ladle on the tiled counter. "René's writing a screenplay, plus working freelance—studio jobs, public-TV stints—and wrapping up her Chicana activist documentary."

"I've never understood where René gets her energy."

"She exhausts me," Veronica admits. Adjusting the flame of one burner on the narrow stove, she adds a bit of water to the spicy arroz con pollo. The aroma is delectable.

"You're a dynamo yourself, Veronica."

She gives a modest shrug.

"Have you finished your novel?"

Disappointment fills her eyes. "No time for it, Toni. To get tenure at Loyola Marymount University, I have to concentrate on publishing research first."

"Is your dissertation published?" I recognize the irony of an ex-librarian having to be informed of an assistant professor's publication history.

She frowns, perhaps agitated by my question. "Not yet. The dissertation gave me the basis for an in-depth analysis of Chicana literature. I have a book contract for that, and I've been working on revising the manuscript. It concentrates on the work of urban Chicana writers. My novel will have to wait."

I sense her conflicting feelings about the postponement of her creativity, but I understand the motivations behind her decision: She needs job stability in an ever-changing academic employment market.

For several moments Veronica is silent. "Let's talk about you," she suggests. "You're being noncommittal, Toni."

My chuckle is bemused. "It took 18 months for this hard-headed woman to discover that life in the woods wasn't what it seemed."

"Sounds like a line from *Twin Peaks*," she says softly. "I'm sorry."

"Me too."

Neither of us speak for an awkward moment. The hair dryer's buzz fizzles. The bathroom door opens. My tension increases.

"Remember Pat is one of René's best amigas," Veronica advises. "Don't let her pounce on you."

"Preciosa—" we hear René call in exasperation. "This damn cabello isn't falling right. I look like Woody Woodpecker."

Veronica's dark eyes glint. "Let me take a look, René." She gestures for me to stay where I am as she leaves the kitchen.

While she is gone I am tempted to sneak from the apartment and slither back to Mama's. Am I a masochist? Do I think no one will question my abrupt breakup with Pat and my subsequent return? Not everyone will be as simpática as Veronica. Of this particular group of friends, she is the least judgmental because she has known me the longest.

Before I have time to formulate a plan, René Talamantes strides into the kitchen, clad in black except for a silver-and-red embroidered vest. Her ebony hair is shiny with mousse, tufted like a modern-day version of an Azteca.

"Stumbled out of the Cascades, huh?" she jokes, eyeing me. "Hijole, Toni. Que pasó, eh? Must have been a rough life. You have more gray hair than mi mamá."

"Ay, René," Veronica murmurs at her lover's candor. "What a way to welcome Toni."

I laugh in spite of myself. René's greeting is less antagonistic than anticipated. "You've forgotten I'm 40. Last time you saw me was two birthdays ago."

"Middle-aged spread y todo." René studies me. "Elastic waistband too? Pat's gonna gloat."

At that I flinch.

"René, stop it," Veronica snaps. "There is no need to be rude."

"I'd better go." Though I feel the sting of tears, I refuse to cry in front of René.

She looks me in the eye as I begin to pass her. "Look, Toni, I don't want to see Pat hurt anymore, entiendes? It's New Year's Eve, end of el año viejo. People get sentimental and all that shit. Have some respect for her, eh?"

"Do you think I came to taunt her?" I face René, anger replacing sensitivity. "She's much safer here than I am. You're making that very clear."

"Listen," Veronica begins.

The abrupt opening of the screen door interrupts her. A group of women whooshes in at once, some familiar, some not.

Michi Yamada, Marti Villanueva, Alicia Orozco, and many others tumble toward us, chattering all the while, offering dozens of champagne bottles and numerous trays of desserts. Behind them is the one I have been dreading—and longing—to see.

In the doorway, slim and slinky in a cobalt-blue shirt, black jeans, jet hair shorter than she's ever worn it, Pat Ramos remains alone. Her gaze is unwavering. All I can do is stare.

Pat

Toni's in one of those loose Pier 1 Imports–type outfits, a multicolored thingy. It would've hung on her when she was skinny. I always associate that kind of getup with aging flower children. With her cabello negro parted in the middle, graying at the sides, that's what she looks like. Except she isn't a '60s throwback; she's la mujer I've loved for over ten years, la Chicana who threw me over for a country dyke. Now, Toni seems trapped against the kitchen wall. Serves her damn right.

The more I look at her, the sicker I feel. Bile shoots up my throat, hot and bitter. I push Michi out of the way and make a beeline for el escusado. I barely have time to lock the door before I upchuck my late lunch of a cheeseburger and fries. After a few dizzy, disgusting moments, I lean on my haunches and take lots of deep breaths.

"Carnala, let me in," René insists at the door.

"Not unless you want to get sick too," I mutter. "I need some 7 Up."

"Be right back."

René's true to her word. Seconds later I crack the door when I've flushed the toilet. She elbows her way in and hands me the can of fizz.

First René shuts the door. Then she leans across the bathtub to crank the louvered windows all the way. Cool air wafts in, scented by night-blooming jasmine.

"Pat, Veronica's trying to talk her into staying. Myself, I think Toni's a goner. You OK, mujer?"

"Humiliated more than anything," I murmur. The soda slides down my throat. Taking off my shirt I hang it on the doorknob. I splash cold water on my face.

"Sexy bra," René teases, one eyebrow raised.

"Shut up."

"Just tryin' to make you feel better, esa."

I dab myself with a towel and close the toilet seat. Plopping on it I take more deep breaths and chug the 7 Up. "Staying home would've worked."

René sighs. "Mira, machita, you love her so much she makes you sick."

"Don't repeat that, OK?"

"You have my word, loca."

"Is my shirt messed up?"

She glances at it, holds out one edge. "It's suave. Pat, take it easy. You're so pale you're liable to turn white."

"Ni modo."

We both laugh at that.

"Your sense of humor's intact, anyway." She eyes me. "Know something? You're a fine lookin' mujer. Toni looks so old now—like she's been gone ten years instead of almost two."

"You're exaggerating, René. When she left, she already had some gray hair," I remind her. "Toni's put on a little weight, that's all. She's tall enough to carry it. Damn it, I still think she's beautiful. Why do you think I feel so shitty?"

"She did you wrong. Big time. Get that through your thick cabeza." René is exasperated. She points to the 7 Up, urging me to drink more.

I press the cold can against my face. I seem to be reviving a bit. Doesn't matter. I'm ready to bolt.

René reads my mind. "Pat, I'm worried about you. Stick around so I can keep watch."

"Yeah, sure. What's the point? What's to celebrate? Lost my lover, lost my appetite. Mexican food's too much for my stomach right now."

"There's menudo in the fridge. I'll warm some. That'll do the trick."

"I'd rather split."

"Don't let her win," René urges.

I avoid her piercing eyes. "Go. I have to pee."

Toni

Veronica follows me to the second-floor landing. I am about to rush downstairs when she reaches for my arm.

"Toni, please. It's only an hour till midnight. How can you fly out of a New Year's party?"

I shake her fingers off my shoulder, but she presses them there again. Turning around I meet her concerned brown eyes. "I've made her miserable, Veronica. Can't you see? I care too much to hurt Pat all over again. I never should have come."

With a sigh Veronica puts her other hand on my right shoulder. "Toni, I asked you because you're my friend. Knowing what you had to face, it must've been extremely difficult for you, but you have as much a right to be at our party as Pat does."

Evading her candid eyes, I slump.

Veronica is not easily dissuaded. She tries another tack. "Remember when I used to hang around the reference desk? I was so proud to know Toni Dorado, that brainy Chicana librarian. I still am."

With a moan I lean against the rough stucco wall. "Did you see how she looked at me, Veronica? How can I go back in?"

"I guess Pat didn't expect to see you tonight—or at least not right away. Personally I think it's better being among friends." Veronica squeezes my shoulders. "Come on, Toni. Don't make me beg. Can't you even take a hint, mujer? I need your help in the kitchen."

For a few seconds I avert my gaze. "All right," I say quietly. "I'll stay till midnight."

Someone has dimmed the lights. Melissa Etheridge blares from the stereo. Veronica blazes a path through the throng of dancing mujeres. I don't see Pat anywhere.

⌐ CHAPTER FOUR ⌐

December 31: Almost Midnight
Toni

Half an hour passes. In the tiny kitchen I serve mounds of frijoles, warm tortillas de maíz, simmering arroz con pollo. Veronica scoops up each plateful and rushes to serve her guests. I am somewhat grateful to her for keeping me occupied and out of sight. Soon I won't be able to postpone facing everyone else.

René shows up to prepare the plastic champagne glasses for the New Year's toast. Affixing the halves of each glass together, she keeps a running commentary.

"Híjole, wouldn't be a real Chicana party without some mitote goin' on, huh, Toni? Pat's barfin' her brains out, and you're in here makin' like everybody's mamá. Ought to get out my camera and document the whole damn night. Might turn out to be a new segment of my Chicana activist film."

As I serve another heaping plateful, I blow a strand off my forehead. "Is Pat all right?"

"Más o menos. Guess you still have an effect on her—not

exactly a positive one." René's brown hands move deftly, setting the plastic glasses on a woven tray.

"I'm not planning to stay long," I mumble.

"Long enough to say something to her, I hope," she counters in no uncertain terms. "It'd be damn anticlimactic if you sashayed out without some kind of plática."

"I don't want to ignore her, René, but I'm worried about her reaction."

"You ought to be."

Veronica returns for another plate. She glances at us warily, gauging the kitchen's emotional barometer.

"No te apures, preciosa," René murmurs, kissing her lover tenderly on the cheek. "I'm behavin' myself so far. Has Pat shown her face yet?"

"She's on the sofa. She said you promised her menudo."

"I'll get it for her," I offer on impulse.

René's ojos de india scan me. "There's a bowlful in the fridge. Don't make it too hot. And watch your step, Toni."

Turning my back I open the refrigerator and busy myself with heating the menudo for Pat.

After René leaves with the trayful of glasses, Veronica approaches. She sets a stoneware bowl and a tablespoon on the counter. "How are you doing, Toni?"

I shrug. "I'm edgy. René's right, though. Wouldn't be fair to leave without some sort of exchange." I pour the steaming menudo into the bowl. "Veronica, I've never stopped loving Pat. I only needed to go away—from here, from everything."

Veronica sighs. "She hasn't been able to understand that."

"I know."

Veronica touches my arm. For a moment I lean against her. Sorrow and grief have molded her into a caring mujer, willing to listen and not judge.

She takes a deep breath. Her voice is barely audible above the rock beat pulsating from the living room. "Maybe what will matter most to Pat is you've returned—alone."

With a reflexive smile I raise my eyes to her steady brown ones. Picking up the bowl of menudo, I rejoin the party with more resolve than I arrived with.

Pat

"Sure is weird havin' a party without the Latin Satins," Michi Yamada says with a wistful smile. "I'm so used to hearing their new material whenever we all get together."

"Girl, where've you been? The Satins went to San Francisco," Marti Villanueva reminds her. "A paying gig at a dyke bar for the holidays. Shit, I miss 'em too."

"Chic would be hittin' on everyone by now," Michi adds with a laugh. "The bedroom door would be shut. We'd be checking to see who was going in and out."

"Kind of boring without Chic, huh?" Marti agrees.

"Ay, don't let René hear you say that," Alicia Orozco cuts in. "She thinks she's the life of the party."

The chismes y locura, the gossip and craziness, goes on all around me. Light-headed, I'm wondering if I ought to pack up and leave. Not exactly in the partying mood after that bathroom scene. I sip the 7 Up and once in a while turn my head to belch. The stereo's cranked so damn high no one notices my bad manners.

Michi jumps up when a cute Latina I've never seen before asks her to dance. Alicia and Marti snuggle on the other end of the sofa, away from me. Do I reek of vomit? I feel like the local pariah, the loneliest dyke in town. Ex-lover's in the kitchen, and everyone knows it.

I turn my head to sneak another belch. That's when I spot Toni again. She's carrying a giant bowl of menudo. Her cabello negro swings with that easy stride I love to watch. She makes a tantalizing picture, like a slow-motion fantasy. The aromatic cloud of steam wafts around her face like phony cinematic vapor. She seems like a 20th-century Mary Magdalene, for Christ's sake: Chicana-style, tu sábes, with thick black hair, glowing brown skin, flowing Pier 1 outfit. That pinche René. No matter what she said earlier, I can see her conjuring this up. Hope she's not behind me videotaping the whole damn scene.

Every mujer in the packed room gapes at us, but Toni seems oblivious. She keeps her glimmering eyes on mine. In one graceful movida, she kneels in front of me and offers the bowl of menudo. I take it with shaky hands, careful not to spill any on my shirt. For a crazy second I wonder if she really is doing the Mary Magdalene routine. Will she bathe my suede boots with her tears and wipe them with her cabello negro? Even if she does, will I forgive her?

"I'm sorry you don't feel well," she murmurs instead. Her fawn eyes, full of apologies, rip my heart to shreds. I feel dizzy again. She helps me steady the bowl and hands me a spoon and a paper napkin.

Selena's "Amor Prohibido" plays so loud I almost have to read Toni's lips. It seems safer to focus on her mouth instead of her eyes. Sure don't want her to see how wet mine are. Alicia and Marti must've drifted off to dance because Toni moves beside me on the sofa.

"I'll hold the bowl," she mouths. "Don't rush, Pat. Eat slow."

For some reason, I listen to her. I have to concentrate on

sipping the menudo. My mind whirls, trying to make sense of this. Toni skedaddled 18 months ago with a white ex-lover who conveniently popped into her life. Now she's back. Does this maricona loca think I've been in suspended animation all that time? Can't she see the emotional chingadera I've been in? Adjusting to being alone after ten years with her has been the ultimate killer.

I keep my eyes down, not wanting to see her in entirety. Even staring at her gentle hands steadying the bowl is almost more than I can take. Those same brown fingers once turned me on, caressed me through the night, made me wet for her—and finally pushed me away.

The menudo glides down my throat. With its healing powers, it starts to soothe my queasy stomach. The hominy puffs floating in the broth dissolve in my mouth. Will my resentments melt as easily?

Toni doesn't talk, but her tenderness is unmistakable. Why can't she be cool, distant, staying as far away as she can? I want to scream and yell at her, curse her for abandoning me. How can I do that while she's being downright docile? Is she on her best behavior because of where we are? What would it have been like to bump into her on the Promenade, in a coffeehouse, in a dyke bar?

I don't want to make a scene, not in this crowd. So I agree to play this temporary game, whatever it is. How long can I keep my cool? Shit, I have to be honest with myself, conflicts or not. Damn it all to hell. I *love* esta mujer.

Toni

I study Pat's firm jawline. Her tension is evident. She keeps herself reined in, yet her acquiescence surprises me. I had expected her to back away, to refuse any close contact. The pale tinge of her ordinarily mocha skin confirms her queasiness, her nausea. Maybe I have taken advantage of that to come near her. I would have been foolish to do otherwise.

Her brushlike eyelashes, foreign to curl, jut over her lids, hiding her eyes. I let my gaze roam over her, admiring her prominent cheekbones, her aquiline nose, those thin but expressive lips. Slicked behind her ears her black hair, without a trace of gray, has an unruly forelock overhanging her brow. Que grapa la Pat. How could I have ever left her for Amanda Wyler? That question will haunt me forever.

"I'm finished." At last she raises her eyes. They seem bewildered, pained, yet direct.

"Do you feel any better, Pat?"

Not answering, she surrenders the bowl. I place it on the carpet next to my feet. Our eyes meet again.

"Why are you back in town?"

My voice catches. She is right to the point, as usual. I don't want to lose my composure, and I don't want to shout over Selena's exuberant voice, but I do want Pat to hear what I say. Carefully, I enunciate each word. "Because everything is here."

The music stops. René and Veronica distribute the plastic champagne glasses. Foil-wrapped bottles appear, corks pop in all directions. Laughter erupts in corners. Michi begins the countdown to midnight. Everyone joins in, a joyous welcome to the new year.

Mujeres grab each other, kissing and hugging. I smile at Pat. Feeling impetuous, I begin to lean toward her.

"Don't," she warns. Her voice is clear and firm, her eyes ferocious.

Someone taps me on the shoulder. I find myself wrapped

in Veronica's arms. When she releases me I glance around. Pat is gone.

Midnight
Pat

No way am I about to give in to that bullshit año nuevo sentimentality. I make a fast getaway. At the foot of the apartment stairway, I feel shaky, head and stomach out of whack. The brisk January air helps clear my head. Shit, what a time to forget where I parked my car. I take out my keys and hope for the best.

Halfway up the block I figure my bearings are cockeyed. I head back the other way. By then Toni stands by her mother's Escort, watching me with a quizzical expression. She thinks she's totally discombobulated me. Damn it, she's right.

"What's so funny?" I frown, about to pass her.

"Nothing. Want a ride to your car?"

"No."

"Pat, we need to talk." She studies me. "Sometime."

I stop in my tracks. "No way. You'll have me puking again. I have to get home."

"Oh. Well, I…"

Part of me wants to cuss her out, the other wants to squeeze her close. "What?"

"When and where can we talk?" Her voice has a quiver in it.

I'm wary. I jangle my car keys. She almost shimmers in the midnight mist, backlit by the pinkish tinge of the condominium lamps across the street. Why does she have to look like that right now? Fuck, I wish I could walk away and forget this bullshit. I don't want to do anything I'll regret either.

"Somewhere in neutral territory," I hear myself suggest. What was in that menudo, anyway? A behavior modifier?

Her laughter is a tension releaser. "Isn't that a line from *West Side Story?*"

I shrug. "The '90s version, California Chicana-dyke style. Life on the Westside, trying to keep sane in the middle of the class struggle, the race war."

"I suppose," she admits. "Listen, I'm staying with my mother—for the time being."

"Gabi told me. I don't want to go there."

"No privacy."

"For one thing, yeah. You know how Adela is. She'll have us back together in no time—in her head, anyway." I can't resist that dig.

Toni averts her gaze and says nothing.

"Tell you what." My head tells me one thing, but my mouth does another. "I'll meet you at the beach tomorrow morning at 10."

She stares, probably convinced I've totally lost it. For a moment her hesitation throws me off.

"Come on, Toni. Who's going to be on the beach New Year's morning? We'll have the place to ourselves, verdad? Plenty of privacy."

Our old passive-aggressive patterns have taken over. One would push, then the other till someone finally gave in. I have to admit she would usually relent, just like she does now. "That makes sense...I guess. Arizona Avenue Bridge?"

I nod and start to move.

"Hasta luego, Pat. Hope you feel better by then."

"If not, I'll phone. Be sure you answer," I call over my shoulder.

Locked in my car, I'm sweating and feeling chills at the same time. Tears smear my face. At any second I'm liable to start bawling. I'm still dizzy. Why the hell did I agree to see her? I won't get any sleep tonight. When 10 o'clock rolls by, I'll really look like shit.

Adela

I must have fallen asleep during the New Year's Eve broadcast from Times Square en Nueva York. After las muchachas grew up and left home, Juan and I made a habit of turning on that program at the end of every year. Our own tradition, but it used to be better when Guy Lombardo was alive. After the bandleader died and those younger ones took over the New Year's celebration, the show did not seem the same.

A few years after that, Juan was gone too. Now nothing is the same for me. Still, I find myself tuning in to see the happy crowds in snowy Times Square. I remember how we would sit on the sofa, besando at midnight like newlyweds. This year I must have dozed off during a commercial.

"Mama, it's late," Toni whispers when she kisses my forehead.

Almost expecting to see her father, I open my eyes quickly. Ay, her eyes are so much like Juan's, oscuros, speaking more than words.

"Que hora es?" I am embarrassed to be found in the easy chair, prayer book in my lap. During commercials I read some prayers. Tonight I must have been too sleepy.

"Past 12:30." She smiles and caresses my cheek. "Happy New Year, Mama."

"Feliz año nuevo, mija." I reach to kiss her. "Estoy muy

feliz because you're home, Toni."

"At least someone is," she murmurs. She turns off the TV.
"Eh?"

She tosses her long hair over her shoulder and squats beside my chair. "No one at the party—except Veronica—
seemed very happy to see me."

"Y la Pat?"

"Well, she threw up," Toni says in a low voice.

"Ay, Dios! Pobrecita."

"I suppose I should've expected that."

"Her heart was broken, mija." I lean over to raise her chin.
"Did you talk with her?"

"Hardly. Pat has her guard up." Toni's eyes blink as she
tries to hide her tears. "I still love her, Mama. What an idiot I
was to leave."

It hurts me when Toni is being hard on herself. "You had
your reasons, eh? She was one of them, verdad?"

She sighs. Before she gets up, she pats my knee. "What
time are you going to Mass tomorrow? Early?"

"Sí. I want to watch the Rose Parade when I come back."

"I'll have breakfast ready for you, Mama," she says, helping
me up. "We'll watch the parade together, OK? Last year I felt
so homesick, and Amanda doesn't even have a TV. Can't believe I was actually nostalgic for the silly Pasadena Rose
Parade."

That makes me smile. "Ay, Toni. Remember all the times
your father and I took you and Sylvia to see it? All those
beautiful floats. Ay, all the colors and the flowers."

Toni winces. Is she thinking about how different our family is now? Her father is gone. Next door or not, so is
Sylvia.

The Hours Before Dawn
Toni

Amanda believed herself an expert on animal and insect totems. Raised in the Pacific Northwest—and a librarian to boot—she acquired some of this knowledge by necessity. That did not permit her, however, to shower anyone—particularly me—with her so-called interpretation of encounters with certain animals or insects.

These quirky thoughts ramble through my head as I try to fall asleep. The wait until 10 o'clock seems endless. While I don't want to think about Amanda, of all people, on this New Year's morning, I can't help imagining what she would say about the plump spider presently suspended in the far corner of the bedroom ceiling.

"Spiders are creators, Toni," I can hear her advise me. "They weave illusions. They also determine your fate. They teach you to balance your past with your present. Do you feel caught in a web of your own making? Are you trying to break free? Are you becoming scattered in the process? A spider totem encourages you to recognize your life patterns and reflect on them before you're ensnared for good."

"Shut up," I say aloud.

Rolling over I bury my head beneath the pillow, blotting out the memory of her breathy voice. For long moments I inhale, exhale, hoping to make myself drowsy, while worrying about the black arachnid dangling above.

I have always been squeamish about spiders. As a child I would scream if I found a daddy longlegs in the bathtub or a tiny one hovering over the kitchen sink. Years after moving out of my parents' home, I would sometimes phone my father and beg him to rescue me from a trespassing spider. Daddy would always indulge me by coming over, teasing me as if I were still that scared muchachita. Abashed, I would offer him a cerveza, a snack, anything to make his visit seem less impromptu. In retrospect, I realize we had our best conversations during those times alone, undistracted by anyone else in the family. We called them our "spider talks." I miss them.

When Pat and I lived together, she became the spider catcher extraordinaire. At first she would kill them, smash them with her boot or squash them against the wall. When I protested such violence, she good-naturedly became adept at snaring them in a plastic cup and dumping them into the ivy outside. She would tickle me with the ends of my coarse hair, whispering that a black widow was after me. We'd giggle and wind up making love.

Tonight she would not have caught a spider for me. No, tonight Pat probably would have liked to smash *me* against a wall or squash *me* under her boot. She held herself in check admirably. I know those signs of self-control all too well: her attempts to joke, her sarcasm. No matter how she restrained herself, I know I made her sick, made her stomach churn. I caused her mouth and throat to fill with bitterness, the sour taste of indelible memories.

My body contracts, muscles tighten at those candid thoughts, those harsh realities. I pull my legs up to my chin like a trapped spider in a protective stance. The tears come. They dot whatever web I am constructing, flickering crystals glowing in the dark.

In Fir View the shadowy corners of Amanda's cabin offered convenient havens to a variety of spiders. Whenever I swept the pine floors, I'd probe the broom into corners and hope the spiders would meet a sudden demise. I remained too squeamish to check for evidence. I postponed telling Amanda about my fears until one particular night.

She lay on her side, the paleness of her flesh opalescent in the muted light of the glass lamp. The rosy tip of one breast lay inches from my mouth. My tongue played with her, coaxing her pink nipple to respond. Amanda moaned, edging closer. She guided herself toward me. I accepted willingly, my mouth taking her in. Her saltiness in my mouth, I wrapped one leg around her broad hip, grasping her nearer.

"Oh, Toni." The startling sapphire of her eyes aroused me further.

I touched the satiny skin of her thigh. My fingers made little circles there. She moaned again, encouraging me.

Her breast was in my mouth. My eyes were half shut, but from the corner of one, I managed to see a darting movement on the unclothed surface of her skin, directly above where my leg wrapped around hers. Amanda uttered dovelike sounds. My gaze widened at making eye contact with a large spider perched on her ample waistline.

"Holy shit!" I recoiled so quickly her breast bounced from my mouth. I almost fell off the bed.

"Oh, my God!" Amanda stared at me in horror. Immediately she sat up. "What is it?"

I was speechless, halfway across the room, clumsily pulling on sheepskin-lined slippers and a flannel robe. Beside Amanda the spider remained still. I pointed to it.

Perplexed, she followed my gaze. With a nonchalance that unnerved me even more, she flicked off the spider as if it were a clump of lint. "Is that all? Toni, these spiders are all over. Don't tell me it's the first time you've seen one in the cabin?"

Keeping my distance I wondered where the creepy culprit had disappeared. Shivering, I hugged myself.

"Honey, it's all right. My goodness, you're phobic."

"Funny you should notice," I muttered. "Where did it go?"

"Back to its hiding place. Come on, sweetheart." She offered a coquettish glance. "You've left me in a very compromising position."

"Sorry." Try as I might, I could not blot out the picture of that ugly creature on her usually desirable body. "No way I can get back into it now."

"What?" She knelt on the bed, breasts beckoning, thighs slightly apart. From where I stood I could see her wetness.

"I can't handle it, no way."

When she attempted to persuade me, then berate me, I ducked into the bathroom. Humiliated yet determined, I stayed there for over an hour until I heard her steady breathing. I emerged with a flashlight and searched the area around and under the bed. Not a trace. There was nowhere else to sleep—the living room seemed even more ominous. Finally, I climbed into bed next to Amanda.

Hours passed before I slept. In the morning I found three distinct spider bites—oval and scarlet—on my left thigh, dangerously and provocatively close to my vulva. Repulsed, I began to consider that spidery episode as the beginning of the end of my sojourn in the Pacific Northwest.

Wiping my eyes, I glance at the ceiling. The spider is motionless. Is it sleeping?

"Stay there," I command.

With a sigh, I turn off the lamp beside the bed. I crave rest but end up clenching the edge of the sheet all night.

⟡ CHAPTER FIVE ⟡

January 1: Before Dawn
Pat

The ironing board creaks. I press the warm plancha to the magenta-and-purple flannel shirt. I have already ironed five. I swear it's a Latina thing. Have to look sharp, no matter how lousy we feel. Still don't know which shirt I'll wear to meet Toni on the beach.

My abuelita used to work in a laundry. Before I started first grade, she taught me how to use the old Sunbeam on my school-uniform blouses.

"Do the collar first, mijita, entonces the sleeves," my grandmother would say. "Asi verás. Go on to the sides and back."

Abuelita praised my skill once I got the hang of it. She began parceling out my Dad's bandannas, Mama's flowered aprons, my brother Carlos's T-shirts. I never played much with dolls. Instead, I had a toy ironing board set up next to Abuelita's big one. We were partners, Abuelita and me. While we ironed she would tell me stories about growing up in México. I wish I could remember them. I think I've blotted out the poverty, the violence. At least I haven't forgotten how to iron just the way she taught me.

Ironing's the one thing that soothes my nerves. Toni used to tease me about it. Whenever I'd haul out the ironing board and unleash the Black & Decker's coiled cord, she'd smile and toss a few items into the pile (usually tank tops and cotton panties) to make me laugh. If I didn't even crack a smile, she would pretty much leave me alone till I'd gone through the stack. The size of the pile—and how fast it dwindled—pretty much gauged my mood.

My stack's almost reaching the ceiling right now. Flannel shirts mostly, some turtlenecks, a few pairs of jeans, a couple of sweatshirts, even a fleecy pullover. You can never tell how cold it'll be on the beach.

I choose a lavender turtleneck to go with the purple plaid shirt. I really don't need to iron the whole thing since it'll be under the shirt. I have to keep busy. Otherwise I'll flop on the bed in a panic till it's time to meet Toni.

I'm queasy again, partly due to barfing at the party. Everyone had to know what I was going through. Can't believe I reacted like that. I hate making a scene, but my body sure wasn't in sync with my head. I thought I had more control than that.

My grip on the iron is so tight my wrist is getting sore. My head whizzes with thoughts of the party: Toni tried to defuse me with her humble act. After ten years together, she knows me, reads me better than anyone. I hope that means she has a clear-cut idea of how fucked up I am over her. How could she have left me for that whiny Amanda? The white chick offered her a way out—that's what I figure. Otherwise I don't get it at all. Only thing I know for sure is I'm damn glad they didn't stay together.

Sylvia

The red numbers on the clock sizzle like flares the cops use at car crashes: 2:35 A.M. Zalo wasn't here when I got home from working the double shift. He must be mad at me for doing overtime on New Year's Eve. Probably off sulking somewhere. You'd think we had big-time party plans, but Zalo never takes me anywhere. Doesn't like crowds, he says. Holiday or not I figured working late wouldn't make any difference to him. Shit, we need the extra money.

I got home an hour ago and can't sleep. Wonder what time Zalo left. Where could he be? In a bar somewhere, celebrating the New Year? Or with some woman, una sin vergüenza?

"No," I say out loud. "He's happy about the baby. Why would he fuck around? He's just mad I wasn't home."

Rolling over I turn my back to the mocking numbers on the clock. My shoulders are tight with tension. I want— need—to sleep. My cold fingers surround my belly and grip the growing roundness. I hope the baby's a boy, to make Zalo happy.

Gabriela thinks I should have amniocentesis to be sure the baby's normal. What does that smartass girl know? Probably borrowing crazy feminist ideas from Toni. Would they both tell me to have an abortion if the test showed anything abnormal? I'm 37, not 47. I'm not about to let those two talk me into anything. The baby's health doesn't make me worry. What makes me jittery is how Zalo will react if it's a girl.

Before I went off duty, the hospital celebrated the birth of the first New Year's baby: a pretty niña with wisps of blond hair one of the nurses decorated with a pink bow. The parents are in their 40s. This is their first—probably only—baby. The father's one of those clean-cut types, a professional, some white-collar job. The mother's a plain-Jane and looks her age. Her outright joy got to me, a real happy ending/new beginning deal. I was glad my shift was almost over. Those parents remind me too much of the Brandons. No wonder I never fit into that family.

Jeff and I would celebrate New Year's Eve usually at a party or club. He was the outgoing type, loved to dance, booze it up—not like his stuffy parents—which was what attracted me in the first place. Great body, sun-streaked hair, sea-blue eyes. I'm glad Gabriela inherited Jeff's eyes. It adds to her looks, whether she likes that or not.

Whenever I see Jeff these days, which isn't often, he isn't the same. I think he grew up after his accident. Too bad it took that much to make it happen. Being stuck in a wheelchair would change anyone, I guess. He can't surf anymore or dance or make love like we used to. Shit, I was already out of the picture by that time. Just as well, since no way would I take care of Jeff for the rest of my life. Forget that.

I roll over again. 2:55. No sign of Zalo.

Morning
Gabriela

"Yesterday Zalo drove out of the driveway so fast he almost hit my car. He looked furious," Grandma whispers to me on the church steps. "His truck is still gone, Gabi. He's been out all night."

I take in this latest tidbit. "Have you seen my Mom yet?"

"No, mijita. She worked overtime last night."

With Grandma's arm through mine, I walk with her into Saint Anne's. "Bet Mom isn't sleeping."

"Don't mention any of this when you see her today, eh?"

"Don't worry, Grandma. I'll play dumb."

We settle into a pew. Somebody's carved "Li'l Felix" on the seat. Gang marks in church. What's next? I put my shoulder bag over them. I'm not the most religious person in the world, but I've come to early Sunday Mass with Grandma ever since Grandpa died. We both like our weekend routine. This morning I hoped Toni would come with us, but she was still in bed when we left. I think she's backing away from replaying old scenes, traditional ones like this. I'll see her at breakfast anyway.

When Mass begins Grandma prays out loud in Spanish with the rest of the parishioners. I should practice Spanish pronunciation, but I only go through the motions. Phil says my Spanish is worse than his. Maybe we're both too assimilated. I don't even look Mexican. If I didn't say anything, no one would know, but I'm not that type. I'd never get away with the "passing game" anyhow, not in this family.

Right now my mind stays on my mom. Suppose Zalo is playing tomcat? The thought almost makes me laugh, 'cause he's no prize. Who would want him? Some dumb chick. I almost feel sorry for Mom—but not quite.

In some ways she's like Toni, picking someone completely the opposite, just like Toni went off with Amanda. Maybe there's something to this sibling rivalry stuff. Mom and Toni try to be so different from each other, but they really are alike in some ways. Neither of them would ever admit that. I'm glad I don't have a sister. Sure wouldn't want to get caught in that trap.

Grandma nudges me. "Canta, muchacha."

I pick up the hymn book and flip to the page she points to. "Noche de paz, noche de amor," I sing off-key. "Silent Night" in Spanish. At least I know the tune.

Her rouged lips easing into amusement, Grandma checks me out. I smile back, but my thoughts drift back to Mom.

If Mom got rid of Zalo, she could keep living next door to Grandma. Sure, she'd be unhappy for a while. Once she figured out she was better off without him, she'd turn into her old self. I'd have my Mom back. Maybe she and Toni could even make up. Maybe things could be like before.

The hymn ends. We sit for the sermon. My mind wanders. Grandma squeezes my hand. I smile and lean against her shoulder. I try not to think about Mom, but I can't help it.

Adela

"Que bueno. Toni's cooking." As I open the door, I turn to wink at Gabi. "Don't say anything about Zalo, eh? Let's eat in peace. Start el año nuevo off right."

Gabi nods. She follows me into the kitchen. "Hey, Toni," she says. "Happy New Year."

My daughter glances away from preparing the delicious chorizo-and-eggs combination. She whisks her niece into her arms. "Same to you, chula. What good timing. Breakfast is almost ready."

"Ay, que luxury." I smile at Toni and give her a quick kiss. Her long hair is wet. She has a peach-colored towel draped como rebozo around her shoulders. She wears cornflower-blue sweatpants and a long-sleeved pullover shirt. The bulky clothes make her look cuddly.

"Both of you sit," she insists. "This breakfast is my treat."

She has set the table and poured orange juice into small glasses. The TV cart is next to the table and tilted at the best angle for viewing the Rose Parade.

"Wow. I could get used to this," Gabi teases. "I love being

waited on." She slides into a chair next to me. "How was Veronica's party, Toni?"

"I'll leave out the gory details…I'm going to see Pat today."

In surprise I gaze at my daughter. Last night she said nothing about this. Gabi nearly spills her juice. Toni continues forking the chorizo and eggs into plates for us.

"Pat and I are long overdue for a talk. We have a lot of unfinished business to settle."

"Talking's a start, right?" Gabi says.

Toni shrugs. "The whole thing freaks me." She switches off the burner and hands me a heaping plate. "Almost time for the parade. Does channel 5 still have the best coverage?"

The plate before me, I lean over and turn on the TV. Toni is not ready to share any more information about Pat, and I know better than to get too snoopy.

We watch preparade events: interviews with out-of-state marching bands, local celebrities on beautiful horses, designers of fancy floats. Gabi makes funny remarks about all of it. Ay, these muchachas. They say they love the Rose Parade pero todo el tiempo they poke fun at it.

In the meantime Toni serves Gabi and herself. She leaves a cloth-covered basket of warm tortillas in the middle of the table, a platter of pan dulce beside it. Before she joins us she fills our coffee cups. When she is about to start eating, I interrupt.

"Vamos a dar gracias a Dios por tu bien viaje y por el año nuevo."

Obediently, both bow their heads and pray in silence with me for a happy new year. Gabi is the first to look up. She's hungry. When Toni has her fork to her mouth at last, we hear Zalo's truck chugging into the driveway. "About time," Toni mutters. "Does that idiot always stay out all night?"

Gabi and I do not answer. We don't know what to expect next.

Toni

For the first time since coming home, I hear that intimidating male rumble.

"Damn it, Sylvia. You in there? I'm fuckin' hungry."

The door of the neighboring duplex slams. Not a sound from my sister. Mama and Gabi remain motionless. Their eyes show fear.

"No one answered me," I remind them. "Does Zalo do this all the time?"

"Once in a while," Mama admits in a whisper. "Ay, hija. Stay out of it, eh?"

"Do you think I want to barge over there and tangle with that sleazeball?" Appetite gone, my stomach contracts with anger and apprehension. Did Pat feel like this when she saw me last night? "Does he beat Sylvia? Tell me the truth."

Gabi looks down. Mama avoids my eyes. No one needs to verify my suspicions.

"Mama, how could you let them live next door?"

She gives a helpless shrug. Her eyes are on the TV screen, not on me. An orchid-covered float swirls by while kimonoed women flutter ornate fans. The yearly spectacle is a gaudy cliché—an annual ritual that rarely changes. Watching it almost pacifies me.

"Maybe it's better to have Mom near. We can keep an eye on her," Gabi suggests, her blue-green eyes concerned.

The silence next door is ominous.

"If I hear or see anything, I'm calling the police. Understand?" I glance at their scared faces. "No matter what, I'd never sit still and listen to him beat Sylvia."

"Ay, mija, we don't even know for sure if—"

"Have you heard him yell at her? Have you heard her cry?" I shoot back. "Have you ever seen bruises on her? Don't shut your eyes, Mama."

"Grandma, Toni's right." Gabi is very close to tears. "Think of it as our Christian duty. I don't give a damn about Zalo. Mom's the one I care about."

Mama says nothing. She moves a clump of chorizo across her plate. She has firm beliefs about the sanctity of marriage. In her heart, however, she must know Zalo Anchondo does not share—or deserve—her sentiments.

"Toni, if you phone la policiá, Zalo could come after all of us."

"That's the risk we have to take. You should've thought of that, Mama, when you let them move in."

Rising, my mother carries her unfinished meal to the sink. Without another word, she enters her bedroom and shuts the door.

"Denial," Gabi says in a shaky voice.

"She's never had to deal with machismo up close. Your Grandpa was the gentlest man in the world. Mama can't even imagine what Sylvia's reality is like." I study my niece. "Gabi, why didn't you tell me?"

She nudges her plate aside. She buries her head in her arms and erupts into sobs. With gentleness I bend and lift her head. Her wavy hair is silky. I let her lean against me. It's been too long since I've held my niece and comforted her. I've missed Gabi so much.

"I'm sorry. You were gone, and Mom just won't listen to me, Toni," she whimpers. "I keep telling her to get rid of that asshole. What makes all this even worse is…she's pregnant."

Those two words bombard me. I feel limp in the chair.

Gabi looks up to assess my reaction. "Mom told me on Christmas. I think Grandma knows. I wasn't supposed to tell anybody."

"I'd find out sooner or later." With a sigh I smooth her hair again. "Welcome back to the delightful Dorado family. Maybe I should've gritted my teeth and stuck it out in Fir View."

Gabi wipes her eyes with her fingertips. "You mean that?"

I shake my head. "No. I hated that place." Sliding away from her, I dump the rest of my breakfast into the trash. So much for the first meal of the year. I lean against the sink and glance at the clock. I have to meet Pat in about an hour, and I'm already exhausted.

Gabi stays where she is for a few minutes. Brow furrowed, she keeps looking toward the window facing the other duplex. In a sudden motion, she goes to it. "It's too quiet, Toni. I'm going to see if Mom's all right."

I flinch. "You might walk into something you can't get..."

My niece has the Dorado stubbornness. When she heads for the front door, I hurry after her.

Sylvia

He has me cornered in the bathroom, pressed to the cold yellow tile. His sweaty face is unshaven, his breath rancid. I smell female stink on him, but I won't say that out loud since I don't want him to hit me again. I can barely see out of my right eye. It swells fast.

"You hear me, bitch? Make me breakfast. Now!"

I close my eyes. Starting to feel sick.

He figures what's about to happen and backs away. "Don't

puke now, cunt. I want to eat!"

I turn my throbbing head away, retch into the open toilet, too miserable to care what he does next. Zalo is like a furious boar, stomping out of the bathroom like the one I imagined crashing out of Tio Manuel's barbecue pit.

"Stupid slut. Can't even get a meal around here anymore. Where's the cash? Fuckin' cunt."

Squatting at the toilet I vomit again. I want to flush myself down, disappear into swirling water, glide through rusty pipes, spin through smelly storm drains all the way to the ocean, far away from Zalo.

He rips apart dresser drawers searching for hidden money. My head aches and reels, and I can hardly hear his shouts. The yellow linoleum looks closer. I sink to it.

"Mom! Oh, my God! Toni, what if she's dead?"

Gabriela's shrill cry makes me shiver awake. My eyes open into painful slits. My head feels huge. An ugly, sour taste fills my mouth.

"Thank you, Jesus," Gabriela whispers close to me. She starts to lift my head. I sense Toni kneeling next to her.

"Sylvia, can you hear us?"

I move my head a little. Hurts like hell. Think I banged it against the floor.

"Where's Zalo?" I murmur.

"Do you really think he'd hang around? He nearly ran over us in the driveway," Toni says with disgust. I know she wants to add a lot more, but she's being careful because of Gabriela.

"Let's help Sylvia up, Gabi. We'll take her to the bed."

They hook my arms around their shoulders. I feel lopsided. My daughter isn't as tall as Toni. I let them move me in an off-kilter way. Don't have the energy to stop them.

Soon I'm flat on my back in bed, with my dizzy head supported by pillows. Gabi tries not to cry. She puts a cold washcloth on my swollen eye.

"Shhh," I whisper. "I'll be OK, honey."

"Mom, I can't stand this!" She peers into my messed-up face. "Are you going to let him kill you?"

"Gabi, stop it," Toni says in a tired voice. "Don't make your mother feel worse."

"Since when are you so understanding?" I barely manage to ask.

Right away Toni turns snotty. "I prefer to stay out of your business. Believe me, Sylvia, I don't appreciate this shit happening next door."

"Maybe you shouldn't have come home," I mutter.

Toni sucks in her breath. She would really like to lay into me. Under the circumstances she's keeping herself in line.

"Don't fight. Please, don't fight," Gabi begs us. "Isn't there enough of that already? Mom, come over to Grandma's. I don't want to leave you alone. No telling when that asshole will be back."

"Listen to your daughter. Hang out at Mama's for the time being." Toni sounds fed up. "If you have any sense, you'll get a temporary restraining order against him. Then divorce the bastard."

While she's mouthing off I put my hands over my face. "I don't want Mama to see me like this."

"It'll make her face reality, if nothing else will." Toni lets out a long sigh. "Sylvia, you're pregnant, for Christ's sake. You can't be alone. Come on," she urges. "I'll help Gabi take you over there. Then I have to leave."

For a few minutes I stay quiet while my daughter's hands

rub my shoulders. I bite my sore lip. "OK."

"You really ought to see a doctor, Sylvia," my big-mouth sister adds.

"Keep out of this. It's none of your damn business."

Pat

Shit, she's late. Either that or she's chickened out. I'm such a sucker. I even brought an extra beach chair for her. I haven't learned a damn thing in 18 months.

Today the sand is damp. It's freezing out here, with a stiff ocean breeze. I'm glad I decided on the lavender turtleneck, plaid shirt, purple jeans, hiking boots, and fleecy pullover. I'll give Toni another 15 minutes. I'm not waiting any longer than that.

I even brought a thermos of coffee. I sip from time to time. Pretty soon I'll have to pee, but I'm not about to go into those public toilets. No telling who or what's holed up in there.

I check my watch again. Toni's half an hour late. Damn! Am I gullible or what? I lower my sunglasses to stare at the gray water. Fog's floating in; the air even cooler.

If my friend Jessica Tamayo were around, she'd tell me what those silly shorebirds are, the tiny ones that run with the tide and back. I feel like such a total fool. I'm ready to bird-watch just as an excuse for being on this ice-cold beach on fuckin' New Year's morning.

All of a sudden I hear someone call me. Real nonchalant, I turn around. Toni's on the Arizona Street bridge, waving like a maniac. Her long hair flaps like black wings. Seems like a strong gust could carry her out to me. I could catch her, lie with her, make us both warm.

"Yeah, sure," I grumble. "Be an idiot again."

No matter what I say to myself, I wave to Toni. I hold up the thermos. She counters with a large plastic sack. She better have a good excuse for being so late.

She arrives breathless and slumps to her knees next to me. She looks disheveled—brown face flushed, hair tangled.

"I ran all the way, Pat. God, I'm out of shape. Sorry." Her words rush out. "I left as soon as I could. Zalo beat up Sylvia."

"Fuck." I stare at her. "Is she all right?"

"Black eye, busted lip. She was really out of it when Gabi and I found her on the bathroom floor." Toni eases herself into the empty beach chair. She tries to catch her breath. "She's pregnant."

"Christ!"

"Yeah." She gives me a rueful look. "Did I land into a soap opera or what?"

I shake my head and pour her a cup of coffee. She takes it gratefully. Better get a grip on myself and ignore being pissed. Shit, I'll have to be supportive of her family problems instead of dealing with my resentments about the breakup. My luck never changes.

I gulp down my coffee. "Toni, did you call the cops?"

She sighs. "No. Gabi and I took Sylvia to my Mom's. I left the rest up to them. Zalo took off anyway. Who knows where he went. He was gone all night."

"Fuckin' asshole."

"I'm too numb to process this now, Pat. We were having breakfast when he drove in and started yelling at her."

"How's your mother taking it?"

"Distancing herself as much as she can. Gabi's the one I really feel for. Can you imagine seeing your mother in a situation like that?"

Shaking my head again, I gaze at the Pacific. "Well, I guess you're not in any mood to talk about us."

At first Toni doesn't say anything. I glance over. Her face starts to pucker. I recognize that look. She's trying to get hold of herself. Tears are real close.

"Pat, I'm so scared he's going to kill her," she says in a strangled voice. "Sylvia looks terrible. That damn Zalo barreled out of the driveway in such a frenzy he almost crashed into Gabi and me." Her dark eyes challenge mine. "What can I do?"

"Be there for Sylvia."

"She hates to take my advice."

"Don't give any. Just listen to her."

"Like that's so easy. You know how Sylvia is."

"Damn it, Toni, you asked me what to do, and I told you. What the hell do you want from me anyway?" I glare at her and zip the fleecy top up a few notches.

"I'm sorry," Toni mumbles. The wintry wind nearly carries away the rest of her words. "Jesus...I'm so sorry...for everything."

⌒ CHAPTER SIX ⌒

January 1: Afternoon
Adela

La Sylvia is sleeping. Her face is like a smashed tomato. Gabi checks on her every few minutes. I don't know what to do.

In the living room I watch another replay of the Rose Parade. No matter how many times I've seen it, I still don't know who won the Grand Marshal's prize.

"Toni and I should've taken her to the emergency room. How do we know if she's sleeping or unconscious, Grandma?" Gabi paces around my chair, arms wrapped around herself even though I've turned on the furnace.

"Your mother doesn't want anyone from the hospital to see her like this."

"Grandma, who cares! We could've taken her to Santa Monica Hospital instead of St. John's. She'd probably be better off in a non-Catholic hospital anyway."

"Mira, muchacha, be careful what you say." I frown as I rub the rosary beads in my apron pocket.

Gabi stops pacing. She sits on the sofa arm. "The Catholics

would tell her to go home and be a 'good wife.' You know that, Grandma. I wish Toni were here."

"Do you want to phone your father?"

She sighs. "I've thought about it, but I'd hate to get Dad involved. Do you think for a minute Mom would listen to him?"

"No, mija. I meant for yourself. You should talk to him. Jeff es un buen hombre. Es verdad que I didn't always think so. Your mother never should have divorced him."

"No argument there," Gabi agrees. "I'll talk to Dad when I'm home. Right now I'd better stay here. I can't leave you alone with Mom."

"Ay, no." I cringe at the thought. "Pero what could you and I do against Zalo?"

"Phone the police, like Toni said."

"She left in such a hurry."

"Grandma, she had to meet Pat." Gabi breaks off a piece of pan dulce from the platter she moved to the coffee table. "Otherwise I'm sure Toni would've made the phone call herself. I'm glad she left. It's important for them to talk."

"Sylvia is her sister, mija." I hear the quiver in my own voice. "How could Toni rush out at a time like this?"

Gabi gets up again. "If you want the truth," she says before heading to the bedroom, "I think Pat matters the most to Toni."

As she leaves I dab my eyes with the edge of my apron. I don't know what happened to mis muchachitas. My daughters were so pretty, so smart, not always well-behaved, but they were brought up en una casa católica. Juan and I did our best with them. Now one is a lesbian, the other is in a horrible marriage. All these years later I don't understand what went wrong.

Gabriela

Every time I look at Mom, I start bawling. I've never seen her like this, beaten and helpless. Grandma told me about hearing Zalo yell at her. I had suspected more would happen—or had happened already. But whenever I saw Mom, she seemed fine. A couple of times I noticed black-and-blue marks on her arms. Sure, she had excuses for them. Otherwise she was as sassy as ever, always ready to defend that monster.

When they were together, Mom and Dad would argue sometimes. Dad never hit her, as far as I know. I don't think he has it in him. He's pretty easygoing. That's why it's so easy to talk to him. Grandma's right, I really do need to do that. Maybe he'll help me put this in some kind of perspective. I feel guilty for not spending New Year's Day with him, but he knows I like being with Grandma. I never figured the morning would end up like this.

Mom's face looks unreal. The skin over her right eye is turning darker, and her lip is puffed out—and she's really pale. The henna rinse in her hair makes her complexion look as light as Grandma's white pillowcases.

I have the phone in Grandma's bedroom. If I even hear Zalo at the front door, I'm calling 911. I don't want that son of a bitch to come near my mother again.

Moaning, Mom stirs in her sleep. I put my hand on her shoulder to soothe her. Instead she reacts with a start. Her battered eyes fill with terror.

"It's me, Mom. You're at Grandma's. You're safe."

Compared with the rest of her face, her eyes seem the most like her, except for that scared look. It gives me the willies.

"Gabi, I have to get home. Zalo will be even madder when

he comes back and I'm not there."

"Tough shit." I stare at her in disbelief. "You owe him nothing. You're not going anywhere."

She winces as she tries to sit up. "Help me, Gabi."

"No way." I slide off the edge of the bed.

She seems shocked. "Are you refusing to help me?"

"I've already helped you by bringing you here, by cleaning you up, Mom, by keeping you in bed." My voice gets loud. "If you want to let that asshole turn you into meatloaf again, you'll have to do that by yourself. I'm not available for that."

She moves her head as if she is hiding her own tears. She sobs into the pillow. Her shoulders shake like she's having convulsions. The sight is too much. Crying 'cause she wants to go back to him. I grab the phone.

Grandma looks worried when I dart into the kitchen with the phone. Setting it on the cluttered table, I push the familiar numbers. I'm calling Dad.

Toni

She balks about strolling with me on the shoreline. No doubt it seems too much like a Hallmark-card reconciliation, lesbian-style: two romantic women walking side by side on a deserted beach.

"Pat, it's too cold to sit. We'll warm up if we stretch our legs," I suggest with what I hope is a sly grin.

She shoots me a withering look. "You have a helluva lot of explaining to do."

I admit that. I'm so anxious about being with her that my fists are balled tight within my denim jacket pockets.

"I don't expect you to cover everything today," Pat adds. She reluctantly trails me toward the shore. "I know you're uptight about Sylvia. You need to go home before too long."

"I'm glad you realize that," I murmur, bowing my head as the wind kicks up. I walk in silence for a few minutes, wondering where to start. Although I have played this scene in my mind countless times, I am unnerved because she is actually beside me, willing to listen.

"Well?" Pat cocks her sleek head at me. She has her jacket collar turned up, its purple fleece in sharp contrast to her jet-black hair. In the mist she is enchanting, her coppery face startling in the grayness.

"I was very confused—about everything," I mumble, wanting to cry more than talk, to nestle against her instead of walking next to her. I struggle to maintain my composure. My words stream forth in measured cadences. "When I lost my job, I lost my identity too. I began questioning my whole life, my motivations and choices. Nothing felt right anymore."

"I figured that," she concedes. "That part makes sense. The rest doesn't."

"Amanda?" When I say that name, I don't look at her.

"Right." Pat kicks a clump of kelp out of her path. Tiny flies swoop up, encircling it, landing again.

I take a deep breath. "She gave me a way out. I thought she was the answer. She wasn't."

"Go on."

My eyes question hers. Does she want a racial/ethnic/social class analysis? Does she want me to say I wasn't satisfied being with a white woman? That only another Chicana could love me as I longed to be loved? When Pat returns my gaze, she seems unflappable.

"Why wasn't she the answer?"

With a sigh I turn my wet eyes toward the Pacific. Repetitious waves swirl in, ebbing and flowing.

"She isn't you."

Pat's jaw clenches. She pauses to pick up a few pebbles someone has stacked for a partially completed sand castle. She curves her slim body into an athletic stance and hurls each small rock into the waves. I wonder if she wishes she could throw me in with them. When she finishes, she uncoils herself and moves ahead. I take long strides to catch up.

"I never loved her, Pat. I love you."

Pat

"Fine way to show me. Run off with someone else." I know my words sound bitter, but I have a to right to feel that way. What the hell does she expect, anyway?

"I wanted to escape." Toni touches my arm. I'm walking faster than she wants to.

"From me?" I halt in the deep sand. When I do this she drops her hand to her side.

"Yes. From being unemployed, from Sylvia's accusations and her remarriage, from the L.A. tensions. Most of all, from your expectations."

At that last phrase I eye her with candor. "Now you're getting to the point, Toni."

The frigid breeze lifts the ends of her hair. The gray strands seem silvery, almost part of the mist around us, while the rest of her is etched in stark relief. No matter what, she's hermosa—that regal mestiza face. I wonder if my eyes hint at that.

"I honestly thought you wanted me to be someone I'm not. My attempt at being an on-the-job activist backfired. That seemed to sour everything."

"And the white chick offered a way out."

Toni nods. Her ebony eyes are sad. She lets the wind grapple with her hair. The black tangle provides a convenient shield from me.

"The worst mistake I've ever made," she says so quietly I almost think I've imagined it. "I wanted to be far away and safe, but I wasn't. Instead I hurt you, Pat."

"Took you a while to find out, huh?"

"Not too long, actually." Toni almost smiles. "At first I didn't have the nerve to return. I thought maybe I should stick it out. Amanda's not a bad person, really. I just don't love her. I found out I couldn't pretend either. I'm not that much a hypocrite."

I don't trust myself to make another comment. I wish there were seashells to bend over and grab. Not much on this beach, though, not anymore.

"Pat, I thought about you constantly, what you were doing, thinking, saying. You didn't even answer my letters."

Clearing my throat, I stare ahead. "I didn't know what to say, Toni. All you did was write about life in the damn woods, about the books you finally had time to read. Nothing about regrets—nada. What was I supposed to say—'nice knowin' you, adios'?"

She wraps a chunk of her hair around her neck, one of her stressed-out habits. "I didn't know how to ask you if I could come back. When I couldn't stand it any longer, I simply...came back." She looks away fast when she notices I'm watching her. "I'm ready to take the consequences."

"Hell, I'm not planning to murder you," I mutter.

She dares a sudden smile. It fades as abruptly. "I know, Pat. Do you still have the apartment?"

"No way I'd give up a rent-controlled pad just 'cause you

left," I say more roughly than intended.

For a moment she turns her back to me. Her shoulders seem tense, her black hair billowing around her. "How do you feel?"

"Better than last night. Not barfing all over the beach, anyway."

"I mean, about me...about us," she clarifies.

Stepping closer to her, I notice my voice grows hoarse. "Do you need an answer today?"

She half turns, black eyes as misty as the air. They almost flood over. "I'll be patient," she whispers.

On impulse I reach over to catch a tear. She lifts her face toward me. What the hell's gotten into me? I stop myself before touching her.

Sylvia

Things are too quiet. I can hear the TV from the living room, and that's all. Is Mama alone? Did Gabi go home? Will she tell Jeff what happened this morning? How come my know-it-all sister isn't giving me a piece of her lesbo philosophy to chew on?

And where's Zalo? With the same tramp he was with last night? Has he made a habit of fucking around while I'm at work? That's what made him snap. He kept saying he was hungry, and I kept asking where he'd been. I know he has a temper—he's bounced me off the wall before. Never like today. Today he was vicious.

I have a hard time moving even a few inches. I can't see Mama's alarm clock from where I am. She keeps it on the dresser across the room. Doesn't do me any good.

I ache all over. Probably look like shit too. How can I go to work tomorrow? I'll have to slap on a lot of makeup and wear my hair down to cover my cheeks and neck. Don't know what I'll do about my eyes. At least the baby's all right. When Zalo loses his head like he did this morning, he lashes out without thinking. He mostly punched me in the face.

Toni made some comment about batterers hiding their evidence, hitting women in the torso or upper arms, places where bruises won't show. I didn't give her the satisfaction of answering. Zalo really isn't a batterer. He only slips up once in a while. He was too mad to think about hiding anything. He went right ahead and smacked me. Of course, Toni will twist that all around to say he's too stupid to cover his tracks. She never has liked him, never even given him a chance. But she's hard on everybody, not just Zalo.

I really need to go to the bathroom. I don't want to depend on Mama for that. She has sort of laid low. I think she's too embarrassed to deal with it. Well, damn it, so am I. She has it in her head that everyone's marriage can be like hers and Daddy's. Well, get real, Mama. You both came out of another era. Nothing's easy these days.

I stretch one leg out of the blankets and rest my foot on the fluffy throw rug next to the bed. With that to brace me, I grab hold of the edge of the mattress and raise myself enough to lean on that elbow. I still feel woozy. Things would be even worse if I pee in Mama's bed. Real slow, I ease myself up enough to swing the other leg to the floor too. Fine. I'm sitting, sort of. Now to get to the bathroom.

Everything hurts so much. On shaky legs I totter forward a couple of steps, grabbing the corner of Mama's nightstand to steady myself. One more step and I can hold the bathroom's doorknob. I'm in.

For what seems a long time, I sit on the toilet. I'm scared to look at my pee. What if there's blood in it? I'm about to take the chance when I hear a familiar sputter. Zalo's truck.

My heart almost pounds out of my body. I don't want him to know where I am. If he doesn't know, he'll be even madder. I don't want him to hurt Mama and Gabi. No, please God. Better me than them.

Gabriela

"Dad, he's pulling into the driveway." My hands are shaking. I clutch the phone tighter.

"Stay on the line, honey." Dad's voice is steady. I really need to hear him to calm myself down.

"What if he comes barging in here?" I whisper.

"Gabi, baby, get a grip. Can you hear what he's doing?"

I squeeze my eyes shut. Zalo is bellowing Mom's name. I want to blot out that gross noise. She will wake up, and then what?

"He's yelling for her, Dad."

Grandma scurries into the kitchen. She's so scared her brown skin seems a couple of shades lighter. "Gabi, who are you talking to?"

"My Dad. He's ready to call 911 as soon as I give him the word."

Grandma nods, like that gives her some consolation. She moves next to me. Then we hear a huge crash.

"Ay, Dios mio!"

"What's going on?" Dad demands.

"I think he's throwing stuff around, furniture, whatever."

"Where's your mother?"

"Still in Grandma's bedroom."

"All right. Listen, Gabi. Take the phone and your grandma and go to your mother. If the bastard wants Sylvia, he'll have to break into the house. Get it? Multiple charges. I have the other phone right next to me to call the police."

"Dad, I'm really freakin'."

"Baby, do like I say," he urges.

Without even explaining I grab Grandma's arm. I pull her with me into the bedroom. With the phone in my other hand, I shut the door behind us.

Grandma looks stunned. "Where's Sylvia?"

We hear a faint voice from the bathroom. "In here. Where's Zalo?"

"Tearing your place apart. Sounds like an earthquake over there." I give Grandma the phone and sneak over to the window. That's when I see Pat's black Mazda swerve into the driveway.

Toni

"Stay in the car, Toni," Pat cautions.

With a crowbar as his weapon, Zalo Anchondo charges. He storms toward us, swinging the crowbar. Pat keeps her eyes on him and starts to back out the car.

"No. We can't go." I seize Pat's arm. "We have to distract him." Hearing myself say those words terrifies me. What other choice do we have? Otherwise, he will break into Mama's house.

Pat has no time to answer. Zalo kicks the front bumper with his huge construction boot. If she continues ignoring him and reversing the car, he could very well become more violent.

"What've you fuckin' dykes done with my wife?" He rais-es the crowbar over the hood. For an insane moment I wonder if he will smash the windshield.

"Your door locked?" Pat whispers.

I nod, heart pounding. "Not that it'll do much good."

Pat tries another tactic. She leans on the horn. The sudden blast at first stuns, then enrages Zalo. With all his might he crashes the crowbar on the hood of her car, not once but repetitively. The jarring impact shakes the Mazda as if we are on a crazy carnival ride.

"You fuckin' brujas! Where the hell's Sylvia? Where did you hide her? If you don't tell me, I'll kill both of you!"

Pat keeps putting pressure on the horn. The constant ruckus, not to mention Zalo's mad-dog rage, attracts attention. Mama's duplex remains closed and silent, but neighbors on either side peer out. Backyard dogs bark. Pigeons flutter above. I hear a distant siren. Maybe someone had the sense to phone the police.

Not to be intimidated, Zalo attacks the car. He goes bonkers, battling the Mazda as if it were a steel representation of a modern-day Amazon. He yells misogynistic and homophobic slurs. Pat pulls me down with her on the seat. Zalo seems intent on destroying her car, if not us.

Inside, we rock with each jarring blow. If he aims for the windshield, we need to keep our heads tucked. I sense Pat's fear, taste my own. Typically macha, she lies over me, protective, breasts against my back. I am too frightened to speak.

The siren grows louder. Moments later we hear the crunch of fast-moving tires on gravel and an amplified command to Zalo to cease and desist. The cop's voice sounds pumped up. No telling what the unleashed testosterone of police officers and perpetrator will detonate.

"Stay put," Pat advises. "They might shoot the bastard."

"That would solve everything," I murmur.

"Kind of cold-blooded in your old age, mujer," she teases in spite of our mutual terror.

"Only where he's concerned," I add.

"Against the car! Now!" an authoritative voice rings out. In a second we feel Zalo's massive body being lurched over the hood of the car. The Mazda bounces again. Then we hear another voice.

"Don't leave the car until we secure the suspect."

Pat barely raises her head. I imagine her relieved grin. "It's Ron Velez. Never thought I would be so glad to hear that cholo's voice."

Pat

When we sit up we see that bastard Zalo cuffed face down on the Mazda's hood—or what's left of it. He has the damn nerve to spit at Ron Velez while the other cops haul him off to the squad car. The wad lands on the Mazda instead. Damn fool can't even aim.

As Toni and I get out of the car, Sergeant Ron Velez raises his brows in our direction. "Mind telling me who El Gordo is?"

"He's married to my sister. Thank God you got here. You tell him the rest, Pat." Toni gives me a quick hug. Not exactly how I imagined the first abrazo from her in months, but it's not the best time to complain about that. She hurries inside to check on her family.

I'm feeling pretty damn shaky and hope it doesn't show. With a slow grin I look at Ron. "You mean you're not familiar with this character?"

"Not this guy," he says.

"That's a miracle."

I lean on the car hood, noting the million and one crater-like dents on the hood. Looks like it's been bombarded by a meteor shower. Me too for that matter. I'm shaking so bad I don't trust myself to stand on my own. I clear my throat and bring Ron up to date.

"His name is Gonzalo Anchondo. He beat up his wife this morning. She's inside Mrs. Dorado's house."

"That's what I like about you, Pat. Always brimming with info." He gives me the once-over. "Hey, you all right?"

"Shut up," I mutter. "Christ, he really wanted to knock Toni and me around. My poor car got it instead. That asshole better have insurance."

"Consider yourselves lucky. Hang on." Ron moves off to confer with the other officers. By now they have Zalo in the backseat of the squad car. His blubberjaws are flapping, probably cussing them out.

For a while I stand there and try to pull myself together. A knot of curious neighbors gather at the end of the driveway. Pretty soon Ron comes back with his notepad.

"I'm on my way to talk to the Dorados. Coming?"

"Sure."

Inside, Adela has her arms around Toni. They're both crying. So is Gabi, even though she's on the phone. When Adela and Gabi see Ron Velez, they freeze. Only Toni seems eager to welcome him.

Ron nods to everyone. He addresses Toni. "I have to talk with your sister."

"She's in the bedroom. Follow me."

"Ay, Dios de mi vida," Adela murmurs as I approach. She latches on to me, like she hasn't seen me in years. Didn't realize she was strong enough to squeeze me that tight. "Pat, como estás, hija?"

"I'm holding up, Adela. I could use something to drink."

"Como no." She bustles into the kitchen and returns with a tall glass of orange juice.

"Gracias, Adela." I sink next to Gabi on the couch.

The kid leans over to kiss me, phone still to her ear. "OK, Dad. Thanks for everything. You're the best."

Gabi puts down the phone and kisses me again, harder, con gusto. I love this kid. She's the closest I'll ever come to having a niece. For a while, I hang onto her and let her fuss over me.

"Pat, I was never so scared in my whole life. I thought he was going to kill you and Toni."

"Not a scratch on either of us." I slump back on the couch. "Can't say the same for my car. Listen, do you think your mom will press charges?"

Gabi's pale eyes study mine. "How can she not?"

"I'm going to, no question. After what that bastard did to my car." I place the glass of orange juice on the coffee table. "How's your mom doing?"

Gabi makes a face. "She looks horrible."

☞ CHAPTER SEVEN ☜

January 1: Evening
Sylvia

They're in the living room planning their strategy. Nothing ever changes. They always tell me what to do. Even my own daughter is on their side. Shit, I'm no stupid teenager. I don't need their advice. I don't know why Mama always listens to that damn Toni's opinions. Like my sister's life is perfect, right? That smartass Pat Ramos sure doesn't keep her mouth shut either.

Ron Velez was here earlier putting his two cents in. Since when does he have any influence over me, cop or not? When I was a kid, I never paid much attention to that dude. I know his sister Margie; she was in the same class with Pat and me. Ron had already graduated from high school when we were in our teens. He went into the police academy, got hired by the Santa Monica Police Department, and married right after that. A good-looking guy who's very aware of it, he likes to throw his weight around, like most guys. Didn't realize he was palsy-walsy with Pat. Who doesn't she know, being in that rabble-rousing media group she works for?

Damn it, she's going to press charges against Zalo. What a traitor that bitch is! Velez told me about Pat's decision when I said I didn't want to make trouble for my husband. Velez gave me this real condescending look, like I'm some stupid Mexican who doesn't know her ass from her elbow.

"He's already in trouble, Mrs. Anchondo." He ran his slick eyes over me with more than a trace of disgust. "He trashed your mother's rental property next door, he threatened your sister and Ms. Ramos, and he turned her car into a junkyard heap. You should obtain a temporary restraining order as soon as possible to keep your husband off this property. As you well know by what he did to you this morning, he's a dangerous man. Your sister and Ms. Ramos managed to escape being hurt because they stayed in the car. Otherwise he could have assaulted them. Think about protecting your family, all right? Think about yourself."

I glared at him so hard my eyes started to hurt again. When I didn't say anything else, he sat by the bed a while longer. He wanted to know if I'd rather talk with a female officer. I still kept my mouth shut. I didn't answer any of his questions. I ignored his suggestion about hospital care. He stomped out.

Right now I don't want to think anymore. I want to go to sleep for hours—or days. Sure don't want to listen to Toni and my daughter for the rest of my life. I don't need any righteous advice from a know-it-all dyke, even if she is my sister.

The bedroom is dark. Someone moves real quiet. My heart thumps. I feel myself shiver.

"Sylvia, querida, it's me," Mama whispers. "I brought you some dinner, mijita. Do you mind if I turn on the light?"

"Go ahead," I murmur. I try to shield my eyes with my arm.

On the chair next to the bed, she places a tray. Velez sat there hours before. "Enchiladas de pollo, the way you like them. Hay un poco de arroz y frijoles tambien. Let me help you up, mija."

She arranges the pillows and lets me lean on her. I wince while I struggle to sit up. Every bone in my body aches.

"I'll hold the plate for you," she offers.

"Thanks, Mama." I'm not really hungry, but she will feel worse if I don't eat. She's already cut the enchilada into small pieces. I chew them slow. My jaw hurts.

After a few bites, I make myself look at her. "Where is Zalo?"

She's surprised by my question. "Pues, with la policía— in jail."

"Mama, who's going to bail him out?"

At that she puts the plate down. Her usual meekness vanishes. "Mira, muchacha, don't expect me to do that. Isn't it bad enough what he did to you? You haven't seen what he did to the duplex. Broken windows, kicked in doors. Who's going to pay to for all that?"

I stare at her. "Are you saying that's my fault? Mama, are you saying we have to move?"

"Ay, Sylvia! *You* are welcome for as long as you like."

I shudder, trying to keep the sobs in. They push through. Mama holds me, rubbing my neck, murmuring to me.

I wish I was a little girl again. Mama and Daddy would take care of me, patch me up, kiss the hurt away. Daddy is gone now. Mama doesn't have all the answers. I cry harder. Too much has changed.

Toni

My ex-brother-in-law, Jeff Brandon, with several diet Cokes in his lap, rolls his wheelchair out of Mama's kitchen. He tosses one can to Pat, another to Gabi, offers me one, and takes the last for himself. How ironic that tonight Jeff brings a sense of normalcy to this family. Being around him used to annoy me. At one time he epitomized the perpetual teenager—fun-loving, always ready for a good time. The spinal injury at Surfrider Beach years ago created a remodeled Jeff Brandon, the one whose company I enjoy.

He jokes with Pat and Gabi. They share an engrossing discussion about media stereotypes of teenagers. Jeff, no longer tanned, remains handsome in a white-guy way. His wavy blond hair is still on the long side but thinner on top. His eyes are like Gabi's: clear, direct, sea-colored.

After his accident Jeff's wealthy parents came through for him. When he decided to finish college and attend graduate school for a Ph.D. in clinical psychology, the Brandons financed that. These days he has a thriving private practice on the Westside where he counsels troubled and suicidal teenagers. Jeff's persistent boyishness combined with his calm demeanor allow kids to trust him. My niece has an exceptional father…and his quick thinking today saved all of us.

I wonder what Sylvia thinks about him being here tonight. We welcome Jeff as a family member, but we do our best to avoid any contact with Zalo. Through the early years of her marriage to Jeff, Sylvia bolstered his ego by attending his surfing competitions. The rest of us thought her foolhardy to support him emotionally and financially. After years of broken hopes, Sylvia at last ended the marriage. That process had been gradual, and with independence she found loneliness, not fulfillment. She struggled as a single mother, receiving occasional child support checks from Jeff. Meanwhile he suffered his accident and an extended convalescence. Sylvia dated various men and even came close to marriage a couple of times. Jeff went on to a successful career, which helped him become a devoted father to Gabi. For Sylvia, life could have taken the high road, but when Zalo Anchondo became her second husband, she headed downhill.

The realization that Zalo will not be locked up for long makes me very nervous. There's no telling what revenge he might take when he is released. According to Ron Velez, Sylvia has no plan to press charges or obtain a temporary restraining order. I wonder if that really matters. How could a flimsy piece of paper keep Zalo at bay?

I don't want to think about that, so I putter around, picking up forgotten plates and glasses to take into the kitchen. After such an emotion-laden day, I have had no chance to think about my conversation with Pat. Would she have stayed with us for hours, been so supportive and loyal, if she didn't love me? I remind myself that Pat, like Jeff, has been a part of this family for years. Is that why she is still here, keeping us company? I am too tired from what happened today to contemplate her motives.

As I move past her with another stray glass, she grins. "Take a load off, Toni," she urges. "You've been nonstop for hours."

"Yeah, Toni," Jeff agrees. "Listen up. I have a proposition."

"Uh-oh," I murmur.

Gabi giggles. She moves over to give me some room on the sofa. I set the glass on the coffee table and face Jeff.

"Pat says Ron Velez will contact us when Zalo gets out of jail. When that happens—which probably will be soon—

you should all stay at my place."

"That's fine with me, Jeff, but Sylvia will never go for that. Neither will Mama."

"For Sylvia it's a pride thing."

"Grandma won't want to leave the property," Gabi adds.

"I understand that," Jeff says, glancing among us. "But I'm concerned about what might happen otherwise."

I lean toward him. "I totally agree with you. Sylvia and Mama are another story."

"You mean, they won't let me be their white knight in a silver wheelchair?" He smiles over the rim of his diet Coke.

"I doubt it." I'm touched by his generosity; I wish Sylvia would be too. I know better than to expect such a miracle.

"Well, I'll have to talk to Sylvia myself." He looks determined. "Gabi, honey, do you mind seeing if your mother's awake?"

Gabriela

I peek into the almost dark bedroom. "Grandma, how is she?"

"Pues, I'm trying to get her to eat," Grandma says. She doesn't turn when I come into the room. She holds the plate for Mom, feeding her like a baby.

"I can speak for myself, Mama." My mother sounds more like her feisty self. Not a good sign, if Dad thinks he can convince her of anything. "What do you want, Gabi?"

"Dad wants to talk to you."

She winces, probably not from pain but from the thought of being face-to-face with Jeff Brandon. "So you called in the troops."

"We were all real scared today, Mom." I stand by the bed

and stare at her battered face. How can she put on this stupid act? "You better believe I turned to Dad. You weren't exactly available."

"Go ahead, Gabi. Throw the guilt at me too. Everyone else is doing it. Why should you be any different?"

"Ay, hija." Grandma takes the plate away. She seems fed up. I'm not used to seeing her act this way. "For once in your life, Sylvia, will you please be quiet and listen to people who are trying to help you? Don't be impossible, muchacha."

"What am I supposed to do, huh?" Mom's voice is shrill. "Bow down to all of you? Admit I've fucked up again?"

"Don't talk that way to me," Grandma warns. Her face is stern. She leaves the bedroom real fast.

"You need a brain transplant," I mutter.

Mom's bashed face seems even more contorted in the shadowy room. "What did you say?"

I don't have to answer because Dad wheels himself in right at that point. Grandma must have given him the go-ahead. I hesitate by the door, wondering whether or not to stay.

"I want you here, honey," Dad murmurs when he passes. Curious as hell, I nod and lean against Grandma's dresser.

"Well, if it isn't Jeff Brandon, Mr. Do-Gooder himself," Mom says. If she's aiming for toughness, it's falling flat.

Her smartass remark doesn't faze Dad at all. "Other people besides you could have been hurt, Sylvia," he replies. "I want to do whatever I can to prevent any more violence. I'm offering you, Adela, and Toni a place to stay. Zalo needs a cooling-off period. I can recommend a therapist, and—"

Mom laughs like Dad's crazy. "Zalo won't go to a therapist, you dumb shit."

"Then divorce him," Dad says real quiet. "I never beat you, Sylvia. You divorced me."

I wish I could blend into the wall. Mom looks like she's about to cry. Dad makes sense, and she knows it.

"You wanted to play all the time," Mom finally mumbles. "You were a party animal, such a loser, Jeff. I got tired of waiting around for you to grow up."

"I was bad news, no question about it," Dad agrees. "Is this guy any better? I doubt it. His idea of a good time is knocking you around. The violence compounds the problem. Sylvia, he could kill you."

Mom sniffles. "What's your angle, Brandon?"

Dad almost grins. "You and I had a beautiful daughter together, Sylvia. That's the angle. I hate seeing Gabi worried sick over you. She doesn't deserve it. You don't either. I care enough about you to want you to stay alive."

Mom stares at her hands, like she's seeing them for the first time. "He'll come looking for me."

"Let him. Take Sergeant Velez's advice. Get a temporary restraining order. As the property owner, Adela ought to get one too. Velez said he'd personally follow up on this case."

"Yeah, he would," Mom mutters. "I don't know, Jeff. I have to think this through."

Dad nods. He sips his diet Coke and waits.

Pat

This is one helluva new year. Jeff's ex-wife is flat on her back, bruised from head to toe, and her bastard husband's behind bars for the time being. My ex-lover is back in town, and my mangled car's been towed to a body shop. Believe it or not I'm feeling kind of nostalgic about being part of the dysfunctional Dorado family. Hell, that's gotta mean it's time to call it a night.

"Do you want another Coke?" Toni says when I get to my feet.

"Nope. I'm going home." Grabbing my fleecy pullover from one of the chairs, I slip it over my head.

"Would you like some company?" She stands beside me, fawn eyes gazing into mine. How can I refuse?

"Would I have to walk you back?"

She laughs. "No, silly. I'll be fine by myself."

"It's a deal then." Aware of the double meaning of her words, I decide to ignore them. The day has been explosive enough already. I lead the way to the door.

The night is chilly. Toni and I glance at Sylvia's duplex while we walk down Adela's steps.

"Do you think it'll be all right with the furniture against the broken windows?" Toni walks next to me along the driveway. "I hope no one tries to rob the place."

"That's the least of your worries."

Toni's voice is quiet. "I'm really sorry, Pat. You were sweet enough to drive me home and look what happened. Now you don't even have a car to drive to work tomorrow."

"It's alright. I've bussed it before." Although I sound light-hearted, I don't feel it one bit. We move a few more steps, and I take on a more serious tone. "Promise me something, Toni?"

She nods, hands deep in the pockets of her denim jacket.

"Even if Sylvia and Adela stay here, will you please take Jeff's offer?"

"All right." Her large eyes search mine. I figure she is wondering why I haven't invited her to stay with me. Much too dicey.

"You heard what Ron and Jeff said; Zalo won't be locked up for long. He hates your guts—and mine too. The Mazda was a substitute."

She wraps a clutch of hair around her neck. "He wasn't exactly subtle. Sylvia's so damn stubborn."

"Listen, I've had more than enough of your sister today," I grumble, walking faster down Arizona Avenue. "Let Jeff handle her. He's the pro."

"Sorry." Toni sighs. "Seems that's all I've been saying to you today—I'm sorry."

My voice turns gruff. "Maybe I need to hear that over and over."

"I'm sure you do." Toni keeps pace with me before switching gears. "I don't know how I could've gotten through today without you. I really mean that, Pat. You're a true friend."

I look at her sideways. "I've tried to be for a long time. I think you forgot about that."

She nods, not answering for several moments. "If I could change the past year and a half—"

"You can't, Toni. It happened. Who knows why, but it did." I zip up my pullover another notch and duck my head under a low-lying tree branch. "There's no sense in running it into the ground. The question is, What happens now?"

Toni looks unsure of what to say next. Neither of us talk for almost half a block.

"Have you been dating anyone?" she finally asks. I've been waiting for that one all day.

"Nope...too busy with work."

"Oh. Well..."

"Yeah?" I stare right at her.

She acts flustered and blurts out, "I'd like to see you again, Pat—if that's all right."

I keep my eyes on hers. "I thought we were clear on that this morning."

"Well, after—"

"Toni, if I didn't want to see you anymore, I would've hightailed it pronto. Come on." I hear the impatience in my voice, and I don't like the sound of it. Are the months of resentment showing through? The stress of today's sexist and homophobic violence? "Most of the time you're an intelligent woman. Don't tell me you can't figure out why I've hung around."

That gets a rise out of her. "I don't want to take anything for granted, Pat. I thought you'd understand that."

I halt at the corner when a speeding pickup truck slams through the intersection. Damn out-of-state drivers never stop for pedestrians. Walkers' rights of way used to mean something in California. Hell, who can count on anything anymore?

"So we're even." We cross 20th Street together. "Look, Toni, I'm worn out. I need to shut down."

She follows me to the driveway of the apartment building on 19th Street. "Me too. I really don't want us to get on each other's nerves." She hunches her shoulders against the night chill. "Can I call you tomorrow?"

"At the office. I'll be there late."

She wants me to hug her, I know. Being close to her in the car, pressing her underneath me, threw my emotions out of whack again. Lying there while Zalo went on his rampage, I knew I would have died for her, pushed myself in front of her if that asshole had broken into the car. Realizing that scared the hell out of me. Right now I need to put some distance between us. I start to head upstairs.

"Buenas noches," I call over my shoulder.

Her voice drifts up. "Good night, Pat." I can't see her, but I hear the quiver.

I unlock my door. I just want to be alone.

Toni

Jeff and Gabi have gone. Sylvia sleeps in Mama's room. I'm sharing my bed with Mama. I can't remember when I last snuggled next to her, probably not since Sylvia was a baby. The three of us would take afternoon naps together. That was 35 years ago.

Listening to Mama's rhythmic breathing, I had been about to doze off. The very thought of all those years—and their intervening changes—snaps me awake again.

"How did it go con la Pat?" Mama murmurs, to my surprise. "Tan bueno to have her in this house again."

"I thought you were asleep," I whisper back. Sighing, I curl on my side to face her. "Well, it's really hard to tell, Mama. I never expected Pat to stay here all day."

"She cares, mija. How can you doubt that?" Mama tosses a reprimanding glance across the pillows. She has a headful of pink plastic rollers with a white hairnet holding them in place. No matter what she says about my straight hair, I can't imagine the alternative.

"It's late, Mama. Try to sleep."

"You don't want to talk about Pat ahorita, eh?"

"I have to mull all of it over. My brain's overloaded."

She makes no comment about that. "Pues, good night, mija. I'll be careful not to wake you when I get up for Mass."

I lean over and kiss her round cheek. "See you tomorrow, Mama."

Within moments, she is asleep, occasionally emitting a snore or two. Mama has an uncanny ability to drop off when anyone else would be an insomniac. I wish I had inherited her sleepy gene.

Closing my eyes, I concentrate on Pat. I remember her impulsive action in the Mazda, holding me down, shielding my body with hers. I conjure up the crisp ocean scent of her arms, the sleek feel of her jet hair brushing against me. Her strength seemed to embue me, to fill me with the ability to confront the rest of the day with all its ambiguities and conflicting emotions. She held me, kept me safe. She cradled me, whispered to me, calmed me.

At this moment I wish I were nestling with her instead of with my mother. Pat would wind herself around me during the night, spoonlike, her face against my back, one brown arm over my breasts, one muscled leg between mine. I miss her so much. During those months of isolation in the woods, enveloped in Amanda's frigid sheets, I thought of Pat constantly, desiring her and not the woman I had escaped with. Would Pat believe me if I tell her that? Is an 18-month separation too long for any relationship to survive?

Damn Sylvia and that scumbag Zalo. Their violent episode sidetracked my time with Pat. As divided as I felt—trying to keep my family together while focusing on Pat—I failed. In her eyes I fell into familiar patterns and put my immediate family, especially Sylvia, before her.

I know better than to blame the victim. I also know my sister—and her faults. Zalo's behavior is inexcusable; he belongs in jail for a long time. That aside, I'm still aware of Sylvia's sassiness and her tendency to provoke arguments. She must have known Zalo's fuse was ready to blow. Did she incite him further? If so, she is pathetic, caught up in his cycle of violence. I have never seen her in such a depressing predicament. Although she was once hesitant to end her marriage with Jeff, she finally did. Is her self-esteem in such ragged shape that she cannot see the danger around her?

Lying motionless, I try to banish her from my thoughts.

Bad enough she invades my waking hours. I keep seeing her wounded face before me, her bloody mouth, her terrified eyes. Whatever happened to my precious little sister?

Mama's loud snores add to my wakefulness. Silently I slip out of bed, grab the granny-square afghan, and tiptoe into the living room. Settling on the sofa, I curl up and wrap myself in the afghan. A sudden sound alerts me.

"Who's there?" I say aloud.

"I'm going to the john," Sylvia hisses. "Can't I even pee in peace?"

I rouse myself and step closer to the bedroom. "Need any help?"

"Fuck off, Toni."

Her bitter words stab me. I return to the sofa and lie still. The night is endless and lonely.

Part II

You know what the earth does, how it opens up and unfolds a life. How it can break apart, a sun-stroked puzzle in your fingers, dissolving back into itself.
—From "Gitanerias"
by Alicia Gaspar de Alba
in *Three Times a Woman*

⟅ CHAPTER EIGHT ⟆

January 9: Morning
Adela

Que bueno que I'm leaving today. I even went to Mass last night instead of this morning. Soon I will be on the air-conditioned bus with los otros senior citizens, on my way to Las Vegas for a few days.

Una amiga mía, Consuelo Archuleta, moved there with her family, and I'm going to visit her too. First some gambling, then una visíta con mi amiga. When I phoned Consuelo to tell her I'd be going to Las Vegas, she invited me to stay with her for a longer visit. Pues, cómo no? If Juan were alive, we would do this, verdad? In a few days I am going to fly back to Los Angeles. Ahora, as Gabi would say, "I'm outta here."

Gabi will drive me to the senior center to catch the bus. Ay, this past week has been muy difícil. Sylvia, that hardheaded girl, insisted on going back to the duplex right after the new windows were put in. She said she would clean up the place herself. Zalo's cousin Chava bailed him out. Toni heard this from Sergeant Velez. She packed up like a gypsy and went to Jeff's. I was alone for a few days, but somebody had to stay, no?

When Zalo showed up the day before yesterday, sniffing around for Sylvia, I was glad I had planned this trip. She was at work. I don't know if he went there. I don't want to know.

Mientras, while I'm away, Toni will pick up my mail. I wish she had stayed, but I know she wants be as far away from Zalo as possible. Even so, she promised to come by every day to be sure everything is fine. Pobrecita, she's trying to find work besides. She doesn't say much about la Pat. Toni likes to be private.

I carry mi valise to the porch and lock the door. Que bonita día. Muy sunny, almost like summer instead of January. I smile at a hummingbird buzzing by. El pajarito verde is headed for the feeder Toni hung in the peach tree a few days ago. I think mi hija did that so she will have an excuse to come by often.

It's too early for la Sylvia to be up. She said good-bye yesterday before she went to work. She looks a little better. Who knows what she told the other people on her shift? That she fell down the steps? She missed only one day of work; she said she could not afford to miss any more.

"Looks like you're ready, Grandma," Gabi calls out as she drives in.

"It will be good to get away for a little while, eh?" With some effort I take her extended hand and settle beside her.

"Has you-know-who been back?" She maneuvers the old Jeep backward. It used to belong to Jeff. Now he has one of those fancy vans with special controls.

"I haven't seen him, gracias a Dios."

"Mom's supposed to meet me for lunch at the mall."

"Que bueno. We have to make her feel she won't be alone, eh?"

"Not an easy thing to do, Grandma."

Sylvia

I hear Gabi's Jeep drive off. I would know the sound of that old thing anywhere. Jeff couldn't bear to part with it, even if he can't drive it anymore. No wonder he passed it on to Gabi. I think he gets a kick out of seeing her bouncing along in it. Those two have such a connection. Sometimes it makes me sick.

When Gabi was a baby, I was fascinated with her beauty— the Dorado cheekbones, the Brandon eyes, that golden skin, the wavy chestnut hair I loved to curl around my fingers. I used to think she combined the best of Jeff and me, in looks anyway. Nowadays she has a tendency to see things his way, like I'm an ignorant broad with no common sense. It's hard to take that my little girl's a college student with her own ideas and opinions, that my ex-husband—that rockin' blond surfer—is a practicing psychotherapist, Dr. Jeffrey Brandon. They've passed me up. Worst thing is, all three of us know it.

At this moment I have more in common with my dyke sister. Toni's on the skids too. At least I'm employed. She's living like a gypsy, as Mama says, moving from place to place, scrounging off whoever she can. Bet she has all kinds of hoity-toity conversations with Jeff over dinner. Glad I don't have to listen to that crap. Since when have they ever been friends? Mr. Do-Gooder takes a homeless dyke under his wing. I wonder if Toni realizes how desperate that makes her look.

Pat has laid low since New Year's. I haven't seen her

around here since. Fine with me. Zalo's really pissed that she's pressing charges against him. That damn lesbo needs her head examined. Day before yesterday, Zalo's cousin Chava came with him to the hospital. Chava works an early shift in food service. He was the one who got Zalo the orderly job at St. John's. That's how we met. I wasn't dating anyone then.

Whenever I was on duty, Zalo would stall in the corridors and flirt. He's younger than me, and maybe that's what caught my eye. Made me feel sexy. Who doesn't need that once in a while? We'd meet at break and neck in the stairwells. We almost got caught once or twice, which made it even more exciting. He was rougher with me than Jeff had ever been. Zalo would grope his big hand between my legs, put his hot tongue in my mouth, and all of a sudden we'd hear footsteps.

"Come, you bitch," he'd whisper. I would too—so fast I'd get dizzy.

We went on like that for months, till one of the nurses complained about his "inappropriate" comments. She was on the verge of accusing him of sexual harassment. The nuns never much liked Zalo to begin with. He was too in-your-face for their prim and proper ways. They danced around the issue by giving him a layoff notice.

By then I was so hooked on him that we eloped one weekend. My family was shocked. They didn't even know we'd been fucking for months in the place he shared with Chava. After we tied the knot, Zalo couldn't deal with my dyke sister or my teenage daughter either. That caused all kinds of problems. Gabi would run to Toni, to Mama, to Jeff—anywhere to get away from Zalo and me. It was a big relief when Toni split up with Pat and left town. Gabi solved her problems by moving into Mr. Do-Gooder's fancy canyon digs.

When the honeymoon was over, I learned right away Zalo doesn't like being told what to do. Neither do I. No wonder we get into fights. He's his own man, which proves his undoing sometimes. He winds up out of work 'cause he mouths off to his boss, decides to do things his own way, and pushes his coworkers around. Now he wants to come home and start over again. I don't know. Slapping me once in a while is one thing. Knocking me silly is something else.

I'm meeting him tonight at Chava's, where he's staying. Zalo's kept away 'cause I told him Mama's been really upset about the damage to the duplex. Leave it to Mama—she cares more about the property than about me. Acting like a big-time landlady. I'm glad she's gone. For all her religious ways, she's like the rest of the Dorados—taking off when times get tough.

Toni

On Jeff's redwood deck in Santa Monica Canyon, we sit overlooking half an acre of native plants. His landscaper has created an almost drought-proof environment with various sages and wildflowers. In a few months the area will be brilliant with color.

"Let it go, Toni. You said you have no regrets about leaving Amanda," Jeff reminds me.

"I don't. I didn't expect to receive a letter from her, though. I thought we'd both said enough already." I leave the envelope between us on the glass-topped patio table.

"Maybe she wants the last word." He rearranges his wheelchair to avoid the direct glare of the noonday sun. "Nobody likes being the one left behind. Being alone again shows

Amanda how secluded her life really is."

With a sigh, I pour myself another glass of orange juice. "I wanted to get away from it all. I had my fill pretty quick."

"And what about Pat?"

"She's being wary. A busy schedule is her excuse. I'm sure it's a legitimate one. Anyway, we're going to a movie today." I butter half a croissant and take a bite. "If I could only find a job, I'd feel much better about myself. That figures into this for sure. I hate transitional phases."

"Give yourself some time, Toni," he soothes. "You've been back less than a month."

"Veronica told me about a librarian position at Loyola Marymount. I sent my résumé last week. Waiting to hear about it is excruciating." I glance at my watch. "Well, I have to change. Almost time to meet Pat."

"Want a ride into town?"

I shake my head. "I'll take the Fourth Street stairs. Might as well get some exercise while I'm at it."

At the top of the rickety wooden staircase, I pause to catch my breath. Yuppie types in bright workout garb hurry past, seeming irked that I have come to a virtual standstill directly in their path. The steep Fourth Street stairs are a mecca for fitness freaks. Sweaty people clutching bottled water whiz by. Stepping aside at the top, I move to sit on the curb for a few minutes. When my heartbeat returns to normal, I head toward San Vicente Boulevard, then south to downtown Santa Monica.

Passing a clump of Jeffrey pines that appear incongruous on a beach city street, I ponder a section of Amanda's letter:

I keep asking myself what I did wrong. You grew silent, Toni, so inward, a melancholy stranger. I wanted you to be part of the world I created. Maybe, like you said, you're simply an urban creature, out of your element among nature. I think about your experience with the merlin. It foretold your wish to capture your own needs and desires. Like the merlin, you've flown away. The forest—our nest—is empty without you.

Melodramatic, yes. Untainted Amanda: believing she can mold a perfect world, where everyone and everything—regardless of ethnicity and social class—blends without disruption, without strife. It felt artificial, passionless. In Amanda's utopia I missed Pat's offbeat sense of humor, her jive comments, even her occasional grumpiness.

A long time ago, while reading Hayden Herrera's biography of Frida Kahlo, I was struck by the description of the Mexican artist's mode of laughter: carcajadas. That fits Pat too. A deep laughter that starts from her gut and leaps out of her mouth in unrestrained spurts. Amanda never laughed that way.

I have no regrets about leaving her—only a sadness that my confusion, my bewilderment about the direction in which to turn my life, affected her. My headlong decision to join her offered her a fleeting dream fulfillment: a lover to share her utopian vision. My departure destroyed her fantasy. For that I bear responsibility, but no regret.

Afternoon
Pat

I've claimed a corner spot at Humphrey Yogart, relaxing with a mocha swirl and keeping my eyes peeled for Toni. For the past week I've been bound and determined to limit our time together and not 'cause I don't want to see her. Just the opposite. I'd rather be with her all the time. This time around, I want my head to rule my heart. It ain't easy.

She has a lot to do anyway, now that she's back in town—mainly, start earning a paycheck. That's a major deal for Toni. She'll get bored staying at Jeff's, even if it's paradise compared to that damn cabin in the Cascades. She isn't the type to sit around doing nothing, not Toni.

I twirl the mocha yogurt in the cup, mixing in the sprinkles and chocolate chips. Toni ought to be here soon. It takes a little while to walk from the canyon. Not having a car this week makes it impossible for me to offer her a ride. If this keeps up, I'll see if I can get a loaner. Yeah, this is one helluva year. Have to keep my mouth shut about that. It'd give Toni the perfect chance to suggest we combine forces and struggle along together.

I was on the phone with René last night, and she right away asked if I'd made love to Toni yet.

"Haven't even kissed her, cabrona," I muttered.

"Ay, esa! You know you want to." She moaned suggestively into the phone. "Making her suffer for you, Pat?"

"Shut up." I had to laugh at Rene's exaggerations, although there is some truth to them.

Point is, I'm used to being on my own these days: leave the office, go home, and slam the door on the rest of the world. Listen to music, sprawl on the couch with a magazine or book. Or sit at the desk and work on press releases or fundraising for the coalition. If I feel like talking to someone, I pick up the phone. Otherwise I can monitor my calls, "veg out," flick on the tube, hang with myself.

Sure, I miss sex. Not enough to play the pinche dating game. René says I'm a "professional lesbian," out at work and everywhere else, but basically a stay-at-home type. I'm set in my ways, sure. More likely I'm still in love with Toni.

Right then she strides by, figuring she has a few minutes to spare. Her black hair is caught at the nape with a royal blue ribbon. She wears a pair of navy shorts and a Rosie the Riveter T-shirt that states "We Can Do It!" Spiffy. Looks like she's lost a couple of pounds. Jeff's into Lean Cuisine; maybe he's converting her. A few guys turn as Toni breezes by. Forty or not, she attracts attention. She darts into Midnight Special Bookstore.

I'll stay put. She'll be out soon. I haven't finished my yogurt anyway.

Gabriela

"Let's go to Wok In," Mom announces. She's waiting by the first-floor escalator at the Santa Monica Place shopping mall. "I love their fried rice."

"Great."

Following her, I notice she's starting to look pregnant on all sides. She's wearing a splashy sleeveless dress, the summery, tent-like kind. Not exactly a maternity outfit but close. She's dyed her hair again. It falls loosely to her shoulders. Her face is a little puffy on one side but nothing like a few days ago.

We don't say much in the Chinese food line. Afterward I luck out and find a table off to the side where we can talk.

"Did Mama get on the bus on time?" Mom pokes the sweet-and-sour pork with a plastic fork.

"No problem."

"Bet she was glad to have that chance, huh?"

I shrug. "She likes senior citizen trips."

"Just happened to be this week," Mom adds with a smirk. "What's Mr. Do-Gooder have to say about that?"

"I wish you wouldn't call Dad that." I play with a mush-room before popping it into my mouth.

She laughs and glances around. "Where's your sense of humor, Gabi? Can't you see how funny it is? Your ex-surfer daddy's all of a sudden some big-bucks psychological expert."

"Would you rather see him drink himself into a stupor every night? Would you rather see him suicidal over being a paraplegic?" I make myself face her across the table. "You have a twisted way of looking at things, Mom."

"No. You're being brainwashed by Jeff and Toni." She wipes her mouth with the edge of the paper napkin. "That's obvious. Get this straight, blue-eyed baby girl: I'm the sur-vivor here. Who do you think paid the bills all those years your dad was riding the waves? The Brandons wrote him off while he was married to me. I broke their color scheme. You don't remember that, do you? Once I was out of the picture, they took an interest in Jeff again. He hasn't done anything on his own."

"Yeah, right." I lean back and stare at her. "The Brandons wrote Dad's Ph.D. dissertation, I suppose. Mom, can't you ever give him any credit?"

"Who wants to talk about Jeff Brandon? I thought you wanted to have lunch with *me,*" she mutters, taking on a hurt tone.

"You're the one who brought him up." Exasperated, I ball up my napkin and hoist a forkful of rice into my mouth. I de-cide to be calm and not rile her. "You feeling OK, Mom?"

"That's better," she says with a half smile. "Yeah. If I could only sleep through the night. I don't like being alone."

I wonder what she means by that. For a moment I wish I could change places with Grandma. She's on her way to a fun week.

Mom smiles again. She has a saucy look about her. I don't even want to think about what it could mean.

Toni

We're stuck on the left side of the Odeon theater, closer to the screen than either of us like.

Yesterday, when I mentioned wanting to see *Six Degrees of Separation,* Pat made a face. "You want to see a flick about a bunch of rich white folks?"

Sometimes I forget she's a media watchdog who keeps close tabs on new releases.

"Pat, it's written by John Guare, based on his play." I put on my most persuasive tone. "He wrote *Atlantic City,* remember?"

"At least that one had Susan Sarandon," she grumbled during our early evening stroll to Thrifty Drug Store.

"Stockard Channing's in *Six Degrees.* So are Donald Sutherland and Will Smith." I used the long ends of my hair as enticements and brushed them against her arm.

At my action Pat laughed. "Hell, I guess it'll be all right. Class conflicts supposedly based on an actual incident."

"Terrific!" I scooted around her. I imitated a happy child, almost tripping her in the process. On impulse she chased me to the Thrifty parking lot where we reverted to adulthood again.

In the movie theater I glance at her to gauge her mood. She smiles at some witty dialogue. Both of us like well-written films, even though they're few and far between these days. I enjoy the conversational exchanges between Stockard Channing and Donald Sutherland—her expressive face, his drollness. The audience titters. But their laughter—and ours—

ceases when two thunderous booms shake the theater.

People scream. Several men dash to the front exits. On instinct I grab Pat's arm. "What was that? An explosion on the Promenade?"

"Earthquake," reasons a matter-of-fact voice behind us. "No big deal."

"Felt pretty damn big to me," Pat whispers.

"Should we stay or what?"

She gazes at me with affection. "Thought you wanted to see this."

"I do."

"Shhh," the irritated guy behind us hisses.

"There's your answer, Toni. We're losing a whole chunk of dialogue," Pat remarks. She leans back again and rests one hand over mine.

A few people in the audience straggle out, no doubt unnerved by sitting in the lower level of the cineplex. The rest of us—jaded Californians to the core—settle down, too engrossed in the film to leave.

A bit uneasy, I remain in my seat, very conscious of Pat's soothing hand. It has not moved. As a result, neither do I.

Sylvia

"Zalo went to buy some cerveza," Chava tells me through the torn screen door.

He lets me into the downstairs apartment on Brockton Avenue. A few doors north, on the corner of Santa Monica Boulevard, a shabby liquor store gives a clue about the rest of the block. When I got off the No. 1 bus a few minutes ago, I passed lots of run-down apartments, filled with single Latinos, many of them immigrants. I didn't see Zalo near the liquor store or anywhere else.

Chava's a skinny guy, about a third Zalo's size in weight. He has sad puppy eyes, a graying crewcut, and a scraggly mustache.

"Hot for January, no?" He's barefoot, in baggy shorts and a ripped camiseta. The small apartment reeks of male sweat—Zalo's.

"Thanks for bailing him out, Chava."

I fan myself with my hand and sink into the sagging sofa. My bra is soaked with sweat. The air conditioner on the city bus was broken. With every seat taken and people crammed together, I almost couldn't breathe.

"Pues, Zalo's mi primo." Chava scratches one thin arm and stares at the threadbare carpet. "Sylvia, it's none of my business, but he ought to treat you with respect. You're going to have a baby, eh?"

I don't want to argue with Chava. He usually doesn't say much anyway. I don't want to mess up things between Zalo and him.

"Chava, can I have a glass of water?"

"Sure, sure." He reacts right away and brings me a water-stained plastic tumbler. "Hey, did you feel los temblores?"

"What?"

"A little while ago, Sylvia. Two earthquakes. Ba-boom! Híjole! I was watching football. The TV almost fell over."

I set down the tumbler. "Didn't feel a thing. Must've happened while I was on the bus."

Chava nods several times. He's run out of conversation.

"Mind if I lie down, Chava? The heat's getting to me."

He points to an open doorway. I know the way. I collapse on the rumpled bed. In seconds I'm asleep.

Something cold is against my face. Real slow, I open my eyes.

"I like comin' back and findin' you ready for me," Zalo says. He holds the icy Coors can to my cheek. He leans across me, one big arm against my tits.

"It's so hot, Zalo." I start to raise my head.

"Have some of this." He hands me the can. "Loosen you up."

The beer tastes good. I take a huge swallow and return the can. "You said you wanted to talk. That's what I came for."

He guffaws and presses one meaty palm hard to my nipple. We both feel it tighten. "Yeah? You came to fuck. It's what you always want."

I'm not about to say otherwise, not when he's already straddling me. He's so heavy, I can't move. He flips my dress up, tears off my panties. I squeeze my eyes closed. I wish I could get in the mood, but I don't want him to hurt me again.

"Look at me," he demands. "Watch me do it, bitch."

I stare at his grimacing face. He seems to be having a problem. Too much booze, maybe. *Just get it over with,* I think.

"Tell me what she used to do to you," he insists.

Why did I ever let him know Toni and I used to mess around when we were kids? In those days we shared a bedroom. Before we'd doze off she'd pretend to be my husband. She'd kiss and touch me, and I'd do it back. That's how we had our first orgasms. We didn't know what we were doing. We just knew it felt good.

Now that's all Zalo ever wants to hear. Some stupid macho fantasy that he's fucking a chick who played sex games with her dyke sister.

"You like it better with her, don't you?"

"Stop saying that, Zalo," I mutter through gritted teeth.

"That's right. Keep at it. Get mad so I'll get hard."

He's stuffed one tit into his mouth. He's chewing on it, slurping like its a giant meatball. When his tongue sideswipes my nipple, I finally feel a rush of excitement. He knows he's getting to me. He bites me.

I wince and grab at him, my fingernails digging into his sweaty back. We grapple and tussle. His rough hands are all over me. He pushes one to my crotch. I'm so wet I can hear the bubbly sounds from between my legs. I'm breathing hard, feeling woozy. My legs pull him closer.

"Do it, man. Fuck me."

Evening
Sylvia

In the truck I sit close to the door. "Why do you do that, Zalo?"

"Huh?" He pulls up at the signal on Bundy Drive and Santa Monica Boulevard.

"You know. All that dirty talk about Toni and me? We were kids. Didn't you ever jerk off with Chava?"

Like lightning he lunges across the cab, yanks me against him. I inhale his boozy breath and feel a wave of nausea.

"Don't ever say that to me. I ain't no fuckin' faggot!" He lets me go. I crash against the seat like a crumpled rag doll.

I say nothing till he starts driving again. I'm asking for it, but I keep on anyway.

"If you hate faggots and dykes so much, how come you always want to hear about my sister?"

"Damn it, Sylvia. Shut up, hear me?" He glowers and raises his hand.

I wince.

Satisfied, he keeps driving.

The duplex is dark. I had set the lamp timer, but the light bulb must have burned out. I open the truck door and step to the graveled driveway.

"You think you have a job lined up, Zalo?"

"Looks that way. Driving a furniture truck in the Valley." He stays behind the wheel and eyes me. "Give me a chance, huh?"

I talk to him through the open window. "You need to understand this. I don't want to be beaten to a pulp again. I want this baby, Zalo, whether you do or not. I want to be treated better than I have been. There's no reason for you to shove me around."

He tries to joke. "I'm a young hombre, Sylvia. I fuck up sometimes, all right? I told you I'm sorry."

I sigh, evaluating my options. It would be too hard to raise a baby by myself. Who would baby-sit during my work hours? Mama would not want to be tied down. I can't count on Gabi—she's out of the house. When I divorced Jeff, Gabi was in grade school. Even so, raising her on my own was no picnic. Besides, I might look good for 37, but I'm not getting any younger. Zalo may not be much, sure, but right now he's all I've got.

"When can I come back?" He leans across the seat. He pushes a a thick finger along my cheek. It tugs at my ear lobe and almost feels gentle. Why can't he always be playful like this? Why can't things be steady instead of such a struggle?

I lick his finger as it travels across my mouth. My voice is barely above a whisper. "Before Mama gets home. Otherwise, she'll make a fuss."

⌐ CHAPTER NINE ⌐

January 12: Morning
Toni

When I worked at the library, I always enjoyed going to the farmers' market. Every Wednesday before going home, I'd stroll over to buy an armload of sunflowers for our apartment and select fresh California produce from Santa Maria, Oxnard, Fillmore, or southward from the Imperial Valley. Sometimes I'd join the crowds milling around the food vendors and purchase tamales and empanadas for an impromptu dinner.

Being unemployed gives me a few pleasures—such as browsing at the outdoor market any time of day. This morning the sky is overcast, but by noon the sun will poke through the clouds and offer another unseasonably warm day. For now I enjoy the cooler weather. After making a stop at Mama's to take in her mail and check on her parakeet, Nopalito, I plan to return to the market. I need to stock up on fruits and vegetables because I cook dinner for Jeff to earn my keep.

When I lived with Amanda, I protested preparing her

meals. We divided most domestic responsibilities. Since I stayed home all day, it made sense for me to cook. Isolation, however, intensified my sensitive nature. Being unemployed and the only woman of color for miles around made me even more aware of social inequities. Amanda provided for me, but I was not in love with her. The sexual aspect of our relationship made things even more complicated, and resentments about cooking spilled into our bed. Fortunately, Jeff expects nothing from me except a well-balanced dinner. I'm off whenever he has evening clients.

I stroll through the market, admiring shiny eggplants, golden jars of sage and wildflower honey, overflowing containers of herbs and alfalfa sprouts. The bespectacled guy in the cartoonish fish cap sells tilapia, which he dubs "organic" fish. The tasty South American species is one of Jeff's favorites. For now I buy a bag of oranges to leave in Mama's refrigerator, a treat for when she returns this weekend.

Ambling along Arizona Avenue with the mesh bag of oranges half under my arm, half balanced on my hip, I notice a familiar figure striding toward me. We recognize each other immediately and lunge forward in jerky movements.

"Crystal!"

"Toni!"

She is taller than I am, a big-boned woman in her 50s with a penchant for flowing scarves and jangling jewelry. "You rascal, when did you blow into town?" Her mischievous brown eyes appraise me. She nearly smothers me with her impetuous hug.

"Right before New Year's."

"Family visit?"

Somewhat embarrassed, I shake my head. "I'm trying to prove Thomas Wolfe wrong."

She laughs outright, her frizzy gray hair bouncing in rhythm. "Wonderful! Let's have lunch, darling." She begins to steer me toward the Promenade.

"I can't today, Crystal. I'm on my way to Mama's and—"

She grabs my hand and squeezes it. "It's been s-o-o-o boring at the library without you."

I smile at her comment. "You're probably the only one who thinks so. How are things at the main branch?"

"Marian's on medical leave."

That revelation catches me by surprise. When I was laid off, Marian Cates became head reference librarian, the position that should have been mine.

"She has lung cancer, Toni. Two packs a day caught up with her."

"That's terrible," I whisper.

"Oh, be honest, honey. Since when has Marian given a damn about you? She doesn't like your natural brown color. Her nicotine-stained fingers are the shade she prefers. But when the old bitch kicks the can—"

Used to her candor, I nonetheless begin to protest. "Crystal, that's so—"

"True," she finishes for me, eyes alight. "I'll tell Baldwin you're back. You know she'll—"

"Baldwin?"

"Yes, dear. Ruthann Baldwin's the chief these days. Old man Nelson retired." She clutches my hand even tighter. "Ruthann will give you the slot when Marian's history. You know you deserve it, Toni. All you'd have to do is ask."

I hesitate. Her revelations throw me off-kilter. I had never imagined such an outcome, certainly not at someone else's expense. For a fleeting moment I wonder if Amanda's totem interpretation about the merlin could have been correct—all that gobbledygook about my wish to capture my needs and desires. The very idea gives me goose bumps. Shifting the bag of oranges to my other hip, I raise my eyes to Crystal's gaze.

"Want to have lunch tomorrow at 1?"

"Love to, sweets." She plants a sudden smooch on my cheek and pats my shoulder. "Bring your résumé. Meet me at the Thai place across from the library." She hurries toward the Promenade.

"Glad I ran into you, Crystal," I call after her.

With an exuberant wave she jogs across Fourth Street.

My pace becomes buoyant as I head east on Arizona Avenue. By the time I reach Lincoln Boulevard, however, reality sinks in. Crystal is a perpetual optimist, which makes her the perfect personality type for the circulation desk. Opinionated and humorous, she has never hidden her disdain for Marian Cates. Crystal already has her dead and buried. But cancer can be unpredictable. Marian is ornery enough to beat the odds. Besides, has Crystal forgotten the ethnic-racial tensions that surfaced after the riots? Ruthann Baldwin, whom I had considered an ally, opposed my attempts to include Latinos in the ethnic-racial displays and programs we initiated. She cited low Westside Latino demographics. She would probably hire another African-American before welcoming me back to the reference desk. Besides, do I want to return to the institution that dismissed me?

On the other hand, librarian positions are few and far between. Loyola Marymount has not been in any hurry to contact me. Uneasy about Crystal's news, I weigh my job possibilities: scarce, virtually nonexistent. No matter what Pat and Jeff advise, I would dread a career change. For the time being, lunch with Crystal Delaney seems a sensible move.

Mama has a stack of mail waiting. Propping the bag of oranges against the duplex's rough stucco, I grab the letters from the tin box attached to one of the porch posts. I push aside the screen door and insert my key into the somewhat rusty lock. Entering, I nudge the bag of oranges inside with my foot. Mama's mail is composed of Catholic-charities requests, one utility bill, two mail-order catalogs, a Spanish-language religious magazine. Nothing has my name on it.

Leaving the mail on the little wooden cabinet beside the door, I take the oranges into the kitchen and lay the bag on the refrigerator's empty bottom shelf. I have already eaten whatever leftovers sat there.

In Mama's pantry I find a can of vegetable soup and decide on that for lunch. I reminisce about Crystal and the library while stirring the soup on the stove. My 14 years at the main branch paralleled my coming out as a lesbian, my decade-long relationship with Pat, my father's death, my estrangement from Sylvia—all the landmarks of my personal history. Would returning be a good idea? To my finances, of course. Otherwise I'm not certain.

Startled out of my reverie, I hear Sylvia's screen door slam. Heavy footsteps grind through the gravel.

"Oh, shit," I say aloud.

Zalo Anchondo's hulking shadow passes the kitchen window. Zalo aims himself down the driveway. What is he doing here? With Mama gone, has Sylvia let him sneak back? Or not?

My emotions steam and simmer like the soup I pour from the pot to a bowl. At the kitchen table I make myself eat.

The phone rings midway through my meal. I am tempted to ignore it, but what if it's Pat? Scurrying into the living room, I pick up the receiver.

"Everything OK, Toni? I'm between classes," Gabi says. "Thought you might be there."

I keep my voice low. "Zalo's back. I just saw him, but I don't know where he parked. His truck isn't in sight."

Gabi sighs. "Is Mom home?"

"I don't think so. Look, I don't want to stay long. Talk to you later."

"Be careful, Toni."

I wash the saucepan and bowl and set them on Mama's kitchen counter. Then I give Nopalito fresh seed and water. The little green parakeet does not seem to recognize me. He chirps wildly and skitters from my hand.

Perhaps the running water obscures the sounds of Anchondo's return. A sudden whirring sound shatters the uneasy silence. With some trepidation I peer out the gingham-curtained window.

"I can't believe it!" I say out loud. I stare at Anchondo's bulky form. With an electric saw he assaults the side branches of Mama's prized peach tree, the one Daddy planted when they moved to the duplex. I fly outside without even hesitating. From the porch I shout in his direction. "What do you think you're doing?"

Either deliberately or because he cannot hear me, he disregards my question. He continues chopping off the bare branches. On one is my dome-shaped hummingbird feeder.

"Stop it!"

Perhaps conscious for the first time of my presence, he whirls. His ugly mouth curls into a jackal's grin. "This yours, pussylicker? Makes a sticky mess, just like you."

He reaches for the fallen feeder and hurls it Frisbee-like. The red plastic crashes against the side of the porch and breaks into smithereens. The sugar water splatters.

Rage overcomes me. I clench my fists, wishing I could plummet them into his hideous face.

"How dare you destroy what isn't yours!" I scream at him. "Leave Mama's tree alone!"

He switches off the saw and carries it with contempt by his side. "You leave Sylvia alone. Hear me, fuckin' pervert?"

I back into the house and shut the screen door. He does not come any closer.

"This saw cuts clean through. See that, dyke?" He yells louder when I lock myself in. "Damn branches won't scratch my bedroom window anymore."

Without making a sound, I grab my fanny pack and rush out the kitchen door. His mocking falsetto laughter follows me. Filled with dread, I remember the Spanish word for *branches* is *ramas*—too similar to Ramos, Pat's last name.

Afternoon
Sylvia

Red pieces of plastic catch my eye. They dot the mossy ground by Mama's porch. The afternoon sun makes them shine. The red slivers look like broken pieces of a kid's toy. I pick one up. Gooey liquid seeps on my fingers. Dropping the piece, I rub my fingers together. What has Zalo done now?

Then I notice the peach tree. Last night he complained about the long branches knocking against our window. The swaying sounds can lull me to sleep, but not Zalo. Looks like he carved Mama's peach tree into a spindly skeleton. It's horrible. By spring it'll be full again, but Mama won't be happy to see it like this.

"You were busy today." I step inside and haul the brown grocery bag to the kitchen.

"Yeah. I can sleep tonight," he says. He doesn't glance away from the war movie on TV.

"Did you have to smash Toni's bird feeder while you were at it?" I take an onion from the refrigerator and begin slicing it on the cutting board.

"Fuckin' birds make a shitty mess, just like that dyke." He hoots with high-pitched laughter.

I've never understood why some burly guys—particularly Latinos—laugh in falsetto like teenaged girls. Not exactly a macho trait, but I know better than to mention that.

"She'll be pissed, Zalo." I grab a couple stalks of celery and slice them too.

"She *was*. Turned tail and ran."

"Did you threaten her?"

He giggles again.

I curse to myself before standing in the doorway separating the dinky kitchen from the living room. "I really hope you didn't, Zalo. Ron Velez phoned me at work today."

"Fuck him," Zalo mumbles. "You tell him I'm here?"

"Of course not. He still wants me to file charges."

Zalo glares at me.

"Don't you get it, Zalo? Everyone's watching to see what you'll do next. The more you hassle Toni, the more reason Mama will have for evicting us."

He scoffs at my comments. "The rent control board won't allow it, Sylvia. We're covered."

"No, we're not. Duplexes are exempt from rent control." I head back to the kitchen. Damn hombre doesn't even know the law.

"So what're you telling me?" In seconds he's in my face.

His fast move rattles me, but I stand my ground. "What's the point of staying here? Once you start your job, we'll look for a new place to live. In the meantime, behave yourself."

He presses against me, rough hands on my belly. One slides up and pushes inside my white uniform.

"Is this your only answer?" I whisper.

"The one you know best." He grabs my hair and pulls my head back.

Pat

"Don't go there alone, Toni."

I balance the phone against my shoulder while drafting an article on the office computer. It's a rebuttal to a recent "Counterpunch" essay in the *Los Angeles Times* about the lack of Latino-Latina representation on television and in films. As the article takes shape and I listen to Toni, I can't help thinking Zalo Anchondo is a living stereotype. No way do I want his kind depicted in the media, but his damn macho hermanos get the most airplay.

"I can wait till Saturday morning. Mama didn't have that much mail, Pat. She'll be home that afternoon."

In all the years we were together, Toni rarely phoned me at work. Does she want me to rescue her from this current family revorujo? Is that her underlying message? She sounds damn shook up about this latest mitote with Anchondo, especially the double entendre about branches and my name. I don't know if Zalo has enough brains to make that connection, but it sure hits home. Picturing that pendejo swinging the chainsaw brings up countless antiwoman images from movies Media OutReach has rallied against. I try to shake them out of my mind. If anything happens to Toni…

Rolling my chair away from the computer, I hike my booted feet to the top of the two-drawer filing cabinet beside the desk. Toni keeps talking. Part of me is touched she has called; the other wants to back off from this whole fucked-up scene.

"By the way, Pat, did you know that Sunday's quake was a 3.7?"

I'm glad she's changed the subject. "Yeah? Felt a lot stronger to me."

"The seismologists think it was on the Westwood extension of the Elysian Park fault."

"I would've thought the epicenter was offshore."

"It was. The fault runs from Whittier Narrows through downtown L.A. and along the Santa Monica Mountains to the ocean."

"You sound like a librarian, Toni." I grab my coffee cup and take a sip. "Getting a mixed bag of welcomes, aren't you, from homophobic threats to offshore earthquakes?"

Toni laughs a little. Probably wondering if I'm being sarcastic.

"Jokes aside," I continue, "you should report Zalo's latest blast to the Gay and Lesbian Center in West Hollywood."

"Pat, Santa Monica is—"

"I know—we're in a different city. The point is, the center keeps statistics on hate crimes for the whole county. Be a good citizen, Toni. While you're at it phone Ron Velez too. Bring him up-to-date."

Toni sighs. "I was scared, but—"

"Zalo *implied* violence. I've already reported to the hotline what that asshole did to my car. The hotline guys ask about the perpetrator's ethnicity. They keep track of that too. Seems our macho hermanos are some of the worst homophobes in Los Angeles County. Not too much of a surprise."

"Gives me chills," she whispers into the phone.

"Another reality to cope with in this mesmerizing multicultural metropolis." I edge my chair to the desk again. "Look, I have to finish this article, Toni."

"All right." She hesitates for a second. "Pat, would you like to have dinner with us tonight? I'm making a huge salad, red potatoes, grilled tilapia."

"Sorry. KCRW is interviewing me after work."

"How about after that?" Toni has a hopeful tinge in her voice.

"Rather see you this weekend." I say the words fast, not wanting to hurt her. "I should have the car by then."

Toni's voice becomes quieter. "I miss you, Pat."

"We both have a lot to think about." I bite my lower lip. "Sometimes we each have to do that alone."

Toni

Sliding the patio door open, I wander to Jeff's redwood deck. My hair falls heavy on my back in the afternoon's warmth. Absently, I roll it into a knot at my nape and slump into one of the molded plastic chairs.

I made the phone calls Pat suggested. I left a message for Sergeant Velez to contact me. On the gay and lesbian hotline, I spoke in a monotone voice, unwilling to offer more than the facts. The gay man who took my call asked my ethnicity too. Another depressing statistic about Latina-Latino relations.

A westward breeze sways the rose bushes beside my chair. I notice the silvery threads of an enormous spider web woven with intricate precision in a whole section of the almost bare bush. In the center rests a large amber-colored araña, her many legs hinged to the fluttering web. The honey hue of her body glistens. Repulsed, I move the chair a few inches. Another spider totem to learn from, Amanda would suggest.

"Go away."

I bring my knees to my chin and try to ignore the spider as well as my encroaching thoughts of Amanda. Maybe I have become like a spider to Pat, bobbing into sight like this garden araña, springing into her life, dangling before her. Does she think I am trying to spin a web around her?

Sylvia, more likely, is the one caught in a web. Why in the world did she get pregnant, binding herself further to that cabrón? Is she so afraid of being alone that she is willing to jeopardize herself? Has he forced his way back? I shudder despite the afternoon sun. Glancing at the spider again, I observe a smaller one at the far corner of her web. I turn away from the creepy sight.

Gabi has always wanted a younger sibling, but how does she feel about this unborn baby? My niece, I'm sure, has plenty of opinions, many thoughts perhaps unexplored. She has put off discussing her mother with me, other than expressing her animosity toward Zalo Anchondo. On that we definitely agree. Gabi is busy with classes and her job. As long as I'm here, though, we need to talk more. Aside from Mama we are the two who care the most about Sylvia. I doubt if my sister would ever believe—or acknowledge—that.

Legs stretched before me in white cotton shorts, I sprawl in the chair. Because of the winter heat wave, my skin has browned to a deeper shade. Jeff has teased me about this when he comes home from work and finds me sunbathing. If Pat and I ever get together, I would not want her to see how my legs faded in the Pacific Northwest gloom. She loves mujeres de color. I wonder how many there have been while I was gone. She says none. Is she sparing me the details?

Frowning at that disturbing thought, I let my gaze meander back to the spider's web. The small one, about two thirds her size, skitters along one strand and approaches the female.

She seems oblivious to his nervous approach. Confident of her attractiveness, she lounges in the sun, rocking gently as if the web were a hammock and she were a lady of leisure.

Although the spiders repulse me, my librarian's curiosity resurfaces. I remember a PBS documentary about spiders; the main branch has several copies. Extremely popular with kids, the program is no doubt the basis for zillions of science projects. Maybe I can watch a nature show in person this very afternoon. Besides, what else do I have to do until dinnertime?

The smitten male advances and retreats, undaunted by her indifference. At last la araña inches toward him. She stops, however, testing his courage. He pauses momentarily, then recovers his fortitude. Soon she begins to wiggle her legs at him, seduction in mind. At her beckoning he scampers toward her; I swear, he almost breaks into a jig. There is much fluttering of legs from both parties. I change my posture and lean closer. Does she actually spread her legs for him?

The intrepid little señor continues his wooing, his thin legs tentatively touching hers. At once I realize one of those isn't a leg. Oh, dear, he is about to penetrate her. With voyeuristic zeal, I am fascinated by this erotic mating dance. I cover my mouth to keep from laughing, as if my amusement would intrude on their privacy. In no time they are a quivering tangle of amber legs. It is difficult to tell which is which. Finally they part. He drifts away, then zooms back in seconds as if he cannot bear the separation. They whirl together again, seemingly insatiable. Once more he breaks off. He repeats these sex-crazed maneuvers several times. Their liaisons seem endless. I am impressed by their stamina.

Afraid to blink, unwilling to miss a detail, I continue to stare at the live-action, X-rated minidocumentary. I hold my breath, suspecting the outcome. La araña does not cringe from her assigned role. During the tiny señor's latest advance, she pounces with deadly alacrity and traps his flailing body within the amber prison of her stronger legs. She spins efficient coils of elastic bindings, hog-tying her hapless lover in a fatal embrace. Without a trace of sentimentality, she drags his bound and still body to the opposite section of the huge web.

Exhausted, I lean back in the chair. Pat and I have begun our own mating dance, but I cannot imagine either of us as predator or prey. The spider totem ought to be my sister's, not mine.

"Goddamn it, Sylvia," I state in the silence of Jeff's garden. "Why can't you do that to Zalo?"

La araña ignores my outburst. She is planning her dinner.

Gabriela

Sure, it's unrealistic to even think this, but right now I wish Toni was my mother, not my aunt. Her gorgeous hair is in a French braid down her back—I did that for her. Her face is glowing. She's wearing a crisp white T-shirt and shorts. You'd think she was a hip Mrs. Suburbia. Next to Dad at the dinner table, she serves us a delicious meal and launches into a hilarious story about two spiders fucking on the patio.

Dad chuckles over Toni's on-purpose melodramatics. "First time you've seen the likes of that?"

"With spiders, yes."

"Didn't you say there were armies of them in the woods of Washington?"

She grins at him. "Jeff, this patio is much more conducive to studying insect life. The spiders up north had the nerve to show up on the bed or in the bathtub. Southern California spiders know their place."

"I wouldn't count on that," I cut in with a laugh.

Toni shrugs. Before long she mentions seeing her friend Crystal and tells us about the possible job. A mindblower, for sure.

"Would you want to work there again?" I pour us both a glass of homemade sangría from the pitcher.

"I'm not sure," she admits. "Not many alternatives that I can see, unless I want to get into another field. That really doesn't appeal to me."

"Keep your mind open, Toni." Dad serves himself another heaping bowl of salad. "I know some job counselors if you'd like to follow another path."

"Thanks. In the meantime, I'll talk with Crystal tomorrow." She rolls a red potato from one side of her plate to the other.

Toni's probably thinking about the library job and my Mom, so I blurt out what I turned up. "I drove by Grandma's on my way home. Zalo's truck was in the driveway."

Dad munches his salad, his eyes pensive.

Toni sighs. "I had a run-in with him when I went to pick up the mail." She explains real fast, like she wants to erase the memory. Makes me scared to even listen.

"Pat was right," Dad says when she finishes. "Don't go there alone. That guy really needs counseling."

I roll my eyes at Dad. "I'm so sure."

Dad ignores my action. "I wonder what in his past has caused his animosity toward women. The man needs intensive psychoanalysis."

"Which he'll never get," Toni concludes. "You're trained to study that kind of psychosis, Jeff. To Gabi and me, Anchondo's the degenerate Sylvia's involved with. I don't care if he was teased because he was a fat Latino kid. I don't even care if racism made him into a bully. His background doesn't interest me one damn bit."

"I realize that. I care about Sylvia too. What I'm saying is, people with unresolved issues tend to attract similar types. For whatever reason, Sylvia has self-esteem problems. Years ago I didn't grasp that at all. She was a knockout when I met her, but I found out she's the type of woman who feels unfulfilled without a man. This guy feeds off that." Dad shakes his head at that realization. "I contributed too by not being 'man' enough. Sylvia made it clear she felt more like my mother than my wife."

Dad's upfront remarks sometimes surprise me. He takes responsibility for a lot. Wish Mom would do the same.

"But Jeff, you didn't beat her." Toni stares out the patio doors. "I honestly don't understand my sister. Her behavior scares me."

Facing both of them, I lean on my elbows. "I think she stays with Zalo 'cause of the baby. She thinks everything will be fine when the baby's born."

Dad reaches across the table for my hand. "Honey, if he beats her again, there might not be a baby."

☞ CHAPTER TEN ☜

January 15: Dawn
Toni

The parking lot at Union Station appears deserted. Hauling my luggage, I follow Sylvia and Gabi to Mama's lone Escort. None of us speak. Sylvia slides behind the steering wheel, Gabi beside her. Surrounded by luggage, I have the backseat to myself. Drowsy yet tense, I rest my head on one of the bags.

Sylvia has her window rolled down halfway. She drives slowly to the parking lot exit. Soon I become aware of a commotion at her window. I lift my head. Gabi screams. In the darkness I witness a cherubic-faced cholo. He grabs Sylvia's arms through the window. They struggle. She stops when he points a handgun to her head.

"Give me your money, bitch!" he snarls. His tough tone mismatches his own frightened face. He motions to Gabi and me. "Come on! Give me somethin'."

"We have nothing." I raise my palms upward. Gabi does the same.

"Drive me to where you do have it." He pulls open the back door. "Move it, bitch," he commands.

He shoves me across the seat, then slams the door. I toss my bags to the floorboard. "Drive! You hear me?"

Sylvia obeys. She and Gabi keep their faces forward. All of us stay silent. The cholo glances at me. Does he suspect I am a lesbian? His gaze falls on Gabi. He finds her more appealing. He swings the gun among the three of us to remind us he is in charge.

Sylvia finds the freeway ramp. I lodge myself close to the door.

"Where we goin'?" the kid at last thinks to ask.

"Santa Monica."

"Shit! Out by the beach?"

"We'll be happy to drop you off anywhere," Sylvia wisecracks despite her fear.

"Shut up and drive!"

Sylvia accelerates. Freeway traffic is sparse. Must be later than I think. Unwilling to provoke the edgy kid, I withdraw and keep quiet. In no time flat, Sylvia pulls the Escort into the driveway. The cholo gazes at our childhood home. The three-bedroom house sprawls on the residential lot beneath two fig trees. It seems abandoned. I hope no one is inside.

"Get me cash, jewelry, whatever you have," the cholo demands. He leans over and shoves the gun to the back of Gabi's head. She freezes. I am paralyzed. "Don't either of you get smart on me or the little bitch gets it."

Sylvia and I stumble out of the car. The cholo yanks Gabi out, forces her in front of him. They follow us to the house.

"Everything's locked," Sylvia says from the porch.

"What you talkin' about? Don't you live here?"

"Yeah. They must've forgotten we were coming back. It's locked up."

Beneath the porch light, the cholo, looking more than ever like a confused child, bangs on the door. No one answers.

"Find an open window." He pulls the terrified Gabi along as we round the house.

"We can't let him in," I whisper to Sylvia.
"They're not home," she murmurs.
"Doesn't matter. We can't let him know what's inside."
The eerie hoot of an owl punctures the night.

That incongruous sound awakens me. Soaking wet from the nightmare, I sit up. No uptight, baby-faced cholo is in the guest room at Jeff's house. Only me. Deep in the surrounding canyon, the great horned owl, el tecolote, hoots again. I hear it clearly through the open window. Like the cholo carjacker, el tecolote hunts for unsuspecting prey. I remember Amanda instructing me on the owl's symbolism of the feminine, the moon, the night. My head pounds from the swirling images.

Too unnerved to sleep I slip into my flannel robe and enter Jeff's living room. I curl into a corner of the sofa and gaze through the unadorned wall of glass. The sagebrush-lined canyon is hushed, full of secrets, like my parents' house.

"We can't let him know what's inside," I repeat to myself. In reality, Sylvia disregarded that. She told Zalo about the games we played as children. She told him we used to kiss and hug, play I was Daddy, she was Mama. We would touch each other—all over. Was this typical behavior for a lesbian child? I know it wasn't always my idea. Many times it was Sylvia's. What was her motivation—childhood curiosity? She didn't tell him any of that, did she? No, he would only like to hear what I had done. He calls me a pervert. Other people would too, if they knew. But I never hurt my little sister. I loved her. I thought she loved me too.

How many times will my mind conjure twisted dreams, variations of the same terror-filled scenario? Before living with Amanda, I had numerous nightmares about a looter, a carjacker, a burglar, a rapist—each one of those shadowy figures threatening Sylvia, Gabi, me, and sometimes Pat too. I had thought those dreams reflected my own fears in the aftermath of the riots: fear of social injustice, vulnerability, male violence—especially by homophobic Latinos like Zalo. This most recent dream, however, focuses on a more personal issue: the secrets Sylvia and I shared as girls, the secrets that led her into a turbulent boy-crazy adolescence and me to closeted young adulthood, the secrets that over time sadly fractured our relationship as sisters.

Afternoon
Pat

"How do you like it?" I slide my fingers across the fire-engine-red hood of the Mazda truck, complete with camper shell. I have this loaner for the weekend. Car's still in the body shop.

"It's so...bright." Toni laughs. Her eyes caress me. "Suits you fine, mujer."

"Think Adela'll get a kick out of it?" We hop in the truck and propel south on Lincoln Boulevard to pick up her mother.

"Mama will love it, Pat." She eyes me, kind of flirty. "When we pick her up, we'll have to squeeze together on this seat. I'll have to sit really close to you."

"No lie. I'll have to put my hand between your legs whenever I shift," I tease.

Her gaze is unwavering. "Will you like that?"

"I'm a red-blooded lesberado, Toni. What do you think?"

"Why haven't you done that sooner?"

"Just got this loaner today."

She smiles, edging over. She puts a warm hand on my jean-clad knee. "If I could erase the past months, Pat, I would. I wish so much that things could be like they were."

I don't let her distract me from traffic. "I never wanted you to go…but it was your choice, not mine."

She nods. From the corner of my eye, I see her blinking fast. She cries easy these days. She's more open than I've ever seen her. Tears can be a barrier, though. Whenever she starts in, I don't know what to do except clam up. I cried by myself every night after she left. That went on for months, for more than a year. Every letter Toni sent me opened the wounds all over again. I thought I'd never get over her. Yeah, I wish things were like before too. Shit, it ain't that easy to go back. What about my hurt, my grief?

Guiding the truck into one of the airport parking structures, I break the long silence. "Lucked out with a parking space, anyhow."

Toni blows into a Kleenex and dabs her eyes. "I have to stop this. I don't want Mama to see me all puffy-eyed."

I lock the car and follow her to the terminal.

In her rosy two-piece traveling outfit, Adela looks muy cute as she walks toward us. Her gray hair freshly "done," she holds her valise with one hand, as her beige handbag dangles over the other arm. She kisses Toni first. Then it's my turn.

"Ay que slick, señora," I greet her. I like hugging Adela. She's so open to it. My own mother never was.

"Gabi would've come, but she had to work," Toni explains, kissing her mother again. "You look rested, Mama. No all-night casino marathons?"

"Cómo eres, muchacha. I did my gambling earlier in the week. Un poco de winnings. Tu sábes, I've been at Consuelo's the past few days." She checks us out with a knowing eye. I move slightly ahead to let them chat, close enough to overhear.

Adela wastes no time when she has Toni to herself. "How is everything en la casa?"

For a second Toni hesitates before filling her in.

"I don't want to deal with that man forever," Adela states when her daughter concludes el cuento. "You're right, Toni. I could have a nice viejita as a tenant instead. How happy I was when Doña Filomena lived there."

Toni doesn't get a word in edgewise 'cause Adela won't let go of the subject. "I'm going to talk with el Padre Huerta after Mass. I don't want to be impulsive about this, eh? After all, Sylvia is my daughter, but ese Zalo es un animál, no? I want to see what el padre says. Evicting them would not be very Cristiano, verdad? Maybe Padre Huerta can talk to them himself."

I have my doubts about that. "He could wind up with a bloody nose or worse if he tries, Adela. Do you think Zalo would listen to a priest?"

"Que barbaridad! Ay, Pat, don't say that."

"It's true, Mama," Toni says.

I guide her mother toward the Mazda truck. Adela seems relieved by the distraction. Right away she throws out a compliment. "Se mira brand new, Pat."

"Practically is. Only two years old."

"Why don't you buy it, muchacha? You and Toni could go camping, eh?"

Toni seems agreeable with her mother's suggestion, especially that last comment.

I grin and toss Adela's bag inside the camper shell. As Toni and her mother make themselves comfortable, I close the door beside Adela and round the cab. Toni was right. We're squeezed together, her bare leg brushing mine.

On the drive to Adela's, I'm pretty damn conscious of Toni's nearness, her velvety morena skin touching me. She converses with Adela throughout the ride, probably hoping to prevent her from noticing. Meanwhile, Toni's left arm and shoulder press against me. She's inviting me. That's real clear. I can even feel the round contours of her chichis. I do want her, but I don't want sex to be the reason. I try to take the whole situation in stride.

Adela puts on a prim expression whenever I shift. My hand gets a little too close to her daughter's brown thighs. Can I help that? Shit, Toni's shorts and this truck make my weekend.

Sylvia

"Don't talk to me like I'm ten years old." I'm back from the laundromat, already getting bawled out by Mama. She couldn't wait till tomorrow. Had to let me have it as soon as she's home from the airport. At least no one else is around.

I leave the laundry basket on the porch steps. My arms are crossed. She's pointing to the butchered peach tree, jabbering in Spanish about what a good-for-nothing Zalo is.

"Your precious tree will be full of peaches this spring. And, Mama, Zalo has a job," I interrupt. I'm fed up with her ranting and raving. "That's where he is today—delivering furniture in the Valley."

That shuts her up for a second or so. "How long do you think he'll keep this job, eh? He'll lose his head, Sylvia. You know that. He won't take orders from anyone." She fans herself with the smocklike apron she wears while watering the plants. "Muchacha, you have to think of your future. What will happen when the baby comes?"

Mama has a flush to her face. All I need is for her blood pressure to shoot up over this. Everyone would blame me.

"Calm down, Mama. Things are working out."

"Really?" She doesn't believe me. "Maybe you think so. I'm going to talk to Padre Huerta. I might even invite him for dinner and have him talk to you."

"Forget that."

She shakes her head like I'm the biggest challenge in her life. She squirts the geraniums next to her steps. "What happened to you, eh? You were always mischievous, Sylvia, but you would listen to your Daddy and me sooner or later. Nowadays, you—"

"Hope you had a nice week in Las Vegas, Mama. Don't have time to talk right now." Grabbing the laundry basket, I slam the screen door behind me.

In the middle of the living room, I toss the basket to the hardwood floor. I scoop up a handful of Zalo's boxers and hurl them across the room. Some land on the floor, others on the crooked lampshade, one over the phone. I throw my bras and panties all over, not caring where they wind up. I want to turn on some golden oldies full blast so I can yell at the top of my lungs. Can't even do that. Zalo kicked the stereo to bits on New Year's Day.

Evening
Adela

Padre Huerta gives the final blessing and disappears into the sacristy. I wait a few respectful minutes until the hymn is over. When no one remains en la iglesia, I leave my front pew, genuflect, and enter the side door leading to the sacristy.

"Buenas noches, Padrecito," I begin.

"Doña Adela, cómo estás?" He finishes draping the green brocade chasuble over a padded hanger.

I have known him since the time he was fresh from the seminary and became assistant pastor at Saint Anne's. Now he is pastor of our parish of mostly Mexicano families.

He winks and gives me a big hug. "Did you luck out in Vegas?"

"Enough to buy a seven-day candle to la Virgen de Guadalupe."

We laugh together.

"La Virgen will be happy with that."

He is dark and thin, with tar-black hair un poco longer than necessary. Thirty-six years old, he is younger than both my daughters. If Juan and I had been blessed with a son, I would have liked him to be like Padre Tomás Huerta.

While he puts away the rest of the sacerdotal vestments, I bide my time.

"Pues, Padrecito, would you like to have dinner with me? Tengo unos tamalitos."

Padre Huerta looks grateful for my invitation. The parish housekeeper, Hortensia Montaño, has Saturdays off. "Sounds better than overcooked hamburgers. Gracias, Doña Adela."

"Pues, I have some little things to discuss too."

"Cómo no?" He offers his arm on our way to the parish parking lot.

"It's very quiet tonight." I watch with pleasure as el padre douses his tamales con mucha salsa picante.

He is from the Eastside, much more inclined to like spicy foods than my daughters. Like Juan, Toni and Sylvia are pochas, California native-born. Juan would even get hiccups from chile picante. Por eso, I always cook milder family meals. El padrecito finds la salsa tasty.

"Is Gonzalo home?" he asks.

"Not yet. Sylvia told me earlier he has a new job delivering furniture."

"He's a strong young man, Doña Adela. Maybe this company will keep him on."

I sigh. "That would be a miracle. I can't believe my daughter wound up with ese hombre. I'm worried about the baby, Padre. What if she doesn't get it baptized?"

He pats my shoulder while popping another chile verde into his mouth. Quickly, I pour him a glass of ice water. He downs it right away, drops of perspiration on his smooth brow.

Padrecito Huerta makes me smile. His company always does my heart good. When he catches me studying him, he chuckles.

"That one was very hot." He drinks more water. "Right now, Doña Adela, I'm more concerned about Sylvia's safety. The baby will be born when?"

"I think in June. She hasn't even told *me*, Padre."

He munches un pedazo de tamal. "What you said about the possibility of evicting them—you would be justified, verdad? Gonzalo beat your daughter and destroyed your property. Not only as a Christian who has to think about the safety of yourself, your other daughter, and granddaughter, but also as a responsible neighbor. I wouldn't want him living next to me either."

"Pero, as a mother—"

"I understand, Doña Adela. You have tried to help Sylvia, many, many times. You let her live in the duplex when Gonzalo didn't have a job. You took her in when she was injured. Time and again you have behaved in a Christian manner, no question. Pero, mira, you have been an excellent mother to both your daughters. On several occasions we have discussed this. You cannot control their lives as you did when they were children. They have their own minds, their own modas de vivir. You are getting on in years, Doña Adela—no offense. You should not have to worry over the possibility of violence next door. You have your own health to think about. Besides, why should the other neighbors be subjected to Gonzalo's foul temper?"

I listen to el padrecito, a holy man I respect and cherish. This afternoon Toni said almost the same words to me.

"Padre, what if Sylvia and Zalo move away and he hurts her again? How would we know? What about el niño?"

"That's a definite consideration, Doña Adela."

I hear the fright in my own voice. "I don't know what to do."

"You don't have to make a decision tonight." El padrecito eats another tamale. "Would you like me to speak with them?"

Wiping some dribbles of salsa from the table, I feel myself tremble. "I'm afraid Zalo would harm you, Padre. Y la Sylvia uses bad language. I don't know where she gets that from. Juan and I did not raise her to be disrespectful."

"Gonzalo and Sylvia are in great need of spiritual guidance, Doña Adela."

I nod. He continues to eat con gusto. He is a fine young man, but he has told me nothing new. May God forgive me. Padre Huerta has no more answers than I do.

Toni

"You had Thai food when you had lunch with Crystal."

"Can't get enough, Pat. Didn't have any for ages." I slide

one section of chicken satay from the wooden skewer at the Thai Flavor restaurant on Santa Monica Boulevard, where Cloverfield Boulevard ends.

"One of my favorites too." Pat dunks a sliver of the chicken into a glob of peanut sauce and swirls it. She wears indigo jeans and an African motif vest over a red T-shirt. The colors accentuate her mestiza complexion.

The wiry hostess approaches our table. I am caught off-guard. When we arrived a few minutes ago, she was not on duty. With a huge smile she bows to me.

"Good to see you again. Gone long time."

"Great to be back, Kin." On impulse, I reach over to hug her. Through her rayon top she is thin. She makes me feel enormous in comparison.

"Back in library too?"

"No." I wonder how much, if anything, Pat has told her. Leaning back, I let Kin pour us jasmine tea. "How's your reading in English coming along?"

"Much better." She nods with vigor. "Library sees me all the time. I read many magazines, books, check out tapes."

"That's wonderful."

Kin beams with pride. "Sorry you not there."

"Maybe one of these days."

Kin offers another radiant smile and dashes off to the kitchen.

"Her English really has improved. I'm glad she's still around," I remark. "Remember how scared she was during the uprisings? She kept talking about going back to Thailand."

"Living near Koreatown did a number on her." Pat pokes at another skewer of satay. "Whenever I'd show up for take-out, Kin would try to make conversation. It felt weird 'cause you were friendlier to her than I ever was. She'd always ask about you. All I'd say was you moved to another state."

"We never came out to her, Pat. By now I wonder if she's put two and two together."

Pat chews a crunchy cucumber slice and shrugs. "Tell me what Crystal said. What are your chances of being a Santa Monica librarian again?"

I meet her steady gaze. "You know Crystal. Such an optimist. She took my résumé, promised to give it to Baldwin herself. To me the scenario seems morbid, you know? So bloodthirsty. Marian's terminally ill, and I'm maneuvering to fill her job."

"*Your* job, Toni. You were next in line."

I sigh and lift the tiny tea cup to my lips. "I know. Mama says it's God's will if I wind up working there. It still feels off-kilter. Everything does, actually."

"Including you and me?" She arches a brow and maintains eye contact.

"You probably know more about that than I do, Pat."

She glances away at that comment. "I've never stopped loving you, not even when I was close to hating you. Does that make any sense?"

"Unfortunately, yes." I keep my voice low because the dining booths are close together. "I almost hated you when you kept pushing me to switch careers. I wish I'd realized you were the only stability I had. You stood by me through all of it—when Daddy died, Mama went into mourning, Sylvia flipped out, Gabi floundered. L.A. seemed to consume itself, and I wound up jobless. Whatever faith I had in 'the system' shattered. You were the only one who didn't change, Pat."

"You said I pressured you," she reminds me.

"Right. I misinterpreted that. You were only trying to bolster me." I lower my eyes to the table's formica surface. "At the time I thought you wanted to run my life."

"Sounds like one of your sister's excuses."

I make myself face her again. "Do you think we have that in common? Do you think I'm as self-destructive as Sylvia?"

"God, no. Not hardly."

With some relief, I study her. "You mean that, Pat?"

"If I didn't, I wouldn't be here."

After dinner we are too full to go to the video store right away. We stroll instead to the small park on 26th Street and Broadway. Flanked by palm trees and narrow aspens, it occupies the corner of a midcity intersection. When developers wanted to transform that property—which had long ago been the local dump—the Santa Monica city council agreed, after much wrangling, with the stipulation that a section of that land become a neighborhood park. Unnamed but frequented by nearby residents, the park is one of the cleanest in the city, with tennis and basketball courts, a children's playground, an unpaved walking track—and round-the-clock security guards.

On arrival after sundown, we find ourselves the only ones on the lit track.

"The trees have really grown," I marvel while we make our first round.

"I jog here after work. No traffic hassle, easier on the feet too." Pat picks up her pace. "Come on, Toni. Let's circle at least three more times at a good clip."

I groan. Pat is leaner than I am and speedier too. If I ever want to kiss her, I'll have to catch up with her first.

Night
Pat

Toni isn't really watching *Final Analysis*. She likes Richard Gere films, but tonight she's too distracted. Her eyes are all over the place, not on the TV screen. Some of the time they're on me. I pretend not to notice. Ever since she walked into the apartment a couple of hours ago with the videos under her arm, she's been checking out the pad, trying not to be obvious. She's curious to see if everything looks the same, if I've changed any of it.

About the only difference is I've spread my stuff over the second bedroom, where the TV is. Media OutReach files and promo materials cover the desk in the corner. The framed photo of the two of us is stuck in a drawer somewhere, not on display like it used to be. I've hung a movie still of Sonia Braga from *The Milagro Beanfield War* over the desk instead. The glossy black-and-white shot is one where Braga's in a white shirt, open-necked, sleeves rolled up, long hair floating around her. Reminds me a lot of Toni.

"Not into this?" I lean closer to her. "Let's flick it off if you're not in the mood."

"And do what?" she asks right away, fawn eyes full of suggestions.

All of a sudden I feel like a gawky kid. "It's late. Maybe you'd rather—"

"No, Pat. I don't want to go—at all." Toni moves nearer. With tenderness she outlines my jawline with her index finger.

The tension I've felt all evening peaks. I can't mistake the desire in her dark eyes—it reflects mine. At the same time a rush of emotions surges through me. Even as I inch toward her, I feel the sudden catch in my throat, the drizzle of tears. I want to kiss her for hours. I can't stop myself from sinking into her arms. In seconds, instead of being la seduction sorceress, I'm bawling like I did every night after she left.

"I love you so much, Toni," I manage to gulp. I am out of control and helpless, like I was at the New Year's party when I barfed my brains out and she wound up feeding me menudo.

"Mujer, I love you too," she whispers. Her black hair wraps around me like a midnight curtain. "I've waited months and months to hold you like this. Ay, machita, you need to get this out, if you have to scream to do it. It's so like you, Pat, to react some other way, to throw up instead of—"

With a long sigh, I press my wet face into the flock of tiny embroidered birds on her cotton shirt. I don't want to move. Her cuerpo, her chichis, are inviting, tantalizing, even softer than I remember. Her heart is thumping in rapid beats. Its rhythm soothes me.

"I've *been* in touch with my feelings," I murmur. "Didn't want to break down like this."

She smooths my hair. "Not in front of me?"

I raise my head a bit to meet her own shiny eyes. "Right."

Toni places a juicy kiss on my brow. "I prefer tears to vomit, mujer."

That makes me laugh. "Good thing. Anyhow, there's no menudo in the fridge."

"We won't have to think about that tonight."

She reaches over me for the remote. When she does, her breasts press through the cotton shirt and against my face. I feel the raisin nubs of her nipples on my cheek, temptingly close to my mouth. The sensation makes me dizzy.

Switching off the VCR and TV, Toni tosses the remote on the carpet beside the futon. Her fawn eyes search mine for a moment.

My fingers twine themselves into her thick hair. On one elbow I lift myself and press my hand to her hip. She smiles at me, her lips moist. She lets me tug her toward me. When we are boca to boca, she surprises me by grasping the back of my neck. She pulls me to her in one swift motion. I keep my eyes open. I don't want to miss a detail. I know the ecstasy on her cara linda rivals mine.

CHAPTER ELEVEN

January 16: Middle of the Night
Toni

Rolling over, I expect to feel her next to me. Her side of the bed is empty, yet the warm imprint and the musky scent of her body remain. I spread myself over that coveted spot. My skin soaks up her essence, each pore craving her again.

We loved each other throughout the night. I tasted her piel morena, her chichis deliciosas, her intoxicating miel de mujer. Our cuerpos arched and curled around ourselves like conchas en el mar, like mariposas en viento. Her brazos fuertes surrounded me as she fed me her mocha nipples, her labios como manzanas rojas. Our moans and cries de amor created música prohibída durante esta noche empasionada. Drowsy but alive with sensation, I lie motionless. Everything is still. Where has she gone? To the bathroom?

Perhaps I doze. I don't know the exact amount of time I stay there alone. A glance at the clock reveals 3:27. Has she become ill?

Unable to bear the sudden solitude, I lean over, opening

one of the drawers beneath the platform bed. My fingers recognize a flannel nightshirt. I slip it on but leave most of it unbuttoned. When I tiptoe to the bathroom, Pat is not there.

In the narrow hallway I notice a sliver of light beneath the closed door of the TV room. I knock, then open it.

She swivels in the desk chair. Her black hair is rumpled, her eyes sleepy. She has bundled herself into a fleecy red robe, one I've never seen.

"Did you have another bad dream, Toni?"

"No. Did you?" I come closer. She has the computer on.

She gestures toward the few paragraphs she has drafted. "Revising the Martin Luther King Day speech I have to give at Santa Monica College tomorrow. All about the necessity of protesting racial, ethnic, and gender stereotypes in the media. You know, my usual spiel."

I frown. "Amor, why are you doing that now?"

She blushes. "I really want to be in bed with you, but I have to rewrite this."

I caress the coarse tufts of her jet-black hair. As I do that she encourages me into her lap. I straddle her, my bare legs tickled by the fleecy robe. Already her lips find my neck, her tongue glides there. I take one of her hands into my open shirt. Her fingers are cool. Their sudden touch at my breasts jolts me. She lowers her head to suck me. Her mouth is moist, hungry.

With deliberate motions I slide the red robe off her shoulders. She is brown and sleek. My hands adore her, etching her burnished image into each fiber of my being. We cannot stop touching and kissing each other.

"Toni, Toni," she whispers.

"Que quieres, mujer?"

"Gettin' a crick in my neck. Let's finish this in bed."

Morning
Gabriela

"Nothing to worry about, baby," Dad says. Coffee cup in hand, he has the *Los Angeles Times* ready for an all-day read. "Toni's obviously with Pat."

"She didn't even phone to let us know she'd be—"

He grins. "Who's being the auntie?"

"OK, OK." I back off with a giggle.

Dad wheels to the open patio door. "Gabi, no need to mention this to Adela."

Following, I make a face at him. I plop into a patio chair, brushing my damp hair before I rush to meet Grandma.

"Matter of fact, I was beginning to wonder if *you'd* come home last night," he drawls. Over the unfurled front page, he peeks at me.

"Oh, Dad." With some impatience I unsnarl the ends of my hair. "You can trust Phil and me."

"I only want you two to be careful."

Having a Dad who's a shrink makes it damn hard to pull any fast ones. "We always use protection."

Now he's all the way behind the newspaper. "Good."

"I won't mention that to Grandma either," I add, giggling again. As I pass him, he reaches for me. Bending, I hug him back.

"Gabi," Dad says, quietlike. He smells clean and fresh. "Things have been tough since your mother remarried. That doesn't mean you have to lose yourself in Phil."

"I know that." I crouch beside his wheelchair. "Phil does too. We both want to graduate, go on to careers after college. Dad, we're in no hurry."

He kisses my cheek. "I'm proud of you, sweetheart."

"You're pretty cool too."

Driving the Jeep up the Seventh Street hill from the canyon, I think about Phil and me the night before. His father and stepmother are out of town for a month. Phil's dad is a structural engineer and does a lot of business travel. Usually Joyce goes with him. Phil, meantime, has the Ocean Park condo to himself—convenient for us.

After work last night we ate at Johnnie's Pizza on the Promenade and decided to skip seeing a film. Nothing in any of the theaters appealed to us. We wound up renting *Basic Instinct*.

"Pat would flip if she knew we were watching this." I snuggled with Phil after he stuck the cassette into the VCR. "Her media group came out strong against this film."

"I won't tell her." Phil grabbed the bag of tortilla chips and the remote. He had an impish look in his brown eyes. "It's supposed to be hot."

"Why?" I narrowed mine at him. "'Cause of the blond?"

"I mean," he went on, "you know, Gabi—the whole controversy."

"The lesbian stuff?" I rolled my eyes. "Don't tell me you're still fixated on that."

"Fixated?" He scoffed. "Not me. Veronica explained that stuff to me years ago. I'm used to lesbians. No big thing."

I poked him in the ribs. "Don't have to get defensive, man."

Real ticklish, he doubled over. He sent the bag of chips bouncing off the sofa. Trying to catch his breath, he laughed and squirmed away from me.

"Hey— " he finally managed to blurt out. "Like, are you done, Gabi? Can I start the movie now?"

Kneeling on the sofa, I helped him sit up. "You're so crazy."

He retrieved the chips and offered me some. Top strands of his hair were out of place, making him even more adorable. "This movie's no turn-on for you, huh?"

"Don't need it." I pushed the bag aside. "I have you."

Phil went shy on me, like he hadn't expected me to come on to him. He didn't figure we wouldn't watch the whole film—or that I'd stay almost all night.

Sylvia

About the only thing Zalo has in common with my Daddy is liking hash brown potatoes. I stir them in the sizzling frying pan while he's in the shower. He says he has more deliveries today, wants to get an early start. I'm not used to him being so gung-ho over work. Maybe he really means what he says about being a "new family."

Mama's being real skeptical. Last night I saw that priest drive off. Who knows what she said to him. I think the old lady has a crush on Huerta. I was at the kitchen window washing dishes when he came outside. Seemed like he looked right at me. Huerta's what I call a "pretty man," probably queer as a $2 bill. No way was I going to open my door if he knocked. I sure was glad he turned down the driveway instead.

Zalo comes in. He's wearing work clothes: gray shirt and pants, heavy boots.

"Think you'll be late tonight?" I ask.

"Time and a half on a holiday weekend."

"Lots of after-Christmas sales, Zalo. No wonder you're so busy."

"Nigger holiday. Shit, I sure ain't goin' to turn down extra bucks."

I decide to ignore his snide crack about Martin Luther King Day. Zalo believes all the bad rumors about Dr. King. In parochial school when King was assassinated, I grew up with a completely different take on the civil rights leader. The nuns thought Dr. King could walk on water. I admired him then—and now.

Taking a plate, I serve a hefty portion of hash browns and scrambled eggs. "Tortillas are on the table. Coffee, Zalo?"

"Stupid question," he mutters. "You know I drink it."

I pour him a cup and sit across from him. "What time should I get your dinner ready?"

"Bitch, that's for you to figure out." He holds up the coffee mug, already wanting more.

I fill it, tempted to pour the whole pot on him. "I have a name, Zalo."

"Saliva, isn't it?" He breaks into spasms of high-pitched laughter. "Sounds like saliva. Maybe something that tastes like saliva, squishy and hot—like your cunt."

Right now I hate him.

"Don't look at me like that, hear me?" He points a stubby finger. "Can't you even take a joke?" He giggles again and devours the rest of the meal.

Seething in the chair, I bite my lip to keep myself quiet.

"Oh, I know what it is." He won't stop heckling. "The cunt's pissed 'cause she didn't get any last night. She didn't get fucked."

"You wish," I say through clenched teeth.

"Huh?" He knocks over the coffee cup when he grabs my arm. The brown liquid makes puddles on the tortillas. He clenches me tight. "I'll fuck you when I get back. Don't think

I won't. You're fat and ugly. Gettin' old, too, but I'll still fuck you damn hard."

He pushes me down and crashes into the living room. As usual, he bangs the screen door. Over and over I rub my arm. It hurts.

Adela

"I don't think Sylvia's working today. Let's invite her."

Gabi has Nopalito, my green parakeet, on her shoulder while she squeezes juice from the oranges Toni bought. "OK, Grandma."

"I'll see if she wants to come."

When I reach my daughter's screen door, I see her lying en el sofa, barefoot, wearing a sleeveless pink nightgown.

"Buenos dias, mija. Have you had breakfast?"

She seems grouchy. She doesn't even smile when she forces herself up and to the door. "I'll pass, Mama. Don't have much of an appetite."

"Ay, Sylvia. Don't you want to spend time with Gabi?"

"Oh, all right." She disappears into the bedroom. She comes back in a flowered quilted housecoat.

"Do you have an upset stomach, mija?" I ask when she follows me next door. "I'll brew some yerba buena."

She doesn't say anything. I stoop beside the steps to gather mint leaves. Maybe she will be friendlier to her daughter.

"Hey, Mom," Gabi greets. Nopalito has fluttered to the top of my granddaughter's head. He likes to play with the plastic barrette she uses to gather the side strands.

"That dumb bird's going to shit all over the table," Sylvia grumbles. She takes a piece of pan dulce and slouches beside Gabi.

"Ay, don't be so mean. Nopalito isn't even bothering you."
I hand her a napkin and a small dish for the pan dulce. Turning my back to her sour face, I fill the kettle with water.

Gabi tilts her head and reaches for Nopalito. When he
perches on her finger, she places him on her shoulder. In seconds he's climbing into her hair again, using his beak and his
little feet to grab hold. Gabi doesn't seem to mind.

"Grandma says Godzilla has a job," she says, a playful tone
in her voice.

Sylvia is in no mood for that. "His name is Gonzalo."

"Gonzalo, Godzilla—what's the difference?" Gabi giggles
at her cleverness. "Either way he's a monster."

"Is that why you want me here, to jump on me again?"
Sylvia starts to get up. I place a calming hand on her shoulder.
She winces. Right away I let go.

"Sientese, Sylvia." I frown at my granddaughter. "Gabi, be
nice to your mother, eh?"

"Sorry," the girl mumbles. She drinks orange juice and
keeps quiet por un tiempo.

"I'm fed up with all your 'I told you sos'" Sylvia starts in.
"Zalo's working—a steady job for one of the furniture warehouses in the Valley. And guess what? We're going to look
for another place to live."

"Mom, why don't you just dump the guy?" Gabi cuts in.

"De veras, Sylvia. Your marriage isn't blessed by the
Church. Zalo's no good for you." My own mother had a favorite consejo—"Better alone than in bad company." I offer it
to my youngest: "Mejor sola que mal acompañada."

My granddaughter adds, "Moving won't fix the situation."

"I don't need any more advice," Sylvia hisses at us.

Gabi gets up so suddenly Nopalito almost loses his balance.
He chirps in fright and flies to my shoulder. Gabi doesn't no-

tice she's scared the poor little bird. She storms into the living room and comes back with what looks like a brochure in her hand. She throws it on the table in front of her mother.

"Read this."

The pamphlet's cover has drawings of hearts, doves, a telephone, a pencil, and strange-looking circles. To the side is a title: "Domestic Violence: The Facts."

Sylvia puts one hand to her mouth. She starts to cry. Her other hand clutches her shoulder, as if to hold herself together.

With no hesitation, I hug her. "Querida, we love you. We don't want you hurt again. What if he kicks you in el estómago o algo asi? What about the baby?"

She is crying so much she cannot talk. Sylvia's body rocks against me. I wonder how long she has been hiding este tristeza inside.

Gabi's eyes are like lakes. She edges closer, one hand on her mother's bent head. "Mom, I'm sorry for yelling. I get so frustrated when I see you like this." She takes a breath. "I picked up this booklet at the library. It's from the Los Angeles County Commission for Women. It has phone numbers inside, lots of information. You need help, Mom. You need counseling, you need—"

"Don't expect me to go to Jeff," Sylvia says between sobs.

Gabi doesn't take her eyes from her. "No one can rescue you, Mom. You have to do that yourself. Start with the restraining order to keep him off the property."

Sylvia tries to muffle more sobs. I feel her struggling as she keeps her head against me. Nopalito is too nervous to stay on my shoulder. He lands on the kitchen counter and searches for pan dulce crumbs.

"If you don't care about yourself, think about Grandma. It isn't fair to her to have that maniac next door. He brutalized you, tore through the duplex, wrecked Pat's car, threatened Toni, chopped the peach tree—"

"That's why we have to get out of here," Sylvia murmurs.

"No, Mom. He's the one who has to leave."

Sylvia looks up, her eyes swollen with tears. "You make it sound so simple, Gabi."

Her daughter is ready to cry too. No one says a word for several minutes. A shrill sound breaks el silencio. It is the phone ringing in Sylvia's duplex.

"I'm on call for the holiday weekend," she murmurs. She wipes her wet eyes with her sleeve and goes outside.

Gabi sighs. "She didn't take the booklet, Grandma."

"Mijita, she needs to think about it."

"How long will that take?" Gabi rushes into my arms.

I hold her to me and whisper unas oraciones to Saint Jude.

Afternoon
Pat

Toni sleeps on the futon while I juggle paragraphs on the computer screen. She looks content tucked into my red robe, her blanket of hair shielding most of her face. A little smile hints of her happy dreams.

We did it so many times during the night, I'm still reeling. My tits are really sensitive right now and hard as chocolate chips too. Believe it or not, my whole body's ready for another go-around. All my senses are in overdrive. Been a while since I've felt this way.

Before Toni left me our nights of lovemaking had become few and far between. Whenever she's depressed her emotions shut down—at least, that's what I remember most about those awful months. I was dedicated to merging my identities—woman, Chicana, dyke—into my role as spokesperson for Media OutReach. Sometimes I was too damn worn out to even think about sex, let alone do it.

After the Los Angeles rebellion, I was in high demand as a public speaker, a triple minority willing to talk about it. All these months later I can only imagine how lonely Toni must have been. While I was off on my media trip, she was coping with low self-esteem, unemployment, family problems. Whether I want to admit it or not, that damn Amanda must've helped Toni feel better about herself. Meanwhile, I was too caught up in my own media whirl.

I can't concentrate on the damn speech. All I can think about is Toni. Doesn't help that she's in the same room, naked under my robe. I could wander over, slide my hand between her piernas chulas, wake her with a hinting beso. Glancing at her, I decide to let her sleep. She's been having bad dreams, but none while with me. La mujer's exhausted from this whole crazy week.

Scrolling through the computer directory, I think about borrowing some other paragraphs from a talk I've already given. How much has actually changed since the so-called L.A. rebellion? Race relations sure haven't improved. The whole county still has its racial-ethnic splits. Everyone is polarized. The inner city is worse off than ever. A couple of months ago, the Malibu fires proved again that government money is more available for rich folks who live on the edge of the Pacific Rim than it is for families of color who squeeze into substandard housing where the only landscaping is concrete and asphalt.

Sometimes—like right now—I question whether working for Media OutReach is the way to go. Civil rights movements or not, Hollywood continues to stereotype people of color, ethnic groups, women, lesbians, and gays. The entertainment industry is populated with the same unrealistic folks who live on the fiery coast, the sliding hillsides—the ones who want it all no matter what the cost. They're hardly the types, liberals or not, who are sensitive to the have-nots. They live out their fantasies and can't understand those who don't, who can't.

Maybe I ought to go back to the grassroots, back to the trenches of community work, women's shelters, literacy programs. Been there, done that, yeah. I used to reach la gente by the direct route in those days, even though I got damn burned out in the process. Nowadays, I'm all over the place, propagandizing about the need for positive images in the media. Shit, do poor people in the community even care about that? Not if they're wondering how they're going to pay this month's rent and feed their kids.

Movies, TV, rap music, even talk radio—all those strategies keep la gente quiet, subdued. Give them a steady dose of glitzy entertainment, and they'll turn on the tube or the radio to forget about their own troubles. Give them a taste of sugar-coated fantasy instead of better schools. Show them a glittery world of dreams instead of a realistic path out. That's the American way, que no?

Toni

A feather flickers near me. Has that pesky falcon returned, spreading its dark wings as it swoops by? I feel another twinge on my thigh. Why would the merlin fly so close? Or is it la araña, the fine hairs of her spindly legs brushing against my skin? I flinch awake.

"It's only me, Toñita," Pat whispers. Her cherished face is inches from mine and her teasing fingers are between my legs. One barely touches my clitoris.

"Thought you were a spider, mujer," I murmur, bringing her closer.

"I am a spider, a black widow who wants to wrap my legs around you and keep you stuck to me."

"We're wet enough to make glue, verdad?" I love her obsidian eyes, the way they widen—soften—when she speaks to me.

"What do you think?" She brings her fingers to my mouth to let me lick my own juice. She leans forward, her tongue greedy for some of it.

"You're the only nourishment I need, Pat."

Throwing off the robe, I bring her down with me. She's wearing a baggy T-shirt and nothing else. My hands slip under it, grasping her chichis. Ay, her nipples are dark brown—tender buttons, as Gertrude Stein would say. Pat helps me pull the shirt over her head. She keeps one hand on me, almost in me. I like to move and feel her fingers there, ready to pleasure me.

"Mujer, did you finish the speech?" I lie beside her, thighs opening even more for her.

"Combined it with old one," she murmurs. Her fingers are inside me now.

With a moan, I fold one leg, lifting it to her sleek shoulder. She turns her head slightly to kiss la pierna, her tongue exploring it. At the same time I clench her brown back, craving those tender buttons. My mouth is full of her, tasting the sea-saltiness of her, inhaling the sultry olor de mujer.

"I love you, Pat."

"I've wanted you like this, Toni, so many times."

"I'm yours, mi amor. Para siempre."

Half laughing, half crying, I reach down to touch her too. Her muscled thighs quiver and part for me. She pants with longing while I play with her curly pussy, spreading its erotic nectar on her legs, all over my hand. She comes before I have a chance to do anything else. Her eyes are like smoky glass, never leaving mine.

Already crazed with desire, I roll astride her. I am over her, open wide. Her fingers never stop titillating me. They dart in and out, upward, around, creating floods, deluges, oceans. The rush of passion overwhelms me.

"Ay, si, Pat. Asi, mujer. Ay, como te amo."

We doze for hours. We have hardly eaten all day. When we awaken we laugh about that. The refrigerator is almost empty. We decide to order pasta from Café 26.

"Jeff must've figured out where I am."

"No kidding." Pat wraps capellini around her fork and offers it to me.

I dip my finger in marinara sauce and decorate her chichis with women's symbols. Then I lick off my doodles, sucking her while I'm at it.

"Jeez, Toni, I'm wasted," she whispers, watching me. Soon she drops her fork and sprawls backward.

Pushing the aluminum delivery containers aside, I crouch down with her. "I'm not leaving," I answer. "I'm all yours. Tomorrow I want to sit in the front row when you give your speech so you won't be able to forget me."

"Ain't never goin' to forget you, mujer," she promises.

She is so relaxed, the way I love her best.

"Did you know you still have clothes in the closet?"

I nuzzle her. "Doubt if they'll fit." Kissing her mouth, I cling there.

"So don't wear anything," she quips when she comes up for air. "Fine with me. The ultimate fashion statement."

Evening
Sylvia

I don't know what Zalo will do when he finds my note. I taped it to the refrigerator door and left a Tupperware bowlful of albondiga soup for his dinner. Being on standby this weekend, I had no idea whether I'd work or not. Never can tell at the hospital. Like he says, who can turn down time and a half?

Before coming to work I stood under the shower a long time. I let the water drench me. Hoped it would clear my head. It didn't—at least, not very much.

Gabi's turning into a do-gooder like Jeff. Too much Brandon influence on that muchacha. While I was in the shower, she stuck that man-hating booklet inside the screen door. She figured it was safe to do while Zalo's gone. Who would've thought my little girl would turn into a bra burner? She does have a boyfriend, though. Not a lesbo like Toni. I should be grateful for small favors.

That booklet with the male and female symbols and all that other junk on the cover is folded inside my purse. At break I'll throw it in the trash. I might look at it first, but I can't leave it at home. If Zalo ever finds it...

He doesn't hit me in the stomach. Mama has it in her head that he's going to. She exaggerates. Too much *Eyewitness News*. Toni and Gabi, of course, feed her all those so-called facts about domestic violence. Don't they realize Zalo was bummed 'cause he didn't have a job? He took it out on me. That makes sense, no? "You always hurt the one you love," like the song says.

I don't want any of them—especially Mama—to know I think he's playing around. That's the real reason he didn't touch me last night. I could smell sex on him, female stink mixed in with his. Zalo can't help it—he's younger than me, on the prowl for tighter pussy. No wonder, 'cause I'm blowing up like a balloon. He'll come around after the baby's born. He'll be home on time then. He'll be a good husband and father. I know he will.

After Midnight
Sylvia

No lights on. No sign he's been back. I tiptoe through the house to be sure. Nothing out of place except my thoughts. I keep seeing him with some cheap callejera—huge tits, big ass, some babe closer to his age.

No way could he be delivering furniture this late. I'm not that gullible. If he isn't home by morning, I ought to phone the damn furniture warehouse. Ay, Dios! I hope he wasn't in an accident. Don't even *think* that.

I take the note off the fridge. I'm starving. Might as well eat the albondigas.

Another thought flashes. Zalo grew up in Pacoima. His Mama still lives there. Maybe he went to visit her or other familia. Shit, who's kiddin' whom? How many times has he told me his mother's "the stupidest broad in the world"? He always says, "She's way dumber than you, bitch."

Part III

This Sunday, as you sit at home in your red robe drinking coffee, think of all the times the earth has given you something to unfold: a star-tipped blade of grass, an onion, another woman's arms. As you watch your warm body turning in the darkness, your fingernails writing on your flesh, remember how the soil whispers.
—From "Gitanerias"
by Alicia Gaspar de Alba
in *Three Times a Woman*

⌐ CHAPTER TWELVE ⌐

January 17: The Hours Before Dawn
Toni

Rattle, rattle. Not noisy dreams, please. Spiders, falcons, and angel-faced cholos are enough. But the continuous metallic sound makes me stir. Not a dream but a reality. The sliding glass window on Pat's side of the bed clatters. I don't remember leaving it open. The glass vibrates again. Must be a windy night.

Fully awake, I hear a distant rumble. No doubt a garbage truck blocks away.

"Damn traffic," Pat mutters. "Used to be a quiet neighborhood."

I nestle beside her. "Shhh. Let me rock you back to sleep."

She curls into my arms, dark head against my cheek. I cradle her and move her gently from side to side.

"Hey," she protests in seconds. "Not so—"

"That isn't me," I whisper in sudden terror. "I think—"

In pitch darkness the platform bed comes alive, transformed into a wild mustang, bucking in fury to hurl us off.

With frantic jolts it bounces and jerks, possessed by the ghostly spirit of un caballo renegado.

"Oh, my Jesus! Pat, oh, Pat—don't try to get up."

The clamor is deafening.

On the levitating bed we hang tight to each other. A thunderous uproar emanates from the earth, combined with the protesting creaks and groans of the wood-frame apartment building. An eerie chorus of breaking glass, tumbling furniture, and screeching car alarms compounds our fears. The bookcase headboard spews paperbacks like bullets against our backs. The betrayal of cherished books frightens me even more. Every object in the bedroom seems propelled by the earthquake's fury.

"Oh, my Jesus!" I scream again.

"Toni, get hold of yourself! Concentrate on what's going on."

"Earthquake!"

"Christ, I know that." Pat's sarcasm masks her own fear. "We must be at the epicenter."

"A consoling thought." My heart almost explodes from my chest.

"I think it's winding down."

Thank God, Pat is right. Gradually the bed becomes still. Not even the windows quiver. The silence proves even more unnerving.

"What if there's another one?" I stare at her in the darkness. We still have our arms around each other, too afraid to let go. "What time is it?"

She turns to glance at the clock radio. "Power's out."

"Oh, my Jesus—Mama! I have to phone her."

"Phones are probably out too."

"I have to see if she's all right." I search the rumpled sheets for the flannel nightshirt. It lies at the edge of the bed. Something prevents me from pulling the shirt toward me. Pat tosses me the fleecy robe instead. She shines a tiny flashlight with a very dim bulb toward the foot of the platform bed.

"The armoire's down," she says with a sense of wonder. "If we'd been stretched out instead of cuddled together, it would've landed on our feet. Your nightshirt's half under it."

The sight of the sturdy armoire tilted over the bed makes me even more alarmed for Mama, alone in her duplex. Pat hands me her moccasins.

"Put these on, Toni. The phone's on the living room floor next to the rattan chest. At least that's where it was. I'll find some clothes."

I stumble through the narrow hallway. Piles of towels and sheets litter the carpet, having slid out of the hall cabinets. I feel my way into the living room and almost trip on the telephone cord. The receiver lies on the floor, but I hear a dial tone. Fingers trembling, I punch in Mama's number. Her phone rings again and again.

"Pat—she doesn't answer!"

"Let's get the hell over there." She joins me with the dim flashlight. She's in jeans, a sweatshirt, and hiking boots. "Here." She gives me thick sweat pants, a long-sleeved T-shirt, a heavy wool shirt, socks, and sneakers. "I have a better flashlight in the truck."

I throw on the clothes any which way. With caution we move to the apartment door, stepping over the fallen bookcases. The ordinarily neat room is ankle-deep in books, mangled picture frames, shattered glass. I turn the double-bolt lock and open the door. Pat is by my side, shining the hazy beacon before us. She whisks it to the right.

"Holy shit!" she shouts. "The stairs are gone."

Our escape route is thwarted. I am close to tears, terrified that Mama is dead.

Pat takes charge. "We'll go out the bedroom window."

I am too stunned to answer. In seconds she nudges me with an armload of sheets. Flashlight propped under her chin, she starts to return to the bedroom.

"Shut the door, Toni. We can't go out that way." She pauses in the hallway, as if giving me time to catch up.

I can hardly see her, but I can imagine the determination etched on her face. Closing and locking the door, I let her voice guide me.

"Let's tie these sheets together. We'll have to swing down." In utter fascination I observe as she rapidly knots one end of cotton fabric to the next.

"Help me, Toñita," she urges.

Her abrupt change in tone snaps me into reality. The sooner we get out of the apartment, the faster we can check on Mama. I grab two sheets and begin to work.

Before I am finished she hustles me into the bedroom. Fashioning a bulky knot on one end of the chain of sheets, she loops that over the top of the door. Satisfied, she anchors the sheets by shutting the door, leaving the knotted side facing the hallway. The trailing remainder is our lifeline.

"Do we have enough sheets?" I whisper, noting the distance from the door to the window.

"I think six will be about right. Give me yours, Toni."

"Do you really think they'll hold?"

"Let's try and see." She beckons. "Come on, mujer. We'll do this together."

She slides the window open as far as possible. She loosens the screen and pulls it into the bedroom. After she props it against the wall, she quickly climbs on the sill, one leg inside, one out. She grabs the chain of sheets to tests its strength.

"Ándale, Toni. Vamanos, mujer."

All I can think of is that Mama's alone. Otherwise I would be too panic-stricken to follow Pat's instructions. Gritting my teeth, I join her at the window. She encourages me to straddle the window sill as she has done. Already she balances herself outside the window, the sheets clutched in her hands. Because of my awkwardness, she has some difficulty positioning me in front of her. I am no athlete. Instead of cursing the darkness, I am grateful for it. If I could see the ground two stories below, I would no doubt freeze in fear. Pat's arms shield me as we inch, rappel-like, past downstairs walls and windows.

"How you girls doing?" a male voice calls. "Who else is upstairs?"

"Next-door neighbors aren't home," Pat yells. "Don't know about the others." She returns her attention to me. "Careful, Toni. We have to jump a few feet. Don't worry—there's grass. Ready?"

"Yes."

We leap, landing hard. Right away we scramble to our feet.

"OK?"

Nodding, I hug her as tight as I can. "Thank you, Pat."

For a second she squeezes me. She flickers the flashlight toward the carports. The supporting pole is at an odd angle. Chunks of plaster cover all of the cars.

"Where's the truck?" I ask in alarm.

"On the street. Don't you remember? Someone used my spot. Lucky for us, huh?"

I shiver. I wonder if Mama's good luck has held out.

Adela

Ave Maria Purísima! The most horrible earthquake! It must be the end of the world! Ay, Dios mio!

The night swallows me. I fall into a dark hole. Everything is black, so black.

I don't know where I am. Soft things surround me, but I am not in my little bed.

Where are my daughters? Ay, Juan, ayúdame, por favor.

At last the shaking y el ruido feísimo stops. Creo que I am on the floor. But where? My hands poke through the dark. I feel something long and thick. My wool coat.

Ay, Dios mio! Estoy en el ropero! How did I ever land in the closet? I don't know if I can get up. I have never been so scared. Gracias a todos los santitos que estoy viva.

I do not stop praying. Ojalá que no hay otro terremoto fuerte como este. Ay, I think my phone is ringing. Cual hija me habla?

I want to answer it, but it stops before I can leave this cave of clothes. I am sitting on the floor of the closet. There are chanclas y muchas otras cosas on top and under me. I have a hard time trying to stand up, but I don't think I'm hurt. The piles of clothes are like soft feathers in a nest.

Ay, Nopalito! Pobrecito pajarito! I hope his cage hasn't fallen off its stand.

I can't see the clock. Ay, que noche de diablos. Where is my rosary? Well, I don't need it. I can pray without it.

Sylvia

Zalo's so furious he's trying to throw the bed—with me in it—out the window. With his burly arms he's lifting it, slamming it down, hoping I'll fall out. Then he'll be sure to come after me.

"Stop, Zalo! I am sorry I ate your dinner. You weren't here—"

Why isn't he yelling? Calling me every nasty name in the book? Maybe he's too busy trying to break the damn bed. He's making terrific noise, being rougher than ever. Yanking it around, scaring the damn shit out of me. He must figure he doesn't even have to yell. I'm scared enough already. If his adrenaline is pumping so hard that he can throw a double bed around, what the hell will he do to me this time?

Where is he now? I hear stuff crashing all over the place, a loud racket from the living room too. He must be breaking everything we own. How can he be in both rooms at once? So damn dark I can't see anything.

I pull the sheets over my head. Curl into a ball in the middle of the bed. My head's between my arms. I'm going to protect myself and the baby. When he grabs for me, I'll stay put, like one of those tube bugs Toni and I used to poke with twigs. Those tiny guzanos would roll up and make us laugh. I'll do the same. Zalo won't be able to hit me in the face or in the stomach either. I'll be like a smart little bug, drawing myself inside, pulling in, and keeping safe.

Gabriela

"Gabi, stay where you are!" Phil shouts from somewhere. "Cover your head!"

I've already done that. I'm huddled in the double bed in the condo's guest room, shaking from head to toe. This quake is huge, unbelievable.

"Where are you, Phil?"

"In the john. What a time to take a pee," he adds, sounding damn jittery himself.

When Mother Nature finally settles down, Phil rushes in. He hurtles into bed like a human javelin. "Stuff all over. You OK, Gabi? No electricity. Transformers must've blown." His body is ice-cold.

Wrapping the sheet around him, I kiss him a million times. "Do you think this was 'the big one'?"

"Forget any jokes about the earth moving," he whispers. "That was more movement than I ever want to feel again."

It's fabulous to have him back in bed with me. Next to him I close my eyes for a few minutes, stoked that he's near. All of a sudden I jerk up.

"Where the hell's my head? I gotta check on Grandma—my Mom too. And Dad—fuck! He's all by himself!"

Phil scrambles up. "I better check on my grandparents. And Veronica and René. You use the phone in here. I'll be in the kitchen."

Pat

The fire station on the corner of 19th Street looks deserted. Those guys are in for a long day. I whiz the truck through the intersection of 20th and Arizona. There are no other drivers on the street.

This is the blackest night I can remember. Not even a moon. Wish I could swivel the headlights to see the damage around us. I sense it. I know Toni does too.

Shadowy figures float under the palm trees outside St. John's. Christ, is the hospital being evacuated?

"Sylvia," Toni whispers. "She might have worked the night shift."

"We'll find out in a few seconds. We're almost there, Toñita."

More than anything I hope Adela's in one piece; Sylvia I'm not so worried about. Toni's scared out of her wits about what we'll find at the duplex. I'm feeling fuckin' wacko myself. Of the two of us, people figure I'm the so-called "butch." Sure don't feel very macha right now. Not one damn bit.

"Do you have Adela's keys?"

"In my fanny pack."

Nodding, I whirl the Mazda into the duplex's gravel driveway. A cluster of bundled-up neighbors sit on the nearby curb. They wave to us. Toni doesn't seem to notice them. She jumps out of the truck.

"Wait." With the bigger flashlight I join her at the foot of the steps. The beam shows the abrupt sag of the porch, the cracked wooden steps. "Careful. Let's go real slow."

She grabs my hand. I wrap my fingers around hers. She fumbles with the keys. The door seems stuck. We put our weight against it and push. The door creaks open.

"Mama—it's Toni. Are you all right?"

We get no answer. I flash the beam toward Adela's bedroom. We keep our hands together, maneuvering around smashed furniture, broken glass.

"The china cabinet," Toni says as we climb over it. "All her precious things."

"Adela, dónde estás, mujer?" I shout.

We hear a muffled voice. "Patricia? Toni? Ay, gracias a Dios!"

With a relieved grin Toni pulls ahead of me. "We're here, Mama. Don't worry. We're here."

"I'm in the closet, muchachas," Adela says with some amusement.

A small dresser blocks the bedroom doorway. Toni and I

shove it back into place. When the flashlight reveals Adela, I laugh out loud. In a flannel nightgown, her gray hair bedraggled, she sits in the middle of one of the messiest closets I've ever seen.

"Ay, Mama. Are you hurt?"

"Creo que no. I thought it was a good idea to stay here por un poco."

"Smart move, Adela." Handing her the flashlight, I squat beside her. Toni's already next to her mother, smothering her with kisses.

"Mijita, I'm fine, de veras. Just help me up."

We get on either side and guide her to the bed inches away. She seems in damn good shape, except for a few bruises.

"You must've bounced right out of bed and into the closet," Toni says with a giggle. "I was scared to death when you didn't answer the phone."

"Well, how could I?" Adela glances at both of us. "Cómo está Sylvia? Y Gabi y Jeff? Y Nopalito?"

"We'll find out, Mama. You were the one I was most worried about. Thank God we were close by."

Adela whisks us aside. "Go see how Sylvia is. Ándale."

Toni nods, shooting me a quick look.

"Stay right here, OK, Adela? The power's out. Your living room's un gran revorujo. The porch is damaged too. You're better off staying put. If there's an aftershock, put a pillow over your head. We'll be back in a few minutes."

"Bueno, Pat. Muchísimas gracias, muchacha."

Zalo's truck isn't in its usual spot. That makes us less wary of approaching the duplex. Sylvia's sagging porch is almost identical to her mother's. The steps are in better shape, though. Toni knocks on the door.

"Sylvia, are you in there? Mama's fine. Are you OK?"
Not a sound.

"Hey, Sylvia," I call toward the bedroom window. "It's Pat
Ramos. Do you need help getting out?"

"Flash the light inside," Toni advises. "Maybe she can't
come to the door."

Moving to the bedroom window, I shine the beam
through. I can see the bed's at a weird angle in the middle of
the room. Sylvia's crouching on it. She looks bewildered, her
eyes like a trapped rabbit's. A shelving unit lies across the
bedroom doorway. Her dresser has toppled. Shards of mirror
spread across the floor.

"I better go through the window, Toni, so I can help
her out. She might hurt herself if she tries to climb over
that stuff."

Toni moves closer. "Can you hear us, Sylvia?"

Sylvia starts to get off the bed. "Nothin' wrong with
my ears."

"Don't walk around barefoot, mujer," I warn her. "There's
glass all over."

She blinks at me. "Don't know where my shoes are, Pat."

Toni and I exchange glances. Like a team of rescuers, we
take off the screen. The window is the old-fashioned kind
that lifts. I raise it as high as it goes.

"Good thing you're long and slinky," Toni murmurs. She
takes a sturdy plastic milk crate off Sylvia's porch. "Stand on
this, Pat."

Using the box to boost me up, I aim one leg through the
window. In seconds I'm inside.

Whether she wants to show it or not, Sylvia is glad to see
me. She's kneeling on the bed, pointing to where she thinks
her shoes are. Personally, I wouldn't choose canvas es-

padrilles, but that's what she wants.

"You need something warm, Syl. Damn cold out there."

She slips on the flimsy shoes and finds her way to the closet with the help of the flashlight's beam. She's wearing a skimpy nightgown.

"You goin' to stare at me getting dressed?"

"Sorry," I mutter. I decide to clear the way out in the meantime.

An aftershock hits while I'm in the middle of making a clear path to the front door. I dart into the bedroom doorway. Aiming the flashlight at Sylvia again, I urge her to stay motionless. She's in a pair of stretch pants, not much else. Damn, her belly's round already.

The old duplex groans and sways.

"Stay away from the window," I yell at Toni.

I hear her shouting to her mother.

"Where's Mama?" Sylvia calls to me.

"In her house. I want to get both of you outside fast. Sylvia, soon as this stops, throw anything on, and let's get the hell out. I don't trust these old buildings."

The shaking halts. I stumble back to Sylvia. She wraps herself in a fake leopard jacket.

"Pat, I'm really scared," she says when I reach her. "Zalo hasn't come home. I don't even know where he is."

"He'll show up." I take her arm. "Let's go."

Gabriela

It's almost like Pasadena before the Rose Parade. People huddle together on curbs, on street corners, keeping warm before the big event. Today it's already happened. Everyone's trying to figure out what to do next.

I leave the Jeep in the street and find Mom in a lawn chair outside Grandma's. No Godzilla in sight. Grandma's in another chair, Nopalito's covered cage next to her. Toni and Pat huddle together on the crocheted afghan. They have a propane camping lantern propped on top of a milk crate.

"Gabi, oh baby—thank God you're here." Mom grabs me real tight. She hasn't hugged me like this in ages. "We couldn't get through to Jeff on the phone. Is he OK?"

All of them surround me, practically suffocating me. I'm so glad to see all of them in good shape. Without even thinking, I blurt out an answer. "Gosh, I don't know. I'm going over there right now."

Toni and Pat look the calmest at my news. Mom's eyes kind of bulge. Grandma looks about to cry.

"Y dónde estabas, Gabriela?" She is the first to ask. Her voice sounds real old.

I move my eyes from face to face. "With Phil."

Toni keeps a matter-of-fact tone. "Where is he now?"

"With his grandparents. Figured his Dad would phone there. Phil wanted to be sure Mr. and Mrs. Melendez were OK. I came straight over when the phone wouldn't work."

"Ay, muchacha. I can't believe you were with that boy all night," Grandma says, real sad.

"Mama, leave her alone," Mom cuts in. "Gabi's old enough to know what she's doing. I'm thankful she's alive. That's all I care about." She hugs me again and rubs my back.

Pat springs up. Seems like she doesn't want to get involved in any family uproar about Phil and me.

"Plan of action," she begins. "I'll go with Gabi to Jeff's. We'll take the Jeep. Toni, you drive the truck to the apartment and take all the camping equipment out of the carport storage bin. Set up the Coleman stove and make some coffee here. We'll be hungry before too long. Gabi and I'll be back as soon as we can."

Toni acts nervous about Pat's plan. Without saying much, she takes the truck keys. Pat gives her a smooch and whispers something. Maybe a good sign.

"We have to pull together through this," Pat says to no one in particular. "We don't even know how bad things are yet."

"Pues, I went to the market yesterday," Grandma reveals. "I have lots of food."

"Me too," Mom says.

"I don't," Pat admits. "Besides, I'll need a ladder to even get inside my place."

I gape at that comment. She pinches my arm. "Come on, Gabi. Let's zip over to Jeff's."

On the way Pat tells me the whole story of helping Mom and Grandma out of the duplexes, of Toni and her dangling from upstairs by tying sheets end to end.

"How'd you come up with that?"

"Saw it in an Abbott and Costello movie when I was a kid," Pat says with a laugh.

"You're the only one getting a kick out of this."

"Defense mechanism. Better to laugh than cry, Gabi. My apartment's a disaster zone," she adds.

"Pat, that can be fixed. I think it's great you and Toni were together."

She nods, like she's not ready to talk about it. "Did Phil get in touch with Veronica and René?"

"He knew they'd go to his grandparents, so he went there too. It was strange, Pat—we both wanted to be with our families."

"Normal reaction. Soon as the phones work, I have to get a

hold of my brother Carlos. So don't sweat it, Gabi. Doesn't mean Phil doesn't care for you."

"I know that," I murmur. "Pat, thanks for helping."

She looks embarrassed. "Hey—you guys matter."

"The Brandons are here." In the circular brick driveway, we can't miss my other grandparents' navy Mercedes sedan.

Pat shoots the flashlight at a bunch of scattered bricks. "Think that used to be Jeff's chimney."

The front door is unlocked. "Dad—" I call.

"Well, Gabriela, wherever have you been?" I hear Phyllis Brandon's refined voice. Sure don't feel like tangling with her. I am glad Pat's with me. We can make a fast getaway if we have to.

Pencil-thin Phyllis is in an expensive-looking jogging out-fit. It has a silky finish, and she isn't a runner. I ignore her question. "Where's my Dad?"

"In the dining room with Stuart, dear." From her position by the crumbling fireplace, she makes no move to approach me but does nod to Pat. "The patio doors shattered. Extensive damage to the house. Jeff came through wonderfully. He simply has a bruise on his forehead from the bedside lamp falling on him. He—"

I don't need to hear anymore. Pat can deal with her bab-bling. They're already making small talk. I only want to see my Dad.

"Oh, sweet baby," he murmurs to me. Balding Stuart Brandon pats my arm and walks off to join his wife. "Gabi, I tried phoning you but—"

"Me too." By then I'm practically in Dad's lap, crying at last. "How did you—"

"I was stunned when the lamp hit me. That might've been for the best because I rode out the quake. Hair-raising, huh? Like a boss wave. The buggy," he says, patting his chair, "rolled right to the bed. I leaned over and pulled it close enough to slide into."

"Dad, I'm so sorry I wasn't here," I sob.

"Everything worked out, Gabi." He kisses the top of my head. "Don't worry about it. Your old man's been through a lot worse."

⌒ CHAPTER THIRTEEN ⌒

January 17: Morning
Adela

We're having a breakfast picnic outside my poor little house.
Neighbors all over the block are doing the same. Toni made
scrambled eggs with potatoes. Sylvia made coffee in the little
percolator Pat had in the camping box. Even if I don't approve of where Gabi was during el terremoto, I am glad she
is with us now. She brought her portable radio, uno muy
grande. We can hear about everything that has happened en
el Valle de San Fernando and all over Los Angeles. But no
one says much about Santa Monica.

Pat went to find out if Santa Monica College still planned
to have the Martin Luther King program. Before she left she
turned off the gas in both duplexes and took Nopalito to the
animal hospital for me. Pobrecito, his tiny wings were bloody
from flapping when his cage fell over. El vet will keep Nopalito overnight.

Whenever we have to use the bathroom, we go through the
back door of mi casita. My porch is very wobbly; Sylvia's

porch is too. Ay, now that the sun is out—que lindo dia, muy bright sun y todo—we can see how awful things really look. Every chimney on the block is down. Cracked walls, lopsided stairs, broken windows everywhere. Gracias a Dios that we're all fine.

"There's enough for another serving, Sylvia. Want more?" Toni holds up the frying pan to show her.

Sylvia nods. "Might as well finish it, if no one else wants any." Today she is un poco amable with her sister. "I wonder if the phone's working yet. Zalo should have called by now."

"Guess that depends where he is, Mom," Gabi says. "If he's in the Valley—they're worse off than we are, according to the radio."

That is not what Sylvia wants to hear. I can tell she is worried. Perdóname, Jesusito, but I am not. Mis hijas are safe, y Gabi y Pat, tambien Jeff y Nopalito. I do not even want to think about ese Zalo. Ay, when he finds out Pat helped Sylvia out, puede ser que el hombre se va volver loco.

"I have to check in at the hospital, but I don't want to leave till I hear from him." Sylvia finishes her breakfast and hands Toni the empty plate.

"After I clean up here, I'm walking over to St. John's," Toni says. "Patients were being evacuated when Pat and I drove by. We couldn't see much in the dark."

Sylvia's big eyes stare at her sister, then at me. "Why didn't you say that sooner? How old's the hospital, Mama?"

"Pues, it was built after World War II—almost 50 years old, eh?"

"Before the current earthquake codes," Toni mumbles.

Sylvia looks even more nervous. "I'll walk over there with you, Toni."

Sylvia

Toni's really into playing big sister. I don't even remember the last time I ate a meal she cooked. Must've been way when she and Pat shared a place. They'd invite me for brunch or dinner. It was a regular thing after I divorced Jeff, when Gabi was a kid. If I was dating, I would leave Gabi with them overnight. Didn't used to think anything of it—then.

I don't even remember why I told Zalo my sister's a dyke. Right away he wanted to know everything. It drove me so crazy I wound up telling him stuff, about when we were kids. No surprise, they clashed right off. I never thought Zalo would tell Toni what I'd said about her.

Even before all that she would put on her snooty librarian face. In other words, she made it real clear she didn't want to deal with Zalo, a blue-collar hombre. Since Pat has a big brother—Carlos—she knows how to deal with guys better. She wouldn't be overly friendly to Zalo, but at least she would act like he's human. Toni looked down on him from the start.

She has her back to me. Never been one for small talk. She's wiping off the blue enamel camping plates with one of Mama's dish towels. Don't know if it's such a great idea to walk to St. John's with her, but I'm damn curious about what's happening at the hospital. I wonder if the emergency generators blew. Our electricity is still off.

Other than a few words here and there, Toni's been quiet ever since Pat drove off a couple of hours ago. Maybe she's trying to figure out where to stay tonight. I'm not sure if I want to sleep inside, even when Zalo's back home. We've already had lots of aftershocks. Nerve-wracking. All of a sudden the lawn chair shakes, the ground growls.

Not as scary as being inside, though.

Gabi and Mama are by the rickety fence, talking to some neighbors who have a battery-operated mini-TV. I stay where I am, even if it's damn sunny. Beats the cold from earlier. I keep waiting to hear the phone ring.

Toni stacks the plates into the camping box. "Sylvia, want to take that walk?"

"Soon as I use the bathroom." I pull myself out of the chair and head to Mama's back door.

I am in there a few minutes when Toni knocks. Can't she wait?

"Someone's here to see you, Sylvia."

I rush out. "Is Zalo back?"

Standing at the back door, my sister looks serious. "It's Sergeant Velez."

"Shit. What does he want?"

"He—"

I wave her off. Damn meddling cop.

He is by the fence with Mama and Gabi. They're shaking their heads at each other. I bet Velez has been all over town. He's probably telling them the city is in worse shape than we figured. What's he wasting time for, coming over here?

"Mrs. Anchondo," Velez moves his muscular body toward me, "I'm sorry to say your husband—"

I stop right where I am. His deep eyes aren't condescending like before. They stay with me. My hand flies to my mouth.

"What?"

"This morning your husband was driving on the Antelope Valley Freeway. His pickup was on one of the overpasses that collapsed in the earthquake."

"No!" My knees feel like mush. Toni hurries to me. Her arm clutches my waist.

"I've come to tell you he didn't survive," Velez finishes.

"No!" I scream. "You're lying! Zalo's *not* dead!"

Toni

In her anguish Sylvia breaks free. Her face is a quivering mask of terror and grief. Sobbing, she nearly stumbles on the graveled driveway. She regains her footing. At the end of the driveway, she turns right and disappears. I think she is on her way to the hospital. Does she think she'll find him there?

"I'll go after her," I call over my shoulder. I try to pick up speed.

Gabi begins to run alongside me. I grasp her shoulder.

"Stay with your grandma, honey. Let me do this."

She hesitates, then relents.

I trail after my sister. She is half a block ahead. Her wails of despair fill the street, echoing through the January morning. Neighbors stop conversations to stare. Sylvia's cries tear at me, reviving memories.

Years ago, heartbroken over Jeff, she would come to me for consolation. I would try to convince her to give him another chance. Sylvia has always been headstrong. She wouldn't listen then—or since. Will she accept anything from me today? I brush off that thought.

At this moment I am not the issue. She is. Panting, cursing myself for being out of shape, I endeavor to catch up.

She zig-zags across Arizona at Chelsea. On the other side of the street, I run parallel. She seems unaware of my presence, no doubt too blinded by tears.

I am becoming winded. Adrenaline fuels Sylvia.

She dashes toward the grassy park adjacent to the hospital's maternity wing. Patients of all ages, on gurneys, in wheelchairs, congregate there. Their faces are either frightened or blank. Nuns and nurses hover over them.

On any other day the outdoor gathering could be a celebration, a morning party in a lovely setting, but the hospital's stark-white exterior shows deep rifts, erratic criss-crosses of structural damage. Broken windows gape. Only the enormous palm trees seem undisturbed.

At the gnarled trunk of one, Sylvia slides to her knees. Her entire body racked with sorrow, she lunges forward, raking her fingers into the earth. She pulls up moist clumps of grass and dirt. She beats her fists into the ground, her shrill voice on the verge of hysteria.

"You killed him! Damn devil dirt! You killed him!"

Out of breath, I crouch beside her. At first she strikes at me, hits me with filthy balled fists, pushes me away.

But I do not go. "Sylvia, please. I'm here."

Her lamenting face contorts even further. She lets herself collapse into my arms. "I can't believe he's dead, Toni. He can't be."

With tenderness, I hold her close. Both of us are oblivious to our surroundings. For several minutes we stay alone until one of the nuns approaches.

"Sylvia?"

Hearing that caring voice, my sister sobs anew.

"Her husband died in the quake," I murmur.

"Oh, my dear girl." The tiny nun kneels beside us. "I'll get the chaplain for you, Sylvia. We will pray together. Such a humbling, horrible day."

Afternoon
Pat

"What the hell was Zalo doing on the Antelope Valley Freeway at 4:31 A.M.?" Noticing Adela and Sylvia in the back seat of the Escort, I keep my voice quiet.

"Who knows? Ron Velez said a woman was with him," Toni whispers. "Maybe she lived out there. Whoever she was, she didn't have an I.D. She was pregnant, Pat."

"Damn," I mutter. Sylvia's bawling. Her mother's hugging her, rubbing her shoulders.

"Sylvia doesn't know any of this. She ran off before Ron had a chance to tell her."

Arms crossed, I lean against the Mazda. "Do you think she suspects?"

Toni shrugs. "Mama wants to handle it. Gabi'll drive them to Chava's in a little while." She touches my hand. "Pat, help me get some clothes together for Sylvia."

I slip an arm around her and guide her to Sylvia's crooked porch. In daylight it looks pretty bad. We go in carefully.

"Hard to tell what broke in the quake and what Zalo smashed," I remark as we pick our way through the living room rubble.

"I'm numb, Pat," Toni says. She heads to the bedroom closet and searches for a suitable dress for her sister. "You know how I felt about Zalo. He was repulsive. Plenty of times I wished him dead. Now that he is I don't know what to feel—besides relief. I can't let Sylvia see that."

"She sure ain't goin' to believe you're sad." I muddle through the closet floor for the mate to the black low-heeled pump I'm holding.

"She's so involved with her grief she hasn't thought about

me yet, thank God." Toni holds up a black flared, V-necked dress. "Is this appropriate?"

"Don't think it'll fit her. Does she have anything looser?"

"You know Sylvia. She's into form-fitting." Toni sorts through more clothes and finds a navy-and-white patterned two-piece pant outfit. "What do you know? I gave her this for Christmas one year, bought it at Pier 1 Imports. Still has the tags on it."

"Figures. Hell, the pants have elastic, the top's pretty big. It'll do."

Toni keeps the outfit over her arm. She leans over and kisses me. "Pat, I'm really happy you're back. You were gone for ages."

I nuzzle her hair and cheek. "Saw a hell of a lot. First thing I did was drive by the body shop. What's left of my car and a whole bunch of others got smashed when the roof caved in."

"Oh, Pat," she murmurs. "My God. At least you'll be insured for that." She shakes her head. "What about the rest of Santa Monica?"

"Saint Monica's Church is falling apart, masonry everywhere, steeples cracked. Santa Monica College has tons of damage—yellow police tape all over. One of the parking structures is a total mess. A black woman who was on the campus, checking out the scene like I was, took a long look around and said 'Dr. King's giving us a wake-up call.' Makes you stop and think, huh, Toni?"

She nods against me.

"Couldn't get into my office. It's cordoned off too. There was a note on the main door of the building from Dennis Reynolds, this year's Media OutReach director. It said to come by tomorrow morning to help take files out. He lives in West Hollywood, so I drove to his place. He lost a chimney.

Otherwise OK. He's not sure if the fire department will let us in. Anyhow, we'll make a try for it tomorrow. I listened to the radio the whole time I drove around. Devastation everywhere. Old street lights on Broadway keeled over. The medical building at Barrington and Olympic is tottering. This side of town isn't getting much airtime. Like everything else, Toni, the news about the quake is slanted."

"I wonder if last Sunday's quake was a precursor."

"Too soon for the seismologists to tell, I guess."

She kisses me again.

"What's that for?" I murmur.

"I'd rather be with you in the middle of this disaster than stuck in a cabin in the woods."

Laughing, I bring her to me. In Sylvia's cluttered bedroom, we hold each other as tight as we can.

Gabriela

I don't know how to act. I say "act" 'cause that's what it feels like. I'm glad Godzilla is dead and gone. Ding-dong, the wicked wretch is dead.

He hated me. That was real plain. Called me a half-breed the first time he laid eyes on me. He made fun of my light skin and eyes. He was jealous 'cause I'm living proof Mom had made it with Dad, a white man from a Pacific Palisades family. Zalo was jealous 'cause the way I look makes it possible for me to move in and out of different worlds—the same worlds he tried to wreck 'cause there was no place him.

Toni and I talked about this a lot before she went away with Amanda. She even gave me a list of books to read. I didn't get very far with them 'cause they couldn't tell me what made Zalo tick, what made him so mean. Even if I knew it wouldn't make me feel sorry for him. Never. I can't forget how he beat my Mom.

This morning his rusty truck flew off an overpass and threw him out of our lives. In those few seconds the earthquake solved a problem that was making all of us crazy. Is it wrong to be happy about that? I can picture Zalo bellowing, mad as hell when his truck goes into freefall. I hope that doesn't mean he's in orbit somewhere, circling for a new place to land.

Sergeant Velez said the woman was young. They know that much about her. Zalo had a sweetie in the boonies. Was she wise to him? Did she know he was married and had a baby on the way? Had he forced her to go with him? Who knows what her story was. I bet she never thought she'd die like that, so fast, without warning.

Wherever he went Zalo made trouble. He should've stayed on the other side of those hills for good, kept his Valley trash far away from us. I can't understand why Mom fell for whatever line he fed her.

This Chava guy seems too nice to be Zalo's cousin. He offered to drive Mom and Grandma to the Valley to meet with Zalo's mother. Does that mean I'm off the hook? I'm not thrilled about going to Pacoima today, even though I said I'd drive. Who knows how long it'll take to get to the Valley on the old Sepulveda route now that the freeways are down. I volunteered 'cause I couldn't let Grandma go by herself with Mom. We all knew it'd be too awkward for Toni and Pat to be the ones to do it. They're having as hard a time hiding how they really feel as I am.

Chava kind of cocks his crew-cut head when Mom says she has to contact the furniture warehouse for Zalo's paycheck. She doesn't know how she'll pay for the funeral.

"Sylvia…they didn't hire him," Chava blurts out. He looks like he wishes someone else could be the one telling her. "Zalo never got the delivery job."

Mom's face is all puffy. Her voice is hoarse from crying. "You're wrong, Chava. He's been working there for the past week."

Chava's basset-hound eyes are real sad. "He lied to you. Zalo can't fool you no more, Sylvia. No more."

Night
Adela

Que noche de tristeza. The weather is cold, but we are warm inside Pat's camper. Esas muchachas chulas brought the mattress from my bed and stuffed it in the back of the truck. They made it comfortable for Sylvia and me. Ay, esa Pat es muy dependable, llena de ideas. Toni looks so happy with her. Esta mañana, I don't know what we would have done without esas muchachas. They make me feel safe.

No one wants to stay in either duplex. Ay, those aftershocks are terrible, so many of them, all day and night. Toni and Pat are in their tent on the lawn. I hope they won't catch cold. Pat says their sleeping bags will keep them toasty. Gabi went to el cañon to be with her father. I think her mother's sadness is too much for her.

Sylvia twitches in her sleep. What a miracle she is able to sleep at all. Pobrecita, she has had a lifetime of sorrow today. I lay beside her, my rosary between my fingers. Toni found it next to my bed earlier and brought it to me.

Ay, Jesusito, I prayed so much for an answer for Sylvia, but I never thought this would be the one you would send. I don't even care if mi casita is crooked, if my china, mis retratos y cositas are in bits and pieces, if I have to sleep like a gypsy in this truck. El terremoto killed many people, most of them inocentes—pero no todos. Zalo is dead. He can never hurt mi hijita again, gracias a Dios. I do feel sorry for Zalo's mother. She looks older than me, but she is much younger. Es una mujer simplecita, no tiene mucha educación. We visited with her and other Anchondo relatives for a few hours. Ay, she wants Sylvia to live with her. She wants them to raise the baby together. Que barbaridad! Sylvia's head almost snapped back when la Señora Anchondo suggested that.

Ay, no. El barrio de Pacoima is in terrible shape. Not only the earthquake but fires and explosions esta mañana. La Señora Anchonodo lives with her niece so she is not alone on the other side de las montañas. Things might be bad here, but they are much, much worse in el Valle de San Fernando.

I haven't told Toni yet because I know she will be angry. I have to lend—give—Sylvia money for the funeral. She can't afford to pay for all of it and neither can la Señora Anchondo. I prayed so hard for an answer for Sylvia, for a way for her to be rid of ese hombre. It seems only right for me to help bury him, verdad?

Toni

"Have to be at the office at 8:30. Let's get up early—like we're going to sleep at all, right?" Pat chuckles to herself. "We'll take your dad's ladder out of the shed in back, go to my place, grab clothes, whatever, bring the stuff here. The duplexes are home base. Makes the most sense, huh?"

Since we nestled into our sleeping bags in the tent an hour ago, she has not stopped talking. Her mind strategizes for the next day at an incredible pace. I am so overwhelmed from all these upheavals I can barely think.

"Pat, that means Mama and Sylvia have to be early birds too. We can't exactly load the ladder into the truck if they're still asleep."

She laughs, una carcajada to punctuate the uncommon silence. "Hell, we'll just throw la escalera over 'em and take off."

Drowsily, I study her. "Loquita. We have to be sensitive to Sylvia, all right? We might have to pick up your things later. Mama will be up early to go to Mass. We might have to wake Sylvia if she isn't up by the time you have to leave. After breakfast I'm walking into Santa Monica. I want to see what state the library's in. Have to stop by Jeff's too."

"Sylvia's gettin' to you, huh?" Pat murmurs, her face inches from mine.

I nod and snuggle closer. "Too difficult to empathize with, Pat. To a certain extent, I can understand her grief—the fear of loneliness, the realities of being a single parent all over again. Otherwise, I have major problems with her mourning the guy."

"Me too." Pat sighs. "I wasn't prepared when she lashed out at me for giving my condolences. She said I'm sorry only 'cause I can't sue him now."

"It's her fear talking, Pat."

"I know. It still hurt." She frowns. "What if I'd said this morning, 'Since you're married to an asshole, I'm not helping you out. You accused Toni of all kinds of shit so fend for yourself.' How would she have liked that?"

"We can't let ourselves fall into those traps." I rub my hand along her flannel-covered arm. "What matters is Zalo's gone for good. We have to show Sylvia we care for her, that we're willing to be supportive."

"What does that really mean, Toni?"

This time, I sigh. "I'm not sure yet."

◠ CHAPTER FOURTEEN ◡

January 20: Morning
Gabriela

Phil squeezes my hand at San Fernando Mission cemetery. I'm glad he's with me at the burial service. I didn't want to ride with Mom and Grandma in that creepy black Cadillac behind the hearse loaded with Zalo's body. Reminds me too much of Grandpa's funeral. Zalo wasn't like Grandpa, no way. Sure don't want to be counted with *his* family. I couldn't stand the asshole, but he was Mom's husband.

A bunch of Zalo's relatives stand with his mother. The old lady and Mom are the only ones crying. Grandma has that look that means she's praying. Her eyes give her away, though. I can tell her heart really isn't into it.

Cloudy day, not raining yet. God, I don't know how these people in the Valley can handle all this commotion at once— the earthquake, aftershocks, explosions, fires, rain. Most of the quake deaths and injuries happened in the Valley. On the way to the funeral, Phil and I saw the parks full of community tents the National Guard put up. Crowds of people—

mostly Latinos, seems like—line up for food and water. Looks more like a news clip from Nicaragua or Mexico City after their quakes. Sure doesn't fit the picture of the middle class 'burbs on the other side of the Santa Monica Mountains.

The earthquake messed up Santa Monica real bad too, worse than we thought. Our mayor stuck in her two cents about it when Bill Clinton buzzed in on Air Force One to inspect the damage. The mayor spoke for all of us 'cause we've complained for days how our town wound up lost in the devastation shuffle.

While I was growing up, Santa Monica changed from boring small town to trendy Westside. It sits about as far west as you can go, on the brink of the crumbling coast. Dad's right on target when he says it's the end of the road for hundreds of homeless people who would rather hang out on the pier, the Palisades, or the Promenade than on L.A.'s skid row. This week there are even more homeless people because hundreds of Santa Monica residents had to leave their wrecked apartments—including Pat. She's been at Grandma's since the day of the quake.

Like everyone else, my life's taken some crazy turns too: Mom's a widow, Dad's house needs repairs, I can't go to school 'cause classes at Santa Monica College are temporarily suspended, and I'm out of a job. The Warner Bros. store where Phil and I worked was wrecked really bad, like scads of others in Santa Monica Place. The lower level of the shopping mall flooded when the water mains broke. The whole place is shut down for who knows how long.

Phil's dad cut his business trip short and flew back as soon as he heard the earthquake news. Phil says the phones have been ringing off the hook at the structural engineering business his dad owns. We're both helping out in the office. Phil figures he owes his dad. I need the money, period.

The wind feels colder. I watch the priest hand Mom the wooden crucifix from inside Zalo's coffin. Mom holds it against her chest and cries some more. Grandma tries to calm her. I'm restless; I'm no actress. This whole thing feels too phony to me. Zalo didn't care about religion one bit. At his funeral everyone's pretending otherwise, from priest on down.

I tug at Phil to follow me. At Mom's side I hug her while she sobs against my shoulder. Phil doesn't know what to do. He pats Mom's arm once or twice.

"We're going home," I whisper. "I'll see you at Grandma's."

She doesn't even try to convince me to go to Mrs. Anchondo's house. The relatives have a big meal planned. Since Zalo's cousin Chava promised to drive Mom and Grandma home, I figure I can make a clean getaway. Grandma gives me a little frown when she notices me leaving. I don't look her in the eye.

"I wasn't real crazy about Joyce when Dad remarried," Phil says when we're alone. "Never hated her, though. Must be weird, what you're feeling, Gabi."

"Yeah." I blow my nose and gaze out the car window.

"You crying?"

I shake my head. "Not for him—for Mom."

Phil concentrates on driving back to Sepulveda Boulevard. Both of us are jittery about being in the Valley since the quake. I stare out the window, seeing block after block of damaged or destroyed buildings, families camping out, hanging tight.

"As soon as she met him, Phil, she put him first. I started getting pushed out, remember?"

He nods, letting me talk.

"A little over two years ago. I was barely 16 and had never been on my own. She didn't give me much choice when Zalo moved in. Toni convinced me to go to Dad for help. I was too embarrassed to admit what was happening." Tears splash my cheeks. I brush them off. Why am I crying now?

Toni

Studying the cracked walls and steps, the jagged ruts in the plaster of the stairwell, I recall the original library on Santa Monica Boulevard between Fifth and Sixth streets. The interior of that venerable structure brimmed with WPA murals detailing the progress of industry and aviation, while the walls of the downstairs children's section re-created pastel versions of well-loved fairy tales. While Mama shopped, taking toddler Sylvia with her, she would leave me in that enchanted cavern to make friends with other children and enjoy the weekly story hour. The only brown child present, I was much too shy to do the former but could not resist the latter. Mama would have to cajole me to leave. I remember sobbing in protest, little arms clenching a beautifully illustrated *Grimm's Fairy Tales,* later a much-thumbed *Black Beauty.* To soothe me, Mama would check out whatever books I craved. I think she felt a secret pride in realizing I had fallen in love with the written word.

A future librarian sprouted in that no-longer-existing main branch. By the time I earned my degree in library science, the original structure with its creaky hardwood floors and fading murals had been replaced by a commercial bank building. A new library, minus the historic murals, sprang up a block east. It was far too sleek and sanitized to inspire true affection. Nevertheless, I grew fond of its open space, its well-lit stacks, its cubbyhole desks. Working there, nurturing younger generations of book lovers, seemed the ideal job. Losing it broke my heart.

"And to think only a few years ago we had to shut down for asbestos removal," Ruthann Baldwin muses. On her way from the upstairs restrooms, she encounters me in the stairwell. "Remember how we were parceled out to the branch libraries in the meantime, Toni? We were all dying to come back here. Now this."

I glance at her fine-boned African-American profile, her graying well-trimmed head. Since the day after the quake, I have volunteered to reshelve books, rearrange furniture, do whatever I can to return the library to operating condition.

When I fail to respond, she gazes at me with what appears to be genuine concern. "How are you, Toni? Is it too much?"

I nod.

"Crystal told me about your sister's husband. Lord, what a catastrophe." She rubs a firm hand across my shoulders. "You don't need to come in every day, honey. Being with the family—"

"Honest, Ruthann, helping out has pulled me through this week. I need to feel useful."

We fall into step together down the stairs. "I want you to come back to work, Toni. As I'm sure you realize, it's a delicate matter. Marian was in St. John's during the quake. She's been transferred to a hospice."

Hearing that makes me more demoralized. The woman is at death's door, and I'm poised to swing through the other way.

Ruthann scans my face. "Don't let that affect you, understand? We've all been hurting since the bigwigs handed you the pink slip. Crystal and I are the only ones who'll admit that. Lord, anytime we have a Spanish speaker asking for information, none of us can make heads or tails of the inquiry.

We need you in this library, Toni Dorado. It'll happen, honey, believe you me. Wish I could tell you when."

"I'll appreciate whatever you can do, Ruthann," I murmur. Too overcome to say more, I hurry to the nonfiction stacks to continue reshelving.

Surrounded by books on sibling rivalry, incest, and domestic violence, I kneel on the carpet, half berating myself for not going to Zalo's funeral, half congratulating myself for opting for library duty instead. Yesterday, at Mama's house, I had explained to Sylvia my reasons for avoiding the service.

Her face had twisted when she spat out, "Do you think I want you there? You hated Zalo. You were always ready to phone the damn cops on him. You drove him away from me, Toni. He couldn't forget what you did to me when we were kids."

Her words chilled me. After a long pause, I managed to form an answer. "Whatever happened between us, Sylvia, was mutual. Please take some responsibility for that. I have. I went into therapy over it. You'd rather blame me for all your problems."

"Therapy? I don't need some expensive shrink to tell me the score." Sylvia looked bloated from tears and weight gain. Her lips curled in derision. "If Jeff Brandon can wind up being a counselor, I might as well get my advice from talk radio."

I rose from the kitchen table and started washing the breakfast dishes. "I suppose it's easier for you to cast blame than to delve inside."

"Cut the high-falutin' talk, Toni. You were older. You should've known better than to play around with me. What were you doing, anyway—trying to make me into a dyke?"

At that, I whirled from the sink. "Listen, I'm two and a half years older than you, hardly an adult perpetrator. What you and I did involved childhood curiosity about our bodies. Accept that. Mama and Daddy never told us anything about sex. Hasn't that ever occurred to you? We were experimenting. I was a child too. For God's sake, Sylvia, I didn't realize my sexual orientation until I was in college."

"I don't care what you say," she snapped. "You were older. It was all your fault."

"My fault that you liked it?" I retorted, trembling.

"Shut up! You sound just like Zalo. He always used to throw that at me! Goddamn it, Toni. I don't have to hear that from you."

Muffling a sob, I stay on my knees. My head is bent over the mounds of books to be reshelved. Alone in the stacks I ponder that conversation. Sylvia is my sister. She is the first muchacha I ever touched. Will she always hold that against me, a distorted secret ever between us?

Afternoon
Adela

Gracias a Dios que we settled in Santa Monica. I don't like the San Fernando Valley. I'm glad Juan and me chose to raise our daughters in a town close to the ocean.

La familia Anchondo doesn't have much, pobrecitos. I heard through family gossip at the funeral that Zalo's father drank a lot. No wonder his son grew up mean, malcriado. How much did Sylvia know about Zalo's background before she became enamorada con ese hombre?

This morning hardly anyone was at the funeral. The peo-

ple in this valley have had much sorrow, much destruction.
Maybe their own miseries made them stay away from the
Mass. Or maybe, like Gabi whispered to me, Zalo didn't have
many friends. Creo que Gabi is right.

Chava doesn't say much, but he is a very kind man. I have
a feeling Zalo took advantage of his cousin many times. After
all, Chava was the one who bailed el cochino—que Dios me
perdóne—out of jail. Chava does not seem like the type of
hombre who can afford to raise a lot of money. He must have
done it out of family loyalty, nada mas. I don't think Zalo ever
did Chava any favors.

Earlier when I went into the kitchen to offer to serve food,
I passed by Chava. He asked to have a word with me. He told
me the girl who died with Zalo was the younger half sister—
ay, only 16 years old—of a distant cousin of los Anchondos.
Dios mio, que escándalo! I am going to keep this secret from
Sylvia. Why cause mi hija any more pain?

Beside me she sits en silencio. She hasn't said much to anyone. When la familia comes by to pay respects, Sylvia nods
and mumbles a word or two. Her Spanish has never been as
fluent as Toni's. In her grief, I doubt she can think of anything to say. She looks so tired. After a few minutes she moves
slowly to the bathroom. Her face is puffy with tears, with sorrow. Everyone watches, their curious eyes on her.

It bothers me that Toni chose not to be with her sister
through esta tristeza. Even Gabi left as soon as she saw the
chance. Sylvia doesn't expect much from either of them. I
cannot believe how both my older daughter and granddaughter cannot bring themselves to put their feelings aside
for one day, to be with Sylvia during este dia de luto.

Toni said she didn't want to be a hypocrite. She told me
Sylvia insisted she keep away. Sylvia doesn't know what she's

saying. She cannot forget how Toni never approved of Zalo. Hay, ese hombre feo caused so many problems between my daughters and with Gabi too. She never felt safe around him. Ay, que está pasando con mi familia? El terremoto has divided us even more.

Sylvia

I feel like I'm suffocating in the musty-smelling bathroom. To revive, I splash my swollen face with cold water. A worn orange towel is all I can find to dry myself with. Old lady Anchondo expects me to move in with her? Zalo had her pegged, all right. She must be an idiot if she thinks I'll park myself and the baby in this shack. She's more than a little loca en la cabeza.

People I've never seen before have shuffled by since the service. They all say how sorry they are that Zalo's gone. My bullshit detector's on alert, working overtime. These relatives showed up to be sure Zalo's a definite goner. They want to see for themselves that his coffin is sealed shut.

Daddy used to tell me stories about funerals he'd gone to as a kid. In Santa Monica Canyon his mourning aunts would hurl themselves—black dresses, widows' veils, and all—on pine coffins and threaten to leap into the graves with their dead husbands. Their families would have to pry the wailing women away. At the cemetery all I could think of was how I'll never see Zalo's big body again. I won't feel him on me, in me. He'll never be around to know the baby and watch it grow up. He won't come crashing out of the pit and escape like I used to imagine Tio Manuel's roasting pigs would. Like them he's stuck where he is. He can never return.

No matter how much I've been in shock over Zalo's death,

I never felt like throwing myself on his coffin. I didn't want to stop it from being lowered into the ground. Ashes to ashes, dust to dust. That expression finally makes sense to me. The earthquake killed him. That damn Valley dirt has claimed him.

The relatives mutter among themselves about why Zalo was on the freeway so early in the morning. Here and there I've heard snatches of conversations. They shut up when they realize I'm listening. Chava must've told them Zalo's lie about the furniture delivery job.

All that explains why I get these pitying looks. Damned if I care. I'll never see any of these sorry-eyed losers again, that's for sure. No way will I stay in touch. Aside from his mother and Chava, Zalo never had introduced me to the other Anchondos. Maybe he didn't want to. Fine and dandy. Moneywise, they can't help me a bit. That's my main worry these days—money. So why should I bother with them? I don't owe any of them a damn thing, Zalo's baby or not.

About to leave the bathroom, I hear a sudden rumble. Real quick I brace myself in the unsteady doorway. Someone in the living room screams. Another aftershock, a hard jolt.

I don't move till it stops. Then I rush to Mama. She looks relieved to see me.

"Let's go, Mama. I can't take another minute of this."

Evening
Pat

With the other impatient tenants, I stand by the carports. We listen to the landlord's string of apologies about the delay in building repairs.

"For insurance purposes," George announces, "I can't let any of you inside until the building inspector approves it."

He's a chubby bald man in his 60s, with a butt so flat his wife, Iris, makes him wear suspenders for fear his pants will slide to his ankles.

Furious voices, including mine, protest.

"The stairs have to be reattached," George explains. He breaks into a sweat. The night air is biting. He's too edgy about our collective reactions to feel the colder temperature. "Who knows what else needs fixing? Hard to tell without an official inspection."

"I demand access to my clothes and other personal belongings," my next-door neighbor insists. Brian's a set designer, into the latest trends. He's ready to have a conniption fit 'cause he's been living in his Miata, forced to wear the same threads over and over.

"I don't like this any more than you do." George's resolve is fading. "Well, all right. You can have 15 minutes each to enter at your own risk."

In no time flat we start clambering to our apartments.

George yells after us. "Upstairs people, use that ladder. Take whatever you can carry—one trip each. I refuse to be responsible for possible injuries," he adds with an uneasy shrug. If Iris were here, she'd snap his suspenders to make him change his mind.

The downstairs tenants have no qualms about his offer. Brian looks wary when he sees me scamper up the ladder. No time to deal with his queeny temperament. Everyone for herself. The other upstairs tenants haven't shown up. I'm already halfway to the second-floor landing before George has a chance to reconsider.

This is the second time I've been inside since the quake. The pad seems even worse than before. All the aftershocks have made the apartment look like some psycho giant decided to play fiddlesticks with my stuff. The living room furniture is scattered, bookcases on their sides, framed posters cut by shards, lamps topsy-turvy. The refrigerator sits in the middle of the kitchen, door swinging open, contents spilled on the linoleum. No time to mourn my losses. I rush into the bedroom, tossing underwear and as many clothes as I can into two large duffel bags. Can't carry the computer. I stick the disk storage box into my jacket pocket. Depressed, I balance a duffel bag strap on each shoulder and make my way down the ladder.

At Adela's duplex I turn off the ignition and sit in the loaner truck. I'm getting stuck on it, thinking of using my insurance money to make the truck mine. Right now I'm inclined to sleep in the camper shell, away from Dorado family tensions. All week Sylvia's been at center stage. Everyone else is a supporting player. I'm too wiped out to hear about the funeral. Between settling into a hastily rented Media OutReach office and restructuring my personal life, I'm damn down in the dumps. Not in the best mood for being around anyone. At least not tonight.

I close my eyes and lean against the seat, ready to doze off. Next thing I know Toni's next to me.

"Hi, Pat," she whispers. She moves closer and kisses my mouth. When she doesn't get much of a reaction, she stares at me. "What's wrong?"

"My life," I mumble. Stroking her hair, I tell her about the apartment's status.

"You know you can stay with us, mujer." Toni touches my cheek. "Unless you want to find another place to live."

"I'd rather take my chances with George. Already been there a dozen years. Hell, in a way, I can't blame the guy. He's playing it safe. Just damn inconvenient. Plus I haven't had a chance to clean up the mess."

"We can do that Saturday," she promises. "I'll help."

"If he lets us in again, Toni."

"We'll find a way." She continues caressing me. "I've saved dinner for you."

With a sigh, I take her into my arms. I kiss her thick hair. Its coarseness is such a contrast to the softness of her body. "Let's run away, Toñita. Don't you wish?"

"I've already tried that," she says with a rueful smile. "It doesn't work."

Laughing, I give her a wink. "Then join me in the back tonight. We'll have privacy."

Toni

Sylvia stands in the doorway while I open Pat's duffel bags. During dinner she was subdued. She watches me remove Pat's clothes and make room for them in the closet. Sylvia crosses her arms. She seems ready to pounce.

"You really fuss over her," she mutters.

I let her comment slide. Leaving the duffel bags on the closet floor, I turn to face her. "Sylvia, would you like me to fix you a cup of tea?"

She grimaces. "Whatever you think, I'm not a sick old bitch. I'm makin' conversation, that's all. Where is Pat, anyway?"

"Taking a bath. She's frazzled."

"She matters more, doesn't she? You ignore me, but you sure can fuss over Pat. All of a sudden, when you have nowhere to land, Pat's it for you. You talk about *me* being a user."

I move from the closet and sit on the double bed. "You've

had a very emotional day, Sylvia. Please don't stir things up."

"Stir things up? Me? Blame the son-of-a-bitch earthquake for that." Instead of leaving she parks herself opposite me. "How do you think I feel? You all say you're sorry about Zalo, but you don't mean it. None of you liked him. You've kept your distance; Gabi couldn't wait to split with her boyfriend. Even Mama's off playing bingo tonight."

"She always does on Thursdays," I remind her. I'm dreading the moment Pat strolls from the bathroom and finds us like this. "If you had asked Mama to stay home, Sylvia, she would have."

"My fault again, right?" She gives me a disgusted glance. "All of you keep going about your business. You're at the library—"

"Volunteering," I emphasize. She talks right over me.

"Mama's doing her church thing; Gabi's either with Phil or Jeff, whichever one needs her most. What about me? Do you know what it was like today, being in that rickety shack in the Valley—Aftershock City? All those damn Anchondos bowing and scraping like they'd do whatever they can for me. Shit! They're the poorest bunch of pochos I've ever seen! What the hell can they do for the baby and me? Meanwhile St. John's shut down the maternity wing, and I'm being laid off. Might as well be out on the street." Whatever bravado she had scrounged up vanishes. She breaks into sobs.

Without hesitating, I take her into my arms. She doesn't resist. When we were kids and she hurt herself, she would always run to me first. Despite our emotional gulf, I wish we could recreate those moments. Maybe this is one time we can.

"Sylvia, we'll survive all this together. Believe me, we will."

Her words are almost unintelligible. "How am I going to raise the baby by myself? How am I going to live?"

I rub her back and murmur to her. "We're your family, Sylvia. Don't worry. We'll help you."

Her sobs become unrestrained spasms of grief. While I hold her I can't help thinking of Amanda. She wanted a baby and expected me to raise it. How ironic that my homecoming presents me with a similar situation. But I won't abandon Sylvia. The difference is, Sylvia truly is my flesh and blood. She is mi hermana, a Dorado like me. Amanda could never be that.

In her red robe, Pat pauses at the threshold. Our eyes connect. I note the compassion filling hers. Ordinarily she puts on a cynical act. She shrugs that off tonight. She and Sylvia were classmates once, not best friends. Even so, they have a shared history and much of it involves me. Pat nods. She heads in the direction of the kitchen. She returns with a glass of water for Sylvia.

"Here you go, Syl."

My sister swallows another sob. Her bleary gaze meets Pat's. "You're the only one who ever calls me that."

"'Cause I've known you since you were a little brat," Pat replies affectionately. "Listen, Syl, I think a hot bath would do wonders for you. Sure has mellowed me. What do you say I get the tub ready?"

Sylvia drinks a bit of water. She seems to consider the suggestion. "I hope you two aren't planning to drown me."

"Ay, Sylvia," I murmur, hugging her again. "Let us pamper you. Isn't that what you've been wanting?"

Clearing her throat, she wipes her puffy eyes. She glances at both of us. "I don't know what I want."

☞ CHAPTER FIFTEEN ☜

January 22: Morning
Sylvia

Don't know what got into me. Toni would say I let my guard down. Whatever it was, I slept through the night.

Toni left a note on the bed. In case I needed anything, she explained, they would be in the truck. Figured my sister and Pat were horny as hell. After that steamy bath I was too damn tired to care. All I wanted was sleep, not hints about their kinky sex habits.

Every day the women in this family spread to the four winds. Mama's been around the most, except when she gets it in her head to help that pretty priest with the parish's earth-quake cleanup. Saint Anne's grade school—where Toni and I went as kids—is red-tagged. It must be a pathetic sight.

Till late afternoons, Toni stays at the library. Gabi comes by now and then. Things are weird between us. Who knows what she's been telling Jeff and vice versa? When he phoned the other night, I hung up. I couldn't deal with his phony sympathy.

Yesterday I made myself go next door. Toni and Pat have been bringing my stuff over since the quake. I swear the duplex looks worse than the day Zalo broke the stereo and furniture. My sister and Pat have promised to help me fix the place up. They make me suspicious—too nicey-nicey. Maybe it's just their way of trying to make me feel better.

Sooner or later I have to spend the night alone. It's crowded at Mama's: the two of us in her bed, Toni and Pat in the other, when they're not in the truck. Maybe Gabi will want to stay next door with me. Don't know how to ask her. I'll be pissed if she says no.

Haven't seen any of them today. The sun's out. No rain for the time being. Another note on the kitchen table. Toni and Pat are poking through the apartment's rubble. Mama's at the parish again.

I hang out in the kitchen, eat half a grapefruit, make coffee and toast. I really don't mind being by myself. Don't have to talk or answer questions. Too bad it's Saturday. Otherwise I'd catch a few talk shows. Watch some fucked-up folks worse off than me.

The phone rings. I'm slapping apricot jam on my toast. Maybe Mama's checking on me. I grab one slice and go into the living room to pick up the phone.

"Hello."

"Toni, it's Amanda." The Woods Woman herself. "Sweetie, are you all right? Whenever I've called, no one's answered. I've been terribly worried."

"This is Sylvia, not Toni." I hear her gasp loud and clear. "Could've pulled a fast one on you, Amanda."

"Oh." She fumbles to recover. "Well…is Toni there?"

"Nope. She's with Pat Ramos." Can't resist adding, "They're cleaning up the earthquake rubble in their apartment."

Amanda can't hide her big-time confusion. "I thought Toni was staying with Mrs. Dorado."

"She was, but disasters bring people together, you know."

"Oh." For a second, she doesn't say a word. "Well, I hope none of your family was hurt." Amanda talks in breathy spurts. "I don't have a TV. Had no idea if your town was affected or not. The radio coverage has been pretty sketchy."

"My husband died on the freeway," I hear myself say.

"Oh, Sylvia," Amanda murmurs in genuine shock. "I'm terribly sorry." I'll say this much for her: So far, Amanda's the only one who sounds like she means it.

"If it wasn't for the baby I'm expecting, I couldn't face the future." All of a sudden I'm about to bawl. Doesn't take much. I let myself drop to the sofa.

"I can certainly understand that." Amanda's probably thinking of what else to say. "Tell me, Sylvia," she begins after a pause, "was Toni aware of your pregnancy before she returned to California?"

"Shit, no," I mumble. "You must know she had no use for me—or my husband."

"Well, Toni loves Gabriela. I know she'll love your new baby too." Amanda sighs. "I must go, Sylvia. I'm sorry to hear about your…misfortune. You needn't bother telling Toni I phoned. I only wanted to be sure she's…safe." Before I have a chance to answer, Amanda clicks off.

"Moody chick," I mutter. I wipe my eyes and head back to my breakfast. By now the other half of toast must be stone cold.

Pat

Over breakfast Toni convinced me to phone my landlord. I was gung ho to use her dad's ladder to sneak upstairs. My plan would've been foiled anyhow. George was wily enough to install a chain-link fence to keep looters out. He wasn't thrilled when I said I needed to go in again. I mentioned I hadn't cleaned up any of the spilled food in the kitchen, and he changed his tune fast. No way does he want cucarachas to take over. He told me to come by for the padlock key and warned me to be careful.

Toni and I have plastic gloves and plenty of cleaning equipment. All morning we've been scrubbing, sweeping, tidying up. A foraging army of ants laid siege in the kitchen, too greedy to realize the sticky blackberry jam and maple syrup would do them in. The kitchen was one hell of a mess, with pieces of glass jars and rotting food dumped around the refrigerator.

Toni stacks books in neat piles in the living room. I pick glass slivers from the carpet. Every once in a while there's an aftershock. Nothing we can't handle. I hate to admit it, but this whole scene reminds me of the day Toni left. As soon as she was out of earshot, I grabbed whatever was handy and threw stuff around. I really raised a ruckus. Wasn't about to beg her to stay; I had my pride.

"Gosh, Pat. I found a baby picture of Gabi in this novel. Wasn't she adorable?" Squatting by one of the downed bookcases, Toni hands me a color snapshot of her niece.

I jolt out of my memories and study the photo. "Get a load of those eyes." I give her a quick grin. "Know somethin'? While you were gone I went to the movies with Gabi lots of times. Dykes in the audience would do a double take. The kid really is gorgeous."

"Yes," Toni murmurs. She takes the picture from me and sticks it in her shirt pocket. "I have to talk with her, Pat. She really needs to spend more time with Sylvia."

"Can't be easy—for either of them."

"I know." Toni sifts through books. She flips pages, maybe hoping to find more snapshots.

For a while I'm quiet. I pick up a few more pieces of glass. "Toñita, how do you feel about Sylvia's baby?"

She glances at me, then away.

I study her. "You know where the sperm came from, mujer. Is that going to make a difference?"

She glides the coarse edge of her braided hair along her neck. "Pat, the baby didn't choose its father." She sighs. "I...well, I'm glad you brought this up."

"Huh?" I toss a large piece of glass from a picture frame into the plastic trash can beside me.

For a couple of minutes, she looks away again before plunging in. "Amanda wanted to be artificially inseminated. She wanted me to take care of the baby, and she'd be the breadwinner."

An unexpected angle in the Northwest saga. I wonder what else she hasn't told me. Sure can't imagine Toni being a frontier mom in a log cabin. Years ago we agreed we weren't June and Ward Cleaver types. Back when we came out, dykes seemed more footloose and fancy free. We sure didn't dream about raising a family. I grit my teeth and make myself ask the next question.

"Is that why you came home?"

Right away she shakes her head. "I'm back because I love you, Pat. Because I couldn't stand being away from you. Don't you believe me?"

"I want to, Toni."

"It's true," she insists. "When Amanda told me her plans, I knew my procrastination had to stop. Right away I decided to pack up and go." She shrugs. "Now I have a widowed, unemployed, pregnant sister. Must be in the stars, verdad? Looks like I'll help raise a baby after all."

"Zalo's kid," I remind her.

"A Dorado baby," she emphasizes. "A niña or niño who needs some loving aunties."

"Let's hope the kid doesn't look like that asshole," I mutter. "Before you start planning a baby shower, get real, Toni. Sylvia could give you one helluva hard time. Right now she's got the blues. Who knows if she'll take up with some other loser? She ain't bad lookin'. After she has the kid, who can guess what she'll be up to?"

Toni brings a couple of books with her. She puts them on the floor next to me and kneels on them to avoid hidden glass in the carpet. "The point is—aside from Jeff—you and I have had a tremendous influence on Gabi. More than anyone else we've been her role models. Gosh, do you think she'd be in college if we hadn't steered her there? When Sylvia took up with Zalo, Gabi needed someone to care about her: you and me plus Mama and Jeff. That's what I'm imagining for this baby, Pat. I can't do anything about Sylvia—never could, even when we were kids. I'm thinking familia, sabes? Being there for the kid." She gazes at me, her fawn eyes moist. "That's what this is all about."

"*The Waltons*, Chicana-style," I quip.

"Mas o menos," she agrees with a laugh. "You're a very important part of the equation."

"La Tia Pat."

"Don't you like the sound of that?"

"If Sylvia vetoes, it won't even matter."

Afternoon
Gabriela

"Any particular reason why you hung up on Dad?"

Mom glares at me. "Such a Daddy's girl. Always taking Jeff's side." She's on edge. She presses her thumb to the remote. Anything to cut me off.

I tell myself to keep cool. "Mom, he only wanted to know if you need anything."

"Like what, an abortion?"

At that point I go get can of root beer from the fridge. No wonder Grandma's not home. Has she had to put up with this all week?

"Would you like one, Mom?" Right away I correct myself. "A root beer, I mean." Jesus, what a Freudian slip.

She shoots me a superlong glare and shakes her head. She flicks channels till she decides on *Johnny Guitar*. It's a 1950s cult movie, a campy Joan Crawford–Mercedes McCambridge Western. Pat always cracks up when she watches it. She grooves with "the dyke vibes." Does Mom know about that? She probably isn't concentrating on that crazy movie anyhow.

When he hears bird noises on the movie soundtrack, Nopalito twitters. He's been jittery since his cage capsized during the quake. Maybe the little guy needs some personal contact to calm him. Whistling to him, I open his cage door. Green-and-yellow head cocked in my direction, Nopalito perches on the phony branch inside.

"It's only me, muchachito." I touch one of his scaly feet. He almost bounces onto my finger. As soon as he's out of the cage, he climbs all the way to my shoulder. He likes to play with my hair. At least *he's* willing to pay some attention to me.

"I thought you might want some company today," I say to Mom after a while. I'm cross-legged on a needlepoint cushion on the hardwood floor. Mom's seems fixated on Joan Crawford, the stuck-up Vienna character.

"You're supposed to be so damn smart. About time you figured that one out," she mumbles. She doesn't turn her head an inch. "Toni's been a lot more dependable than you."

I feel like tossing the root beer at her to make her chill out, but that'd be a Zalo tactic.

Mom gets up real fast. Scared again, Nopalito flies off my shoulder to the top of the curtain rod across the room. Mom shuts off the TV and stomps into the kitchen. I hear her close the back door. Nopalito's skittish. It takes a few minutes to coax him back to his cage. Fastening the twisty on the wire door so he can't get out, I follow Mom outside. Don't see her anywhere. Next door, I hear the toilet flush. That's when I realize she's in her duplex.

The back door's unlocked. I wonder what she's up to. I tiptoe in; she's heading into the bedroom she used to share with Zalo. The silence makes me nervous. I peek in. She's yanking his clothes out of dresser drawers. A bunch of faded boxers, old socks, raggedy T-shirts. Man, oh, man. He sure wasn't a *GQ* kind of guy.

"Mama left some boxes near her back door. Bring them, Gabi," she calls, like she's out of breath.

Trying to read her mood, I don't move right away. She seems a little spacey, in a daze.

"Mama said the parish is collecting clothes for the homeless and people displaced from the quake," she explains. She's pretty much thinking out loud. "Might as well put Zalo's stuff to good use."

The idea of seeing that big slob's rags on someone else in

town gives me the willies, but I rush out to bring her the boxes.

When I come back Mom has scads of junk on the bed. Looks like she—or someone—has done some cleaning up, swept up whatever got broken. Of course, I haven't been inside since New Year's when Zalo slammed her around. I was too scared to even notice what the place looked like then.

"Don't just stand there, Gabi. Fill up the boxes," she orders. Her back to me, she snatches more clothes from the closet.

Touching whatever covered that ugly body really turns me off. I remember the disgusting way he leered at me when Mom wasn't looking—all the horrible names he'd call me, the mean, hateful things he said about Toni and Pat.

Mom turns around. "You won't get poisoned, Gabi."

"I refuse to touch his underwear," I mutter.

She doesn't seem surprised by my defiance. "You can finish with the closet. There isn't much left."

With a nod, I move away from the bed. She throws his shorts in the wastebasket and the socks and some T-shirts into a box. I wonder what she's thinking.

Only a worn bomber jacket and a nylon windbreaker hang in the closet, plus a few pairs of slacks that look too small to have ever fit him. No suits. It dawns on me he was buried in the only one he owned. I wish we could burn his clothes; too bad bonfires are illegal.

In silence we fill the boxes. She adds a few pairs of shoes, some dirty sneakers, beat-up construction boots. Worn out, Mom slumps on the bed.

"Take them."

"To the parish?"

"I don't care. Get them away from me."

I lift one box and push the other with my foot to the back

door. I leave them next to Grandpa's storage shed for easy loading into Grandma's car.

An evil spirit's been banished from the duplex. The sun shines through the living room windows, lighting up the place.

I hear clattering sounds. Mom's in the bathroom. She fills a plastic garbage bag with Zalo's shaving gear, a greasy black comb with broken teeth, a can of Right Guard. She looks hypnotized, on automatic pilot. When she's finished she hands me the bag. I take it outside to the dumpster.

I almost hesitate to go back. What else can she be doing? She's on the floor of the bedroom, crouched by the dresser's bottom drawer. She seems to sense I'm there.

"Remember these, Gabi?" She holds up pretty little dresses, one crocheted with pink ribbons woven into the neckline, the other eyelet with yellow embroidered ducks on it. "Mama made this. Toni bought this for you."

"I want a little sister," I say before I can catch myself.

That breaks her trance. Her eyes are big with memories and fear. "You might not get your wish, honey."

"Well, a little brother would be OK too—I guess."

Next thing I know I'm with her on the floor. I grab her like I used to whenever I had a scary dream. She's sobbing into my neck. I try to figure out who's doing the comforting.

Adela

I see some boxes filled with clothes near the shed where Juan used to keep his tools. Ay, is Sylvia getting rid of Zalo's things already? Que milagro! I never expected this from mi hija. Que Dios me perdóne, I thought she would try to keep his memory alive to make the rest of us miserable. Since the funeral she has been crying, eating, watching TV, sleeping, nada mas. "Depressed and in denial," como dice la Toni. Pues, que pasó while I was at the parish?

Gabi's Jeep is parked on Arizona. I think she's in the duplex with Sylvia. Puede ser que estàn platicando o algo. It's about time, eh? I have a million questions but no time right now.

El Padrecito Huerta asked one of the parish volunteers to reinforce the porches for me. Of course, I'll pay the carpenter, el Señor Rubalcava. He's taking an estimate today and will be back Monday to start the work. Toni, of course, thinks I should have both duplexes inspected "to be absolutely sure."

What will we do if there is more damage than meets the eye, eh? Where will we live? No, I want Señor Rubalcava to start work on the porches right away. I'm lucky to find an honest man from the parish. I'm tired of all this mess.

Maybe las muchachas have finished cleaning Pat's apartment. Puede ser que they went to a movie. They deserve to enjoy themselves. Pobrecitas, they've worked very hard this week. It makes me happy to see them together, contentas y feliz.

"Señora Dorado, I don't think you have anything to worry about," Señor Rubalcava tells me. "Whoever built these porches did a slapdash job. Looks they were added to the duplexes later. That's why they're pretty much falling apart."

"Ay, verdad?" I wipe my hands on a dish cloth and offer him a can of root beer. "My husband and I bought the duplexes—porches and all—over 20 years ago."

"You were smart to buy them then. Working people sure can't afford anything in Santa Monica these days," Señor Rubalcava says as he pops open the can. "The porches were probably put on after the '71 Sylmar quake."

"Pues, quien sabe?"

Gabi's face appears in the kitchen window next door. She smiles and waves.

"My granddaughter," I explain to Señor Rubalcava.

"Que bonita." He takes out his measuring tape.

Gabi comes outside and I introduce them. Señor Rubalcava nods. Whistling to himself, he begins taking measurements of the porches.

"Que está pasando aqui, mijita? I saw the boxes."

Gabi wanders toward them, away from the carpenter. "Give me your car keys, Grandma. I'll put the boxes in the trunk for you. Out of sight, out of mind."

"Sylvia filled them up?"

My granddaughter nods. "Wasn't about to stop her. Poor Mom. She's taking a nap now, just conked out." She sighs. "You know what, Grandma? She shouldn't live by herself."

I follow her to my car. "Mira, Gabi, don't make any quick decisions, eh? You're worried about your mother, verdad, but remember what she did before? If another hombre malcriado comes into her life, where will you be? Back with your daddy?"

Gabi's pretty eyes stare at me. "Grandma, the baby—"

"Si, the baby. That's what everyone's thinking about. I'm worried too. La verdad es que Sylvia isn't always trustworthy."

"You think I should keep living with Dad?" La muchacha seems shocked. "Leave Mom alone?"

"Pues, I'm next door. Toni's here tambien. You want to be baby-sitting all the time, mijita? Don't think she won't try to talk all of us into that when the baby comes."

Gabi shuts the car trunk on the two boxes. "I can't believe you're saying this, Grandma."

"I'm an old lady, Gabi. I don't like to admit it, pero there were plenty of times when your Grandpa and I spoiled Sylvia. She would bat those ojos lindos at us, tease us into letting her have her way. She was our baby, no? Well, her way hasn't always been good for this family, eh?"

My granddaughter hands me the car keys. Without a word she walks away from me and back to Sylvia's.

Evening
Toni

"Let me help you, Toni." While Gabi lifts the dumpster lid, I heave the unwieldy trash bag into the steel container.

"Thanks." About to return to Mama's, I rub my hands together in the cool evening air. "I'm glad you stayed for dinner."

My niece seems pensive, quieter than usual. "Want to drive around with me so we can talk?"

"Sure." I smile and pat her arm. I'm relieved she's made the first move. "We can stop by the supermarket while we're at it. Let me get Mama's grocery list. "

"Meet me at the Jeep." She jogs down the gravel driveway.

"Lots of tension in that living room," I remark when I join Gabi a few minutes later. "Sylvia's watching *Hard Copy;* Mama's grumbling about it. Wouldn't have been a bad idea to take up Pat's offer to go see that Latina lesbian play at Highways tonight."

Gabi starts the Jeep and swings it into a U-turn. She maneuvers it east on Arizona to the market. "Why didn't you?"

I shrug. "René and Veronica invited Pat to the play long before I came into town."

"They're your friends too, Toni."

"Pat needed a break." I stare out the window at numerous brick piles in front yards, on curbs. No more chimneys in this neighborhood.

"Too much togetherness?"

"Maybe. Why aren't you with Phil tonight?"

"Same reason." She glances at me at the stoplight on Berkeley and Wilshire. "I think he's tired of hearing about my...stuff."

"That happens, but I'm willing to listen. In fact, I've been waiting for this ever since that night at Union Station. I wondered if you were avoiding me."

When the light turns green, she accelerates. Soon she turns into the market's parking lot. "Guess I've been scared you'd take off again," Gabi answers.

My eyes well at her honesty. I put my hand on her arm. "Not this time, Gabi."

In the market Gabi acts silly. She stands on the edge of the shopping cart and rides it while I push. I tease her about not being as lightweight as she used to be. While I browse the cereal aisle, she glides the cart to me, her behavior a bit more sedate.

"Did you know Mom has a whole drawer of my baby clothes?"

Great Grains versus Mueslix loses significance. "Really?"

"Yeah, she showed them to me today. Some Grandma crocheted, some you bought."

"Hmmm. She wants another girl?"

Gabi wastes no time choosing a bag of fat-free granola. She tosses it into the cart. "Mom didn't say. Seemed spacey while she was clearing out Zalo's junk. She wasn't too talkative."

"With Sylvia, actions sometimes speak louder than words. Dorado trait, actually." I signal her to move the cart further along the aisle. "She's worried about making ends meet. Zalo didn't leave her anything, not even an insurance policy. With the maternity wing of the hospital about to be demolished, your mom's in a real fix. She can collect unemployment for a while. That will cover her living expenses, but what about her medical bills?"

Gabi shoots me a nervous look. "Grandma won't throw her out, Toni."

"Of course not. The point is, your Grandma lives off Grandpa's social security, his pension, and the rent from the duplex. Sylvia can't afford to pay Mama. That puts a cramp in your Grandma's style." I select a jar of orange marmalade and Pat's favorite blackberry preserves.

"She told you that?"

"She doesn't have to, Gabi. I know Mama like the back of my hand. She's glad I've filed for my unemployment. I really need a job, Gabi. I'm hoping for the library, but who knows? We have to have regular income—soon. There's no way Sylvia and I can live off Mama. And with a baby coming— whew!" I shake my head, mindful of my niece's reaction.

"Then I really should move in with Mom," she concludes, searching my face. "I mean, I'm working part-time for Phil's dad. At least that's something. Dad pays for my schooling. Whatever I earn I can hand over to Mom."

"That's a big decision, Gabi. Don't jump into it. You really ought to talk it over with your father first."

"Grandma doesn't seem real thrilled about it either. She thinks Mom would use me," she adds, her eyes perplexed.

Moving ahead of her, I ponder my words. "You know, Gabi, I don't like to label your mom. You're aware we still have our ups and downs. What we all need to be conscious of more than anything is she's been through a horrendous experience with Zalo. Whether we understand it or not—and for me comprehending it is the most difficult—he had an extremely negative influence on her. That affected how she responded to everyone in this family. He used divide-and-conquer tactics to turn her against all of us—and she bought into that." With a sigh, I turn to face her.

Gabi's concentration is intense. She stands close to me in the bakery aisle, her sea-green eyes urging me on.

"When we were kids, your mom and I once found a stray cat in the alley. Mama didn't want to let him in the house." I pull a bag of bagels and a package of English muffins off the shelf. "He was a straggly looking tomcat with a huge appetite. Mama let us feed him as long as we kept him outside.

"After school one day, when Mama was doing errands, Sylvia and I lured him inside with a bowl of cat food. By that time he would let us pet him. He would even rub against us and purr. But when we closed the kitchen door, the cat went berserk. He jumped on Sylvia, maybe 'cause she was smaller. He scratched her arms really bad. She started screaming when she saw the blood. I was scared out of my wits. I managed to grab that cat by the back of his neck. He was snarling and kicking, trying to bite me. I opened the back door and hurled him as far as I could. Then I tried to calm Sylvia down, put Band-Aids on her, the whole bit. Of course, when Mama got home, we were in huge trouble. But you know something, Gabi? We never saw that cat again. He disappeared. Sylvia and I used to wonder if he had a scam running from neighborhood to neighborhood."

"You think Mom's like that cat? Not to be trusted?"

I meet her unwavering gaze. "Your mother's been mistreated, Gabi. Abused like that cat had been. It's hard for her to trust anyone. She knows we're all relieved Zalo's dead. She needs us, but she can't completely trust us."

"That means she can turn on us at any time."

I touch her shoulder and guide her toward the cashier

lines. "Honey, it means be wary. When she's backed into a corner, when her life takes a tailspin, your mom strikes out. Her defense mechanisms kick in. She puts herself first."

My niece ponders this as the cashier rings up our purchases. Gabi wheels the cart to the Jeep.

"If that's the way you feel, Toni, why are you willing to deal with her at all?"

"She's my sister." I hear the sudden catch in my voice. "I know that sounds simplistic, but it's the only answer that makes sense."

CHAPTER SIXTEEN

February 1: Noon
Pat

"Hey, Jackie." One hand over the phone receiver, I call to my coworker. "Any ideas for lunch?" I'm on hold for one of my studio contacts. Another sex-violent film to protest. Hard to ignore my growling stomach, though.

When Jackie doesn't answer, I lean over to see if I can catch a glimpse of her. I almost drop the phone when I notice Sylvia's in the outer office talking with her. Toni's sister, in blue maternity stretch pants and a scoop-necked top, must've just strolled in. She scans Media OutReach brochures and posters. Jackie shrugs her apologies and points Sylvia in my direction.

She sashays in and makes herself at home in the chair across from me. No wonder Jackie seems bug-eyed. With her hennaed hair pulled back, Sylvia looks a lot like Toni.

She grabs one of my scratch pads and doodles while I'm on the phone—geometric shapes, circles of arrows. Maybe feeling closed in. "Hey, Syl." I finish my call and put down the phone. "What's up?"

"Want some lunch?" She nods toward the door. "Doc gave me a clean bill of health, so I jumped on the bus and headed this way. I owe you for helping out the day of the quake, Pat."

I have my doubts. Whatever she's really here for, I might as well be open to it. I roll back my chair. "Hey, if you insist. There's a salad joint down the block. That OK?"

"Fine. Let's go."

Jackie winks when we pass by. Probably figures I have in-law trouble.

"My sister treating you all right?" Sylvia starts in while flipping through the menu.

"Huh?"

"Pat, you've been around a lot less. At least not 'sleeping' in the truck as much." She flutters her eyelashes at that last comment.

"Gettin' kind of personal." I shut the menu, toss it on the table. "In the office just now, didn't you see the brochures about stereotypes? Dykes aren't always ready to rip each other's clothes off."

Her brown eyes meet mine and hold them. "I'm joking, OK?" She sips the iced water. "The thing is—I want some info."

At that I frown. "What gives?"

"Tell me about Zalo, and I'll tell you about Toni."

"What the hell is this?" I glare at her and wave to the waitress.

"Tell me about him, Pat." She shuts up as soon as the waitress comes to take our orders.

Tapping my fingers on the table, I keep my eyes on Sylvia's. Adela's been postponing the truth. Typical Dorado tactic. They're the biggest bunch of procrastinators I've ever met. No wonder Sylvia showed up. I'm her best bet, but she figures I'm not about to spill any beans first.

"Amanda phoned the Saturday after the quake."

"So?"

"I was home by myself. Toni doesn't know about it. Amanda said I didn't have to tell her, so I didn't."

I still don't make a comment.

"Pat, damn it! Aren't you curious?"

"Seems like you are more than me."

She fiddles with her hair. She twirls a couple of strands around her fingers, almost like Toni does. Why haven't I ever noticed she has that same habit?

"Why did my sister leave Amanda?"

"Where've you been?" I take a piece of pumpernickel from the basket between us. "Toni realized that whole escape angle was bogus. Being away from here did a real number on her."

Sylvia mulls that over. "Amanda sounded—well, like she's really crazy about her."

"Sure she is."

"Must make you feel on top, huh?" She offers a look that's borderline flirtatious.

"Sylvia," I lean toward her. "what are you driving at?"

"Already told you. I want to know whatever you're keeping from me about Zalo." She fishes a lemon slice from her glass and sets it on the edge of her bread dish. "And I want to be sure Toni's telling the truth."

"About what?"

"Helping me financially with the baby."

"She wouldn't lie to you. She's already promised," I add as gently as I can. Shit, I'm not used to reassuring Sylvia. To be honest, I don't have much appetite for it.

"I know, but—" She breaks off, her eyes already wet. "There's so much we—" She presses the paper napkin to her mouth. She stares at the table instead of me.

"You have to talk to her. Don't put me in the middle, OK? She's your sister. Somehow or other, Toni's willing to let bygones be bygones. If you ask me, she's being damn generous. You need to give in, too, huh? After all those accusations—" I shake my head. "Christ, it's a miracle you didn't accuse her of molesting Gabi while you were at it."

"She'd never hurt Gabi," she denies quickly. "Zalo made me say those things, Pat. I—"

"Hey, stop, all right? Don't lie to me, Sylvia. Toni didn't deserve any of your bullshit, and you know it. She's done plenty for you. I'm damn aware of that."

She keeps her head down, her fist curled around the napkin. "What does it matter if you believe me or not?" Her words fly out. "The first time Zalo beat me was when I said, 'My sister's a lesbian.'"

Swallowing hard, I don't want to hear any more.

"You didn't know that, did you, Pat?"

Slowly, I shake my head. "But I know his type."

The waitress sets our salads in front of us. Neither of us look like we're in the mood to eat. Sylvia forks through the greens. She picks out the mushrooms. For a few minutes she doesn't say a word. "When I left the doctor's office today," she begins, "I thought about going to the library. I wanted to check if the newspaper files have anything about Zalo's accident. I decided to ask you instead. I didn't want to rattle Toni on her first day at work."

"Why didn't you ask Chava?"

"I've cut my ties to the Anchondos. They can't do shit for me."

"Right to the point, anyway, Syl." I chew some sprouts and study her. "Hell…all right." I sigh. "Zalo wasn't alone."

"No surprise." She exhales. She looks like she's relieved. "Did she die too?"

I keep my voice low. "Yeah."

"At least it wasn't me." She takes another sip of water before picking up her fork again.

"Syl, we figured you were hurt enough. We didn't want to—"

"It's OK, Pat. Really." Her eyes are clear now. "You don't have to explain. I needed to know for sure." She gives me a steady look. "How can you do it?"

"What?"

"Take Toni back. Doesn't it hurt to remember what she did to you?"

I'm not about to confide in her. Even so, her questions prove she's noticed my conflicts. I sure don't like being an open book.

Toni

No doubt most of the patrons assume the floral displays lining the reference section are commemorating the library's reopening. Some of them do, but a number are memorials to Marian Cates, and two are congratulatory gifts from Pat and Veronica. Surrounded by flower baskets, I compare my mixed emotions about returning to the main branch to the apprehension of my homecoming a few weeks ago. Relief and sadness coupled with a bit of superstitious trepidation best describes my feelings today. A few regular patrons have confided how much they have missed me. The majority, however, continue to line up at the reference desk, more concerned about obtaining assistance than asking where I've been. Few seem curious about Marian's absence.

"Yoo-hoo, Toni." Crystal flings one braceleted wrist in front of me during the noontime lull. "Where are you?"

With some embarrassment, I laugh. "Wafting around in my head. Sorry."

She beckons me. "Our turn for lunch, darling. More Thai?"

"Gosh, yes." I glide from behind my station to join her.

We amble along Sixth Street to Santa Monica Boulevard. Across the street, the once bustling Pep Boys auto supply store deteriorates behind a plywood barricade. Many businesses on the boulevard—especially those in older, brick buildings—have borne the destructive brunt of the earthquake. Everywhere merchants struggle to keep afloat amidst the jagged sea of rubble. Fortunately the quake hopscotched over half of the block. The Thai restaurant remains unscathed.

Crystal orders her usual Thai iced tea; I prefer a pot of the hot jasmine. We agree on several dishes to share.

"You're in orbit again, Toni," Crystal teases after a few minutes. She claims to be psychic. "What is it—your nagging Catholic conscience?"

"There you go, Crystal. It amazes me."

"It's easy to guess. Take a look at your reflection in the window, darling. Pinched-in cheeks, tight mouth, haunted eyes—undisputed signs of Catholic guilt on the rise."

With no argument, I turn my back to the window. Sighing, I glance at her. "I keep thinking: two deaths and my life has reversed direction. That's spooky, Crystal."

"People die every day, darling."

"Those two?"

She pushes up the wide sleeves of her hand-knit chartreuse sweater. Her collection of turquoise bracelets slips to her plump wrists. "Their time had come. Do you think fire-breathing Marian had any qualms about snatching the job you'd aimed for? Do you think your Sylvia's Neanderthal husband cared about pummeling her to smithereens? One way or another I believe the universe answers us. I couldn't be more delighted with the outcome."

Mulling her words, I gaze at her. "I know you really mean that, Crystal. For me it's more difficult to accept."

"Of course. You're not a pagan—not like goddess-in-the-flesh Crystal. That Catholic guilt's creeping under your fingernails. I can almost see it oozing."

I smile and pour myself a tiny cup of tea.

"How about your mother? Does she feel guilty about praying for an end to Sylvia's beatings?"

"Well, Mama won't say."

"Because you haven't asked her, most likely."

"There you go again, Crystal. You're uncanny."

"I've known you for years, darling." She wraps spicy noodles around her chopsticks and begins to eat.

"I'm trying to be a little more open," I admit. "With Pat and Gabi, anyway. They're more receptive to it than the others are."

"Are you moving in with Pat?"

Turning slightly, I let my gaze wander to the boulevard traffic. "Her landlord's waiting for FEMA money to start the repairs. In the meantime, she hasn't made the offer, but she hasn't insisted on sleeping alone either."

Crystal considers that while dipping a chicken sliver into peanut sauce. "Focus on her, darling. She's why you're back in California. Don't ever let Pat think otherwise. Maybe all else seems to have fallen into place, which aggravates your damn Catholic guilt. Pat, though—she's someone you have to strive for."

Dropping a tangle of noodles on my plate, I glance at her. "Crystal, I'm disappointed. Maybe you aren't uncanny. You aren't telling me anything new about Pat."

"Because I don't need to."

Gabriela

Phil isn't too stoked about my plan. Dad's advice is to listen to my heart. Grandma tells me to be careful. Toni advises lots of communication. I have doubts, sure. Mom doesn't seem to have any.

Maybe her track record isn't the greatest. She's my Mom, though. I'm going to have a little sister or brother—not quite the way I expected, not the fantasy of Mom and Dad remarried. I'm old enough to know that's fairy-tale stuff. They aren't anywhere near the same people they were when I came into this world.

A thunderous wave, one of the most spectacular Dad ever rode, knocked him unconscious one summer day and splintered his spinal cord. He doesn't hate the ocean for that—no way. Dad thinks the Pacific saved him from drowning in a nowhere kind of life. I don't know if Mom's that open-minded about the Northridge fault. On a moonless cold morning, it spun Zalo off the freeway's edge. Weird, isn't it, how both my parents' lives changed in split seconds? Guess that teaches us to make the most of what this water-bound, earthquake-prone land delivers. We really don't have much choice, except to abandon it. Toni swears no matter where you go, your feet get tangled up in your roots, your raíces.

I'm starting to pay more attention to Spanish phrases. In my second semester I'm enrolled in a Chicano literature course, much to Toni's relief. She used to encourage me in her letters "to find out about the culture." Since the liberal arts building took a direct hit in the quake, every other day I sit in one of the temporary classrooms at Santa Monica College, soaking in poems, essays, and stories with bilingual dialogue. Names of writers I've heard Toni mention a zillion times come alive. Cherríe Moraga's my favorite. She grew up in the San Gabriel Valley, not far from here. Like me, she has a Chicana mother and a white father. Like me, she's light-skinned. Like me, she's had problems with that. Because of the way she looks, she's had different experiences than either of her parents. I need to know more about people like me, to read whatever else Moraga's written.

Sometimes when I'm with Mom, I read Moraga's poems out loud. Her first reaction is to poke fun 'cause Cherríe's a lesbian. Mom rolls her eyes and blurts out, "Damn, not another one. What's with all these Chicana dykes?"

But when I start reading to her about Cherríe's feelings about her mother, about violence against women, about racism—hell, about sex—Mom starts to listen closer. She really likes Cherríe's play *Giving Up the Ghost.*

Who'd ever think I'd be reading poetry—even plays—to my Mom? I think she's more surprised than any of us. After I move back in this weekend, I'm going to keep this up. That's for sure. It feels so great to be close to my Mom again, in a whole new way.

Twilight
Sylvia

The chain-link fence protects the slumping hospital from the gawkers, or maybe it's the other way around. I hug myself and stand closer to the fence.

The X-shaped chain links are neater versions of the giant X patterns that span the hospital's north wing. X marks the spot: Each X means structural damage. Looks like some crazy vato took a deadly marker and tagged the hospital for his own. Westside gangs can be bold, but they can never compete with the quake's tagging skills. No, Mother Nature carved these X marks deep into the white plaster. She tagged the hospital and hundreds of other Santa Monica buildings. She claimed her territory and dared us to make a fuss about her wild trip through town.

The February wind is cold. I should have worn a coat instead of this bulky sweater. On the other side of the fence, a few squirrels are scrounging on the already dying lawn. I used to toss them bread crusts as I ate lunch under the palm trees. Hospital maintenance staff must have put the picnic tables in storage. Cranes and tractors have taken their place between the palms. The little park with rosebushes at its center, where nurses would take their breaks, where patients in wheelchairs would visit with their families, is gone. Will the demolition crews bother to feed the squirrels?

"It's like a ghost," Toni murmurs.

She's on her way home from work already. I didn't realize I'd been standing here so long. The hospital has a hold on me. I don't ever want to see that damn freeway overpass—over the mountains—where Zalo and that stupid girl took a dive. That part of my life's over. But St. John's—I can't avoid it. It's right in the neighborhood, like home, like family.

Toni's been talking for a bit. I don't even know what about. Maybe she's telling me about her first day of paid work.

"St. John's was one of the biggest employers in the city," she goes on. "Empty now, so desolate."

My hand clutches the fence. I keep my eyes on those damn X marks, remembering what used to lay beyond. "We were born here. Gabi too."

"Daddy died on the other side of the building, down the hall from the ICU," Toni whispers. I hear the sadness in her voice. "Before I decided to leave town, I would meditate in the chapel and weigh my options. The stained glass windows made the most radiant rainbows. They gave me hope, Sylvia. I loved to sit there in the quiet, all by myself." She sighs. "Never thought I'd see the destruction of this peaceful place. It's too—close."

We keep to ourselves for a little while. A few feet from us, other people pause at the fence. They shake their heads and walk on.

Toni glances at me. "You come by here often, Sylvia?"

"Used to work there," I remind her. Sometimes I can't help being snide with Toni. "Thought this baby would be born here too, like the rest of us." I sniffle and stare ahead. "Birth, death, unemployment—St. John's pretty much wraps up my life."

She nods. "I'm sorry."

"You didn't cause the earthquake, Toni." I wipe my nose on my sleeve and take a look at my sister.

Her dark eyes are calm, no trace of a righteous gleam. "I'm sorry it's taken a disaster for us to start talking."

"Yeah, well, that figures," I mutter. "Like Mama says, we're both such cabezonas."

She smiles at that. "We take after her."

With no one else around—nobody to be referee—it's so hard to talk with Toni. When we were kids I told her everything. She was the one with the answers, the patient one, the one willing to teach me. Nursery rhymes, fairy tales, doll games. About my body too. The places it feels good to touch.

She keeps on, maybe nervous I've stopped. Can she guess what I'm thinking?

"This afternoon, a science writer came to the reference desk. She wanted to see topographic maps of the area." Toni's voice rolls on when she tells a story. "Anyway, Sylvia, while I was out of state, the library acquired updated seismic maps from Cal Tech. I had never seen them until today. We spread the maps over several tables. Fascinating. People began to gather. We were dumbfounded at the myriad of faults criss-crossing the Westside."

I look at her again. Who else but Toni would say "myriad"?

"Remember when all we'd hear about was the San Andreas fault? Seismologists are studying several local faults now." She's rolling along in librarian mode. "One is the Newport-Inglewood fault—the one that caused the Long Beach quake in 1933. The Elysian Park fault, which runs beneath downtown Los Angeles, is one of the main ones they're watching. Where the Mormon temple is in Westwood is the steepest rise of the Santa Monica fault. We live parallel to it. Pretty damn obvious—case in point: St. John's and this whole neighborhood."

"This fault, that fault. One triggers the other, right? Doesn't even matter which is to blame."

"All that tension building below the surface," she adds, her eyes glued to mine. "Sometimes we're on bedrock when it hits, sometimes on soft soil. Sometimes we're not prepared to take the shock. Sometimes we fall apart from the stress."

I grit my teeth to stop them from chattering, to keep the sobs locked in.

"You're safe now, Sylvia. We're on solid ground, you and me. Come on. I'll take you where it's warm," she whispers, one arm already around me. "Earth, Wind, and Flour's a few blocks away. Dinner's on me."

Leaning on my sister, I let her guide me toward Wilshire. After a few steps I change my mind. I shake her arm off. She seems confused at first. When I put my arm through hers, Toni smiles again. "No leaning this time," I tell her.

"And not only talking. Listening too."

"Hours—days—of that," she promises.

Night
Adela

Emilia Salcido sits next to me at the parish bingo game. I don't mind Emilia. She is serious about the game. Some of these other viejitas talk too much, tu sábes. Son metiches, busybodies, always peeking at everybody else's bingo cards. They lose track of the numbers and then bother everyone around them for help. Con ellas I lose my patience. This game takes concentration. It isn't easy watching six bingo cards at once. Pero Emilia es una señora muy amable. She minds her own business—at least most of the time.

"I never see you here on Tuesdays, Adela," she says at the end of one game. She spreads four new cards in front of her and checks to be sure her marking pen hasn't dried up.

"I play on Thursdays, pero mis hijas decided to have dinner together tonight. Why should I stay around the house by myself, eh?"

"They didn't invite you, Adela? Ay, these modern girls— they forget about us so easy." She fans herself with one of the used cards. "They think we're boring old ladies."

"Mira, Emilia, no es verdad. I'm happy my daughters want to be by themselves for a change. I was beginning to feel cooped up en la casita. Ever since el temblór, we've been living like sardines, no? Being in that little house with two grown women—ay, que barbaridad! Gracias a dios for Tuesday night bingo."

Emilia laughs. Puede ser que she thinks I'm a selfish mother. I know otherwise. My daughters have relied on me for the past month. Pues, I have depended on them too, especially Toni y Pat. Pero, soon Sylvia and Gabi will be next door. Maybe Toni will even be con la Pat. Quien sabe? I look forward to being free to come and go as I please.

Everyone quiets down por unos minutos. Padrecito Huerta makes announcements about fund-raising for the temporary classroom buildings. The elementary school needs major repairs. FEMA will pay for part of it, but the parish must raise thousands more. Ay, I almost wish I hadn't come tonight. If I win the $250 grand prize, will I have to donate the money to the parish? Que Dios me perdóne for such thoughts!

The next game begins and ends. Ay, que lástima! Not much luck tonight. Maybe I should leave. Who knows what Sylvia and Toni are up to, eh? Never can tell what's going to happen con esas muchachas. Toni said Pat was working late. Ay, I hope my daughters don't start arguing. Without Pat they could be at each other's throats by now.

"Adela, you missed N-48," Emilia tells me out of the side of her mouth. "Que tienes? Getting tired?"

"Ay, no. Gracias," I mumble. We're playing an M-shape this last time. I notice Emilia needs three more numbers. I have one blank spot on my card. Por favor, Saint Jude, I pray. Half for Sylvia, half for the parish.

"G-72," calls Señor Navarro in his booming voice.

"Bingo!" I shout, my elbow almost hitting Emilia in the eye. Ay, perdóname Jesusito! Sylvia needs all my winnings, no?

Epilogue

Maybe we are safe if we have a family
who forgives every fault, who believes, collectively,
the earth will not move again.
—Brenda Miller,
from an unpublished poem

September 24: Late Morning
Toni

A block from the apartment, we spread the folded patchwork quilt on the curb and settle ourselves to view the "Bouncing Back" Parade. Saturday's sunshine promises perfect weather for St. John's daylong reopening event. Seems as if all our neighbors—and a large percentage of Santa Monica's population—have turned out to celebrate the restoration of one of our childhood landmarks.

"Do you think the parade will start on time?" Gabi

helps Mama set up a lawn chair. "I have to be at work by noon."

Her news disappoints me. "You'll miss the free picnic."

"Ay, Toni. La muchacha has a job, eh?" Mama arranges her straw hat to shield herself from the late summer sun. "I can't stay either. I volunteered to help Padre Huerta with the rummage sale."

"For all the time you put in, you ought to be promoted to assistant pastor, Mama." Sylvia removes a plastic bottle of suntan lotion from the baby's diaper bag.

"Como eres, muchacha," Mama scolds in mock irritation.

Sylvia grins while rubbing lotion on her arms and legs.

"Well, looks like Sylvia and I are the only ones in this family with a sense of history," I remark. "This reopening is a very special occasion."

"I'd really have something to celebrate if I had my job back," Sylvia mutters.

My sister makes an inarguable point. These days she is an independent contractor doing private-duty nursing in convalescent homes. She'd rather be a salaried employee with medical benefits. After the earthquake, the hospital administration decided to downsize its operations. The maternity wing was demolished but not rebuilt. Its replacement is a low-slung outpatient structure.

Seismic retrofitting for the remaining wings of the hospital lasted for months. Huge cranes filled Santa Monica Boulevard and caused numerous traffic problems. Noisy drilling and pounding gave us daily headaches. The result is a gleaming St. John's. Its landscaping seems as lovely as ever, although the rose garden looks spindly. The hospital appears familiar and strange, all at once.

"Donde está la Pat?" Mama nudges me.

"Her brother called when we were about to leave. You know Carlos. He'll have Pat on the phone for hours." I shrug. "Who knows when she'll get here."

As much as I miss Pat's presence, I know she will show up sooner or later—probably later. Meanwhile, I cuddle baby Janelle on my lap, pretending to nibble her little toes. Exactly a year ago I lived with Amanda in Fir View, unhappy and homesick. Unwilling to admit it aloud, I longed for Pat and the rest of my family. Amanda's desire for a child gave me the incentive to abandon the Northwest. Now I sit on a Santa Monica curb holding my sister's 3-month-old daughter. I do enjoy being an auntie again. I kiss Janelle's chunky fingers. She smiles and grabs my nose.

"Toni, you're spoiling her," Sylvia grumbles. Permed these days, her tinted hair is shoulder-length. Her dimples show she is trying not to smile at our antics.

"That's what you told me about Gabi. She's turned out fine." Sylvia sighs. "Except she wants to pull a Toni and split."

"An education is a better reason than mine," I say quickly.

"Mom, give me a break," my niece groans. "What's wrong with applying to go away to school? Why do I have to go to UCLA like Toni or USC like Dad?"

"Between Jeff's damn influence and Phil's dumping you—"

"That isn't true!" Gabi protests. "Anyway, Phil didn't dump me. The breakup was mutual, Mom. How many times do I have to tell you that? It has nothing to do with applying to UC Berkeley."

"Don't yell at your mother," Mama interjects. "Y Sylvia, leave her in peace. This isn't the place."

I agree with Mama this time. Gazing up the street, I am impatient for the parade to begin. But I cannot resist adding, "Gabi has the grades, Sylvia. It would be a terrific experience for her."

Her sidelong glance warns me to mind my own business. Mama gives me another nudge, this one reproving. With a chuckle, I smooth Janelle's dark hair. Thick and straight, it already resembles mine.

Sylvia, however, does not keep her opinions to herself. "That kid Phil never liked the idea of Gabi living with me. As long as she stayed in the canyon with Jeff, being ritzy, things worked out. Phil didn't like her being excited over the baby either."

"You're weird, Mom." Gabi glares at her. "You're so down on men these days. There are some nice ones out there."

"What the hell are you saying, blue-eyed baby girl?" Sylvia sputters.

"Ya basta!" Mama is about ready to knock their heads together. "If this keeps up, I'm leaving before this silly parade starts."

"Yeah, I'll go with you, Grandma. Anytime."

"Will all of you please simmer down? You're scaring Janelle." I rock the whimpering baby. "Listen—I can hear the marching band. Take a look down the street, Gabi."

With some reluctance she leans over and gazes westward. "You'd have to be deaf not to hear those drums."

I check my watch—almost 11 o'clock. "You sound as enthused about the parade as Pat. She thinks this whole celebration is corny. For her the free food is the lure."

My comments make Gabi smile at last.

Sylvia laughs. "Pat felt the same when we'd go to the St. John's Christmas parties. Remember, Toni? Every year the hospital would throw a big shindig for 'underprivileged kids'—all of us at Saint Anne's."

Mama frowns. "Ay, tan criticóna! It was a beautiful act of charity, muchacha. You used to love those parties."

Sylvia disregards Mama and keeps talking. "Pat hated all that razzmatazz. She only wanted the fancy cookies and the Christmas stocking full of candy."

"All these years later," I add, "the three of us are at another St. John's party. If Pat ever shows up, that is."

Sylvia

Janelle Patrice Dorado sleeps in the morning sun. Dorado, yes—not Anchondo. I named my baby after my daddy, Juan, and my sister's lover, Pat—the real men in this family.

Someday I'll tell Janelle about her father. Maybe then my bitter feelings will be gone. Maybe then I'll be able to explain in a way that'll make sense to both of us. Maybe.

During the parade a little while ago, Toni sat next to me. In T-shirt and shorts, hair braided down her back, long legs stretched out, my sister was like an excited kid. Reminded me of old times. Living with her, then next door, during the months after the earthquake has given me a chance to know Toni all over again. It hasn't all been fun and games. We've bickered plenty, yelled at each other, the whole enchilada. But seeing her with my daughter—well, she loves Janelle and doesn't hide it. No matter what that always gets to me, makes me overlook the tension still between us.

When Janelle was born at Santa Monica Hospital, Toni was my birthing coach. We went to childbirth classes together. Those nights she would open up about Amanda over dinner. Toni was flabbergasted that Amanda assumed she'd be happy taking care of a baby. My smarty-pants sister told Amanda flat out she had no interest "in being a child care provider for a white baby." Toni repeated that to me with a superpassionate look in her eyes. No wonder Amanda sounded shaky when I mentioned my pregnancy. She knew Toni would help me.

I never told my sister about Amanda's phone call. As far as I know Pat hasn't either. Why bother? Why remind Toni of those awful months she was gone? I think both of us went crazy at the same time, for different reasons. Why should we dwell on that?

After Zalo died Toni let down her guard. She made a real effort to get close to me again. I wasn't always willing, no way. She made me damn suspicious. I didn't want her telling me what to do, reminding me how I'd screwed up. I'd had enough of that.

I know Pat's jealous of me. I can't help that. Sometimes I feel the same way about her. But as long as I've known her, Pat's proved dependable. She's always here for our family, but she isn't perfect. She thinks Toni's too involved in my life, too attached to Janelle. My sister's doing what she thinks best. I can imagine her with that same passionate look if Pat hassles her about Janelle and me.

During the childbirth classes we were the only sister team. The other couples would comment on our closeness, our commitment to each other. Hearing that made me damn nervous. Toni seemed to react the same as me. We'd glance at each other, like we were figuring out if those people were right. By the time Janelle was born, we knew. We're sisters. No one can ever change that. Even if we don't always agree, don't always think the same, we're las hermanas Dorado. We stick together.

"Sorry I took so long." Toni joins me where we grabbed an ideal spot at the foot of the stage. The musicians are setting up for the afternoon show. "I hope the hamburgers are still warm. So many people in line, Sylvia. No wonder Mama and

Gabi didn't want to hang around."

"Thanks." I take one of the cardboard containers from her. It holds two hamburgers, a bag of chips, and a Coke. "Oh, they had their excuses, but Gabi always gets pissed when I criticize Phil."

Toni peers at the sleeping baby before settling on the quilt beside me. "Veronica told me Phil was having problems with his dad. Frank's opposed to the film-school idea. He wants Phil to be an engineer." Toni bites into her burger. "Obviously the guy's under a lot of pressure. Don't second-guess Gabi. If she says the breakup was mutual, I believe her."

"Whatever. At least she isn't pregnant."

Toni ignores that. She's on another track. "At this point it's better for both of them to figure out who they are—by themselves."

"Now you're talking about me."

"Sylvia, come on. That was a general statement." She opens her potato-chip bag. "Janelle will wake up when the band starts playing," she says after a few minutes.

"If she fusses, I'll take her home." Kneeling, I lean over to check the baby. Brown and chubby, she looks more like a Dorado than Gabi ever did at that age. "It scares me, Toni."

"What?"

"If Zalo had lived, Janelle might not have."

My sister moves toward me to let me know she's listening.

"He was getting meaner, more violent. Only a matter of time before—well, I think he might've started punching my stomach or kicking me. I could've lost her, or she could've been an orphan. Maybe both of us would've been killed. I'm glad he's dead."

She rubs my arm. I close my eyes and let her soothe the bad memories away.

"I wanted to think ahead about raising Janelle. But now that the news is so full of domestic-violence stories, I'm making myself think of all those times Zalo beat me. Before that, even though you encouraged me to talk about it, I wanted to forget my life with him."

"No one's going to hurt you anymore, Sylvia," Toni murmurs.

"I was so crazy. I wouldn't listen to anybody. Not you or Mama. Not Jeff or Gabi. I didn't even want to read that booklet Gabi gave me. Can you believe I threw it out?"

"Don't be so hard on yourself. Sometimes it takes a while to make all the connections." She keeps her hand on my arm. Her skin is so morena compared to my tawny color.

"Talking about it does help. I never thought it would."

"It's like coming out of the closet, Sylvia—with your own issues. Lots of people in this city—this country—are in denial over domestic violence. They don't want to believe that domestic violence is the leading cause of injury to women between the ages of 15 and 44. Except for Mama, everyone in this family is in that age group. Zalo could have targeted the rest of us—he tried to."

"I never meant to put your life on the line, Toni."

She squeezes my arm. "It's over. We've both survived a lot this year."

I reach for my sun visor and put it on. Toni drinks some of her Coke.

"A couple of months ago," she begins, "I wanted to display some books on domestic violence in one of the library showcases. Ruthann and some of the other staff people—and these are educated professionals—gave me flak. But when they realized how many women came into the library requesting books on the topic, I proved my point. The display went up then and there."

"You have the type of job where you can have an impact." This time, I lean closer to her. "Keep doing that, Toni."

Afternoon
Pat

Christ. Running late. Never thought Carlos's phone call would last most of the morning. A San Diego activist, Carlos is mad as hell about that racist anti-immigrant proposition on California's November ballot. Mi hermano's venting made me riled too. I'm ready to drive to the border this weekend to help him with community organizing and voter registration.

I swoop down the apartment stairs—reinforced with steel nowadays. For me the earthquake's faded into history. Toni sees it as a unifying symbol for all of us. That's why she insists I show up at this silly "Bouncing Back" picnic at the hospital today. To her the day means we've come full circle.

Her first morning back in Santa Monica she saw Sylvia smack dab in front of St. John's. A few weeks later the hospital nearly caved in during the quake. Not to mention the emotional aftershocks in Sylvia's life. For Toni, being at the hospital's reopening celebration has special meaning. She believes our lives are back on track. I'm not sure if Sylvia and I feel that positive.

Anyway, what matters to Toni affects me one way or the other. True to my word, I jog up Arizona toward the hospital. Parade's over. Crowds overlap the sidewalk and spill into the street. Toni and her cockamamy sentimentality—how the hell can I ever find her in the middle of this crowd? Looks like the whole town's turned out for the free party.

The food lines—full of joking families, bratty kids—snake around the hospital parking lot. Lots of people of color in this happy crowd. Gives me a great feeling. No racial divisions when it comes to a free meal, I guess. Enough comida to feed a few National Guard battalions. Reminds me of the earthquake food lines, but this one seems much more light-hearted. Instead of letting my hungry tummy rule, I decide to scope out Toni. Makes it hard when so many gente in the crowd have long, black hair.

Not having any luck I cut back through Arizona. Someone ahead waves her arms. I squint and recognize Gabi.

"Hi, Pat. They said they'd find a place to sit by the stage." The kid holds two lawn chairs under her arm. Her grandma is with her. I can tell they can't wait to get home.

"Como te va, Adela. Why are you two leaving?"

"Too many people, Pat. Besides, I have things to do."

"Places to go, people to see," I finish for her.

"Ay, muchacha." She laughs. "Como está tu hermano?"

"Carlos wants me down in San Diego. He needs another hand to fight this pinche anti-immigrant movida."

She raises her brows. "Does Toni know?"

I shake my head.

Gabi shows pity for me. "Toni's mellow right now, but I'd be careful anyway, Pat. I wouldn't spring any news on her today. Watch out for my Mom too. She's ready to raise hell."

"Thanks for the tip." I grin and kiss them both. "Hasta luego."

They wave and continue walking up Arizona to the duplexes.

On the stage at the far end of the parking lot, the local band of Billy Vera and the Beaters are rocking. In a black suit, Billy sweats in the September sun and belts out "Papa Come Quick." Toni's probably loving this. She's so into this hometown scene.

Sure enough, I spot her, Sylvia, and the baby stroller near the stage. Poor Janelle must be half deaf by now. Toni and Sylvia have one of Adela's faded quilts spread on the asphalt. They're doing their own bouncing back routine on it, heads bobbing in rhythm. That old sitting-on-the-quilt-and-rocking number. Pretty damn cute.

For a few minutes I stand and watch them. They're giggling, being silly, like a couple of nutty teenagers. I almost hesitate to interrupt their fun. They're finally on the same wavelength. Sometimes I wonder how—or if—I fit.

The song ends. I debate whether to split or not. Will I be the fifth wheel? I push that thought aside. Why should I be? That's my mujer over there, la Toni Dorado.

Bopping over, I sneak behind them and wrap my arms around their shoulders. The sisters let out surprised whoops. Janelle starts crying. Sylvia picks her up to calm her. Toni gives me a long, delicious abrazo. I feel a helluva lot better already.

Toni

"A welcome like that makes me think I should always be late," Pat teases.

Thrilled to see her at last, I feel reckless. I don't care who in the crowd notices. Her lithe body in shorts and a tank top makes me tingle. I caress her slick hair and kiss her right on her sassy mouth.

"Ooh-la-la," she murmurs against me. "Thanks, Toñita."

"Are you starving?"

One of her hands tugs my braided hair. "Well, yeah— for you."

"Damn horny lesbos," Sylvia cuts in. I think she is annoyed

because I have turned my attention to my lover. "Here's your food, Pat."

Laughing, Pat takes the lunch carton from her. "Gracias, Syl."

"Toni got it for you, not me."

I raise my brows at my sister's candor. Maybe she is tired. The sun is awfully hot.

"Ay, what gives here, huh?" Pat is not about to let the comment pass. "Am I a party crasher or somethin'?"

At that Sylvia breaks into a sudden grin. "A few minutes ago, we told Mama how you hated the St. John's Christmas parties."

"Tryin' to get me in trouble with your old lady?" Pat pretends to be upset while she chews the hamburger. "Thanks a lot, Syl."

Sylvia shrugs; her bad humor seems to have vanished. I have grown used to her abrupt changes in temperament. She turns her back and checks on Janelle.

"Mama didn't believe a word of it, anyway." I open the Coke can for her. "So what's new with el Carlos?"

"My long-winded hermano's stressed to the max about the anti-immigrant mugre." Pat's candid eyes meet mine. "Made me feel shitty, Toni, like I'm fooling around with trivial media stuff while he's—"

"Your work is extremely important too," I remind her. "Don't ever doubt that."

Cross-legged on the quilt, Pat takes another bite of the hamburger. "Anyway, I have some vacation time left over from last year. I'm thinking about zooming to San Diego for a few days. Carlos needs help."

I stare at Pat. Although Sylvia is about to change Janelle's diaper, she pauses, as if waiting to observe my reaction.

"Why would you have to go? Why can't you do some local organizing? El Rescate and other places have—"

"Carlos is my brother." Pat rips open the chip bag. "I haven't even seen the vato in months. It'd be like old times for us, being activists together—even if it's only for a little while."

Is this her reaction to my family involvement? Whether it is or not, I would be selfish to argue. I still remember how torn she felt when Carlos left the Westside to move closer to the border.

Pat studies me. Determination fills her eyes. She seems to be daring me to oppose her plan.

Billy Vera revs up for another tune. As if eager to leave us to ourselves, Sylvia scoops Janelle into her arms. She improvises a dance with the baby at the foot of the stage. With her reddish hair, big sunglasses, and one-piece splashy romper outfit, Sylvia's an eye-catcher. I know she craves the attention. More power to her. Other mothers and kids join in, including couples of all ages.

I sit closer to Pat. My eyes remain unwaveringly on hers. I wonder if mine seem fearful. Hers are very steady. Has she told me everything?

I dare myself to probe. "Are you unhappy with me, Pat?"

At once, she becomes rattled. "Christ, Toni. I'm not leaving you."

"I have to ask. You've been a little tense lately."

She sighs. "I figured you'd recognize the signs. It's a heavy case of activist fever."

I do not know what to say.

She finishes the hamburger and wipes her hands. I know she wants to defuse the situation. "Toni, look at Sylvia and Janelle. That's love for sure."

I edge even nearer and lean her head on my shoulder. "I love you."

"I love you too, mujer," she says with much tenderness.

"What if Carlos tries to convince you to work with him on a regular basis?"

"He's too bossy. Turns macho on me. I can only take so much of that dude. You know that."

I say nothing.

For several moments we survey the dancers. From time to time Sylvia and Janelle boogie by. The music begins to shift. The opening strains of a ballad sound familiar.

"Come on, Toni." She rises in one fluid movement. She takes my hand and urges me up when Billy Vera launches into "At This Moment."

My eyes widen as I join her. "You want to dance—here?"

"You kissed me—here." She jokes, "What's the difference, mujer?"

A slow smile flickers across my face. Our hands clasped, I follow her through the clumps of dancers. We wind up next to Sylvia and the baby. I nudge my sister to allow us room. She rolls her eyes but does not protest.

Pat holds me very close. Barely moving, we lean together. I press my body against hers. She molds herself to me.

"For only one week?" I whisper.

"Nomás una semana," she verifies.

We both smile. We notice no one else. Our lips touch. At this moment, this is the only place for us to be.